I0684858

The Thai Option

(A Major Ren Novel)

By

Richard S. Post

© Richard S. Post 2016/2018

ISBN 978-0-9895608-2-5

Acknowledgements

Many Special Operations and Intelligence community professionals reviewed various versions of the final text, as did the CIA's Publications Review Board after it was completed. I thank them for both their service in keeping the country safe as well as making sure that what I pass off for a story does not inadvertently endanger any on-going operations, sources or methods.

My wife, Penny, was, as usual, a rock in forcing me to keep the story tight, government letter abbreviations to an absolute minimum and the prose crisp. Lynn Smith was instrumental in getting design, book cover and presentation ready for daylight while multiple reviewers forced me to look at the story as much from a spec ops warriors viewpoint as well as a civilian possibly reading about their exploits for the first time.

Special kudos go to Russ, Jay, Tom, Betty, Alan, another Allan, Jim, Ken, Ron, Deb, Art, Heather, Sidney, Kim, Lynn, and several others who by their choice shall go unheralded but greatly appreciated for their insights and commentary.

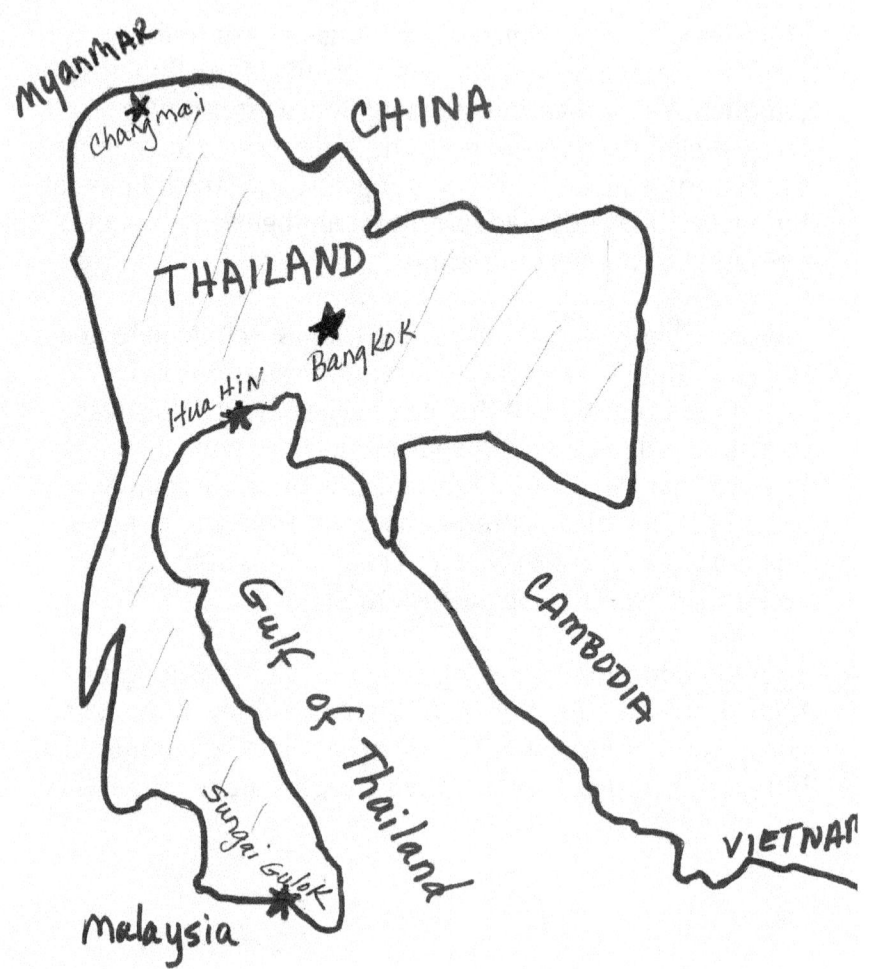

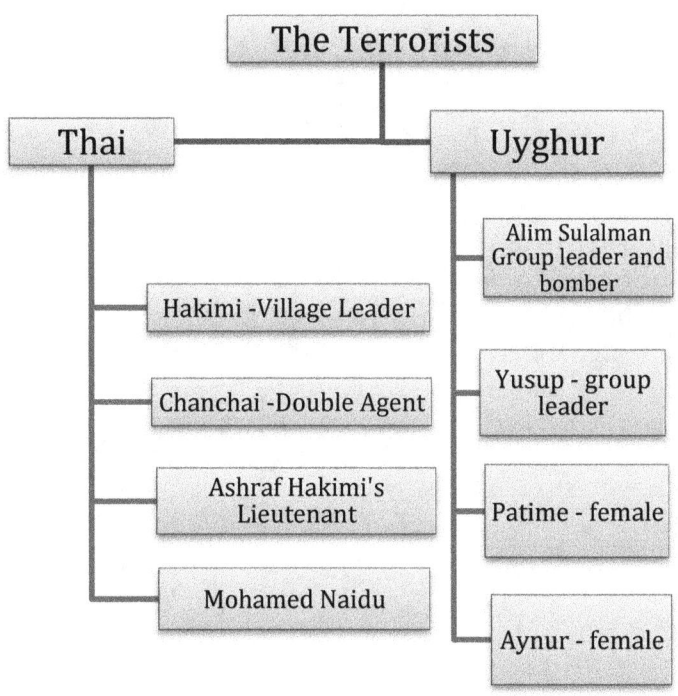

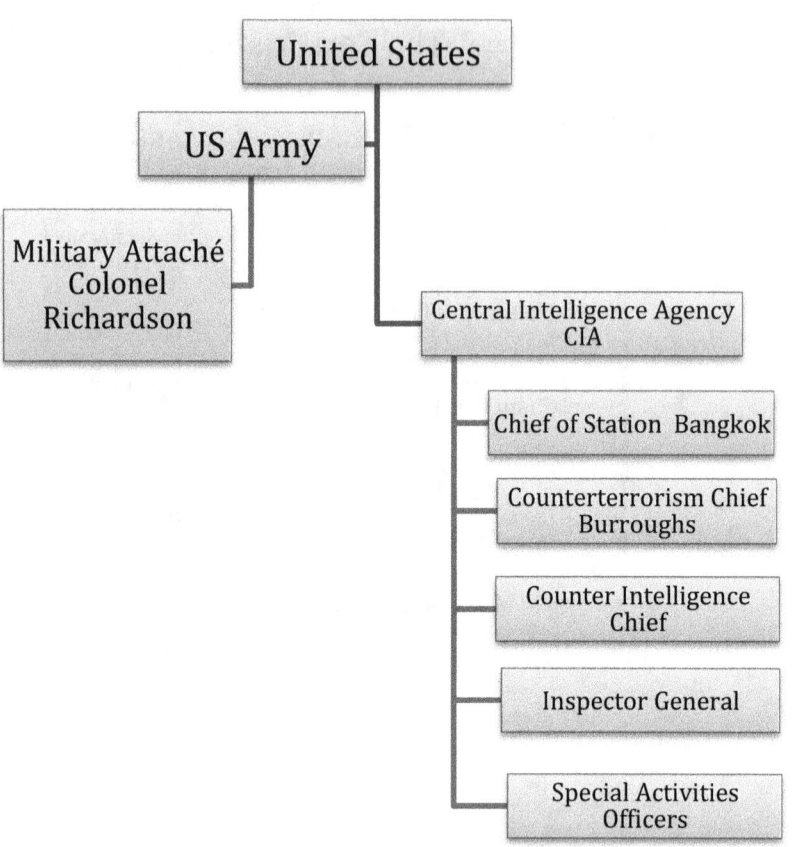

United States

US Army

Military Attaché
Colonel
Richardson

Central Intelligence Agency
CIA

Chief of Station Bangkok

Counterterrorism Chief
Burroughs

Counter Intelligence
Chief

Inspector General

Special Activities
Officers

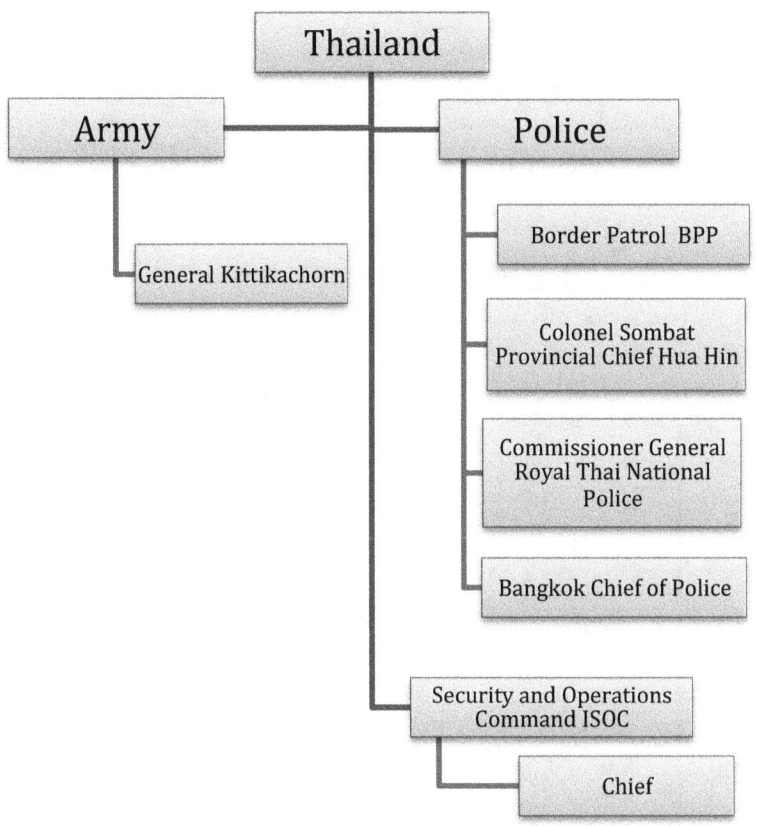

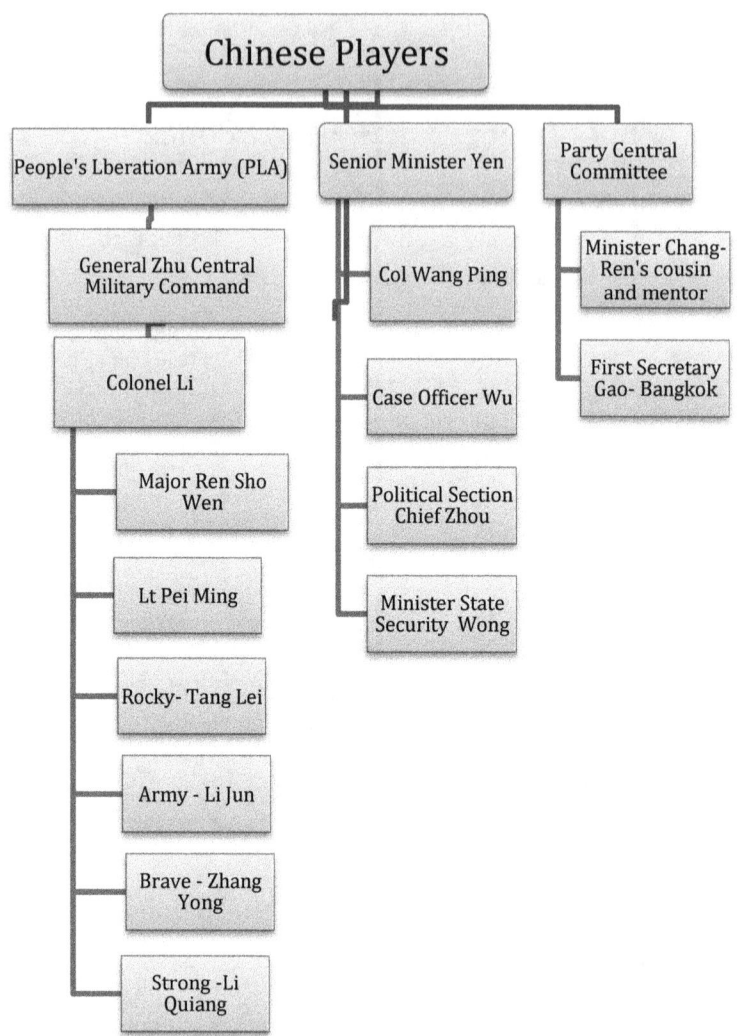

Chinese Players

- People's Lberation Army (PLA)
  - General Zhu Central Military Command
    - Colonel Li
      - Major Ren Sho Wen
      - Lt Pei Ming
      - Rocky- Tang Lei
      - Army - Li Jun
      - Brave - Zhang Yong
      - Strong -Li Quiang
- Senior Minister Yen
  - Col Wang Ping
  - Case Officer Wu
  - Political Section Chief Zhou
  - Minister State Security Wong
- Party Central Committee
  - Minister Chang-Ren's cousin and mentor
  - First Secretary Gao- Bangkok

Chapter 1

Bangkok

The four member Ghost Shadow team moved as one as they closed in on the squat two-story building on the pitch-black narrow street, *Soi* 5 ½. It was more than a block from the traffic noise of Bangkok's major thoroughfare, Rama IV. Here roadway din was little more than the whisper made by the clouds of mosquitoes rising from the sewers placed here and there over the filled in klongs - the once navigable waterways that crisscrossed most of the original City of Bangkok. Now asphalt covered, they were all that remained of the once exotic beauty in this grim residential area where large rats jockeyed for territory along side poor workers, drug addicts and shop stall owners who moved there from impoverished countryside villages.

Major Ren's team blended into the background of the crumbling, soon-to-be demolished building. They carried their silenced weapons up, ready to move forward towards their target for the evening's operation. Just before they struck, Ren halted them for a final situation assessment.

"Looks good from here," reported the team sniper, Rocky, from his rooftop perch. Army, the closest team member to the target, concurred.

Ren nodded, then whispered into his throat mike, "On my command."

"*Lo Ban*, (boss) hold positions," came an immediate response from Rocky over their encrypted network.

"What's happening?" Ren responded, looking around.

"Six armed men approaching from Rama IV."

"Identify?"

"Standby."

"Unknown," came Rocky's reply with an added, "Another six in reserve and five 4x4's positioned on Rama IV

9

just north of the soi (small street); They're all dark green, no vehicle markings."

"Roger," Ren answered. Then to the others in his group he again whispered into his throat mike, "Pull back to Rally Position and hold."

Three clicks from each team member acknowledged the change in plans. They faded silently into the gloom of the deserted soi, away from the target.

Ren continued to watch from his concealed position, as six black clad, balaclava wearing, fit young men silently moved past his hiding place and positioned themselves to enter their target building. He observed one of them raise his fist and sharply lowered it. Instantly the ground floor door crashed open and the team was inside. A muffled scream, shouting in Thai, the sound of furniture overturning and then of bodies being dragged across the floor. These were the only noises in the night. Then nothing. Even the normally loud mongrel soi dogs that roamed these streets knew to keep quiet.

Two minutes later, three hooded prisoners with tie-taped wrists were herded from the building and frog-marched back along the soi under tight security to the waiting vehicles. Ren's sniper-spotter team leader, Lieutenant Pei Ming, reported that they roughly loaded one prisoner per vehicle and immediately spirited them away into the dark.

The lookout position Ren's team occupied atop the four-story shop-house pharmacy building at the intersection of the soi and Rama IV gave them a God-like vantage point. Sniper, Tang Lei, 'Rock Pile' or Rocky for short, watched them disappear, then added over the radio, "These guys are pretty good boss, even the tail-lights of the vehicle were blacked-out."

As the convoy of 4X4's turned a corner and disappeared from view, Pei asked Ren what everyone on the team was thinking. "How did those guys get here before us?"

Earlier that day the Royal Thai police in Bangkok had kicked off "Operation Lock Down the City, Raid the Bandit's Nests." It was a crackdown on crime with a parade of several thousand officers on horseback, motorcycles and on foot. The raid Ren's team had just witnessed did not appear to be part of that public relations effort which yielded 139 suspects, none of whom turned out to be involved in the Temple bombing that had happened the previous week. This was something else. It was a professional snatch operation.

Ren's team was in Thailand to support Project FORWARD operations until further notice. They were dispatched there based on solid operational intelligence, that came directly from the PLA (People's Liberation Army) Special Operations Command.

"Someone will pay for this embarrassment, and it's not going to be us," Ren said quietly to Pei as he scratched at the old white scar on his hand. After Action Reporting was seldom complimentary to the lead officer. He had reviewed operations that ended badly. Now he knew that he had a double handicap: finding the original targets for the night and clearing his name.

Five Days Earlier

Hundreds of visitors pay daily visits to the Erawan Shrine. It is sacred to Hindus and Buddhists alike and especially popular at the end of a workday. Dozens of food stalls dot the surrounding area along with flower vendors selling the beautiful Thai flower garlands called *phuang malai* that are used to adorn the four-faced Brahma statue just inside the gated worship area. The air is always filled with the thick, cloying sweet aroma of sandalwood joss sticks smoldering in the sand filled urns scattered around the temple area. The pungent smell of food grilling at nearby

11

vendor stalls further adds to the festive, yet exotic ambiance for visitors.

On that Monday evening, August 17, there was nothing special happening at the shrine, just another time to pray, reflect and remember loved ones with joss sticks, offerings and meditation. That was until a few moments after 7:00 PM when body parts, shrapnel, atomized bone, and blood once belonging to hundreds of peaceful visitors cascaded into one of the busiest intersections in Bangkok.

The backpack bomb that exploded was filled with three kilograms of TNT and placed near the photogenic shrine. It was indiscriminate with its destruction. There were twenty dead, over a hundred injured. The victims of this violence came from numerous countries but had one thing in common, all appeared to be Asian, more specifically Chinese.

Thai Police investigators pieced together the minutes before the explosion using dozens of CCTV cameras in the area. They quickly identified several suspects, a few of whom were promptly arrested. After several days of follow-up work, what had appeared initially to be the work of a small group of dissidents turned into a maze of conflicting theories, suspects and motivations. The only thing certain was that Thai-Chinese relations had been injured and hundreds of innocent lives destroyed or at least, disrupted. Uyghur terrorists were suspected.

*****

For several years, the Chinese government had globally operated what they termed Project FORWARD to locate, arrest, render or neutralize all activist Uyghur's inside and outside China. There were Project officers assigned to each People's Embassy throughout the region as well as all major Chinese cities. When necessary outside the motherland, Special Operations Commandos were secretly called in to conduct raids, extract suspects and return them to China.

Ghost Shadows, the highly secretive PLA Special Warfare unit, was used only in extremely high value situations. The bombing in central Bangkok was one that certainly called for their involvement.

Major Ren's orders had been very specific, "Uyghur's are trying to put pressure directly on Thailand to stop business and military cooperation with us. It is too important to our Foreign Policy to allow this to happen," General Zhu had warned, then continued, "Over the past three years all Project FORWARD activities were managed from here at Central Command in Beijing. Maintaining stability in the far Western provinces is a high priority for MSS (Ministry of *State Security*), PLA (*Peoples Liberation Army*) and PSB (Public Security Bureau)."

Ren answered, "Yes sir, I'm sure everyone in these agencies takes their work controlling and rounding up Uyghur dissidents very seriously."

Zhu nodded but continued, "A major and highly visible failure would produce ugly consequences for those responsible."

Since that discussion, the Ghost Shadows had been on 'stand-by' and then activated the day after the bombing. They were quickly infiltrated into Thailand on China Southern Airlines in civilian disguise. All their specialized equipment was concurrently sent via diplomatic pouch to the Bangkok PRC (People's Republic of China) Embassy. An MSS safe house, near the Patpong 'red light district' in central Bangkok, had been readied for their use.

0145 Hrs. PRC Bangkok Embassy

A few minutes after the abortive raid and the unexpected 'snatch', Colonel Wang Ping, Project FORWARD's MSS Case Officer, in a secure Chinese

13

Embassy conference room, also asked a similar question, "How could this happen?"

The other intelligence officers around the table remained silent. Ping continued, "Ghost Shadows were on station, on time, our Project FORWARD intelligence accurate. How did the Thais get there before us?" He looked, in turn, at each of his six-member Bangkok station operations team. No response.

"We'll have to answer for this situation," he continued, "All of us."

They had all heard this type of speech before from Comrade Ping and knew that speaking up would bring misery to the unlucky one who raised a negative point, so all remained expressionless, heads bowed, to take the venom that they knew was poised to spew from his mouth. Ping was the worst type of new cadre bureaucrat - quick to steal success or shed any failure like a snake's new skin. While not unlike modern case officers in Western agencies like the CIA (Central Intelligence Agency), this "me first; Party second" type officer had become a relatively new phenomenon in the Chinese Secret Service.

Ping had worked hard to get his position. He was not the offspring of senior party members and daily strove to conform to whatever new edicts were formulated to keep cadres engaged with the latest thinking from the Central Committee. He made sure that embassy hierarchy first and foremost considered him a 'loyal party member' even though he was far from that ideal.

Pressure from the FORWARD program had pushed Uyghur activists to leave China for Central Asia, Turkey and several other Asian countries including Thailand, Indonesia and Malaysia. In these places the sizable Muslim populations gave Uyghur's support and shelter to continue their work of carving out what was once their ancestral territory from the People's Republic. South Thailand and its long running anti-

14

government insurgency was another area into which dissidents could seek a 'bolt-hole' and disappear.

Ping knew that if he did not round them up, wherever they might be, especially since the bombing, it was a sure way to get sent to Tibet to chase 'border hoppers" or dissident monks. Either prospect did not appeal to him. He continually pushed his staff to develop a continuing inflow of new sources that would identify potential targets, dry up support from local groups, and generally make life untenable for Uyghur's who might, for whatever reasons, end-up in Thailand.

0200 Hrs. Bangkok Safe House

Ren's team returned from the failed raid to their safe house in ones and twos using basic surveillance detection routes (SDR's) hastily established prior to the raid. Their gear had been collected near the rally point by an Embassy MSS asset and delivered back to their location in a small-unmarked van. The team was now unwinding in the 23rd floor penthouse condo. It belonged to a Chinese businessman who used it as a residence for his favorite ex-stripper mistress. The two of them were now conveniently out-of-town on an MSS funded-vacation trip to Macau.

"Hey Boss, some great place. I guess they think we are something special to put us in an apartment like this," Army said.

"Lo Ban, look at this city," Rocky added.

"So many lights, almost like Shanghai," Army said.

"Um, every one a place for our enemy to hide," Ren answered.

"Come on boss, not our fault, someone fucked up the Intel," Rocky answered.

"No difference, we didn't get those bastards. They're still out there."

15

"We'll get em, don't worry about it now, let's have a few beers and relax," Brave chimed in.

"Let's worry about it at the debriefing tomorrow. Beer sounds pretty good now," the last of the six men on the team, Strong, added.

"Okay, let's get some food. According to Director Wu, White Pigeon should still be open. He says that their beer is always very cold," Ren answered.

"Come on Pei, time to eat," Army pleaded.

"Not hungry now, I'll go for a run, see you there later," Lieutenant Pei answered as she continued lacing up her cross trainers.

She was the newest member of the team, its only female and the Party Political Officer. With classic Chinese beauty, she often acted more independently than her male counterparts. Though a fully qualified and loyal team member, she often got results differently than the others. Getting through the demanding training while maintaining her poise and well put together body was a major accomplishment.

Consequently they seldom pushed her to join in the horseplay and drinking enjoyed by the others. Rumor of her parent's high Party positions also served to keep close scrutiny of her actions at bay. Ren watched her closely as teamwork was more important than Party correctness when on a mission.

The team waved to her and headed for the elevator. The restaurant was a short walk across the crowded tourist and neon light filled street, under the Sky Train track and down the narrow, poorly lit soi. A cloud of noise, jokes and pushing and jostling followed them all the way to the back booth of the long narrow eating spot. Wu, their MSS Case Officer, had earlier told Ren it was the best late night Chinese food in Bangkok. They hoped, especially after the CF *(cluster fuck)* that evening, that his recommendation on food was better than his operational intelligence.

They each had several beers to start. After six delicious heaping platters of chopped pigeon and lettuce, lo mein noodles, sizzling beef, bok choi with oyster sauce, Shanghai dumplings and steamed fish with ginger and scallions, the verdict was that Wu should be a food critic and not a spy. The food was outstanding. The beer mugs frosted and the beer cold, just like his Intel.

Two hours later the place they had saved for Pei Ming was still empty as they fought over the last scraps from the now mostly empty platters.

Lumpini Park

Pei had followed the noisy group out of the building by a few minutes and turned toward the 142-acre Lumpini Park. She dodged the late evening bar traffic that was clogging the streets and sois around the condo they were using as a base. Wearing a simple figure- hugging spandex outfit and cross trainers she jogged slowly away from Patpong's lights. With no pedestrian overpass, it took almost ten minutes to get across the street that was filled with chaotic evening traffic and into the park. Even at this time of night the park was still jammed with walkers, tai chi groups, weight lifters and assorted people out for a late night stroll in the cooler, slightly less polluted air.

As the walkers on the paths thinned out, she jogged deeper into the park maintaining her steady six-kilometer per hour pace: four laps around the tree filled park was her plan. On the final lap she noticed that three young Thai men had begun following her. She quickened her pace as she reached the far side of the park and further increased her speed for the last dark section of the trail. Suddenly, two more Thais appeared in front of her blocking the trail. One brandished a knife.

"Hi honey. Far from Patpong, aren't you?" one shouted.

"Come on, we won't hurt you. We just want to fuck ya," the other laughed.

The three running from behind were quickly upon her. She stopped, turned and attacked. Within seconds the three behind her were in a heap on the ground moaning and writhing. The one who made some half-hearted Muay Thai defensive moves would never use his right arm properly again. One of the other two likely had a mild concussion and the other some major knee joint damage.

She turned to face the other two. The one with the knife came first. He lunged at her with the blade down and low. She stepped away from the thrust, locked his arm, turned it against him and pushed the six–inch blade into his stomach. The look of surprise on his face told the story. He silently collapsed holding the handle with both hands trying to remove it. She then lashed out with her left leg and solidly connected with the throat of the final assailant. He dropped, gagging, and within seconds was unconscious.

Satisfied that all the attackers were disabled, she scanned the area for witnesses. Finding none, she turned and began her jog back to the condo. She could feel the adrenaline begin to drain from her body and a slight tremor pass though it. *Glad the others aren't here to see my weakness*, she thought as the shaking began to subside.

"Strike first, strike hard, strike often," was the unofficial mantra of the Ghost Shadow team. Unlucky for the Thai toughs, she was well practiced in all the martial arts. Once again her study of Wu Shu since the age of six proved invaluable. She was an All China National Champion at eleven. Even her slight build did not deter competing against, and besting males twice her size. Physically and mentally she

18

was superior in all forms of the martial arts. She still lacked the combat experience of the others, but was slowly closing the gap.

As her action induced stress slowed down, she realized there was some blood spattered on her arm that needed cleaning and her blood-soiled pants would need to be replaced before dinner. Hopefully, the darkness in the park and along side streets would continue to be her friend on the return trip home. Drawing attention to herself was not a good idea just now.

I need to be more careful handling the knife next time. Clothing is expensive. He won't be happy, but maybe I can talk Major Ren into some replacement trousers tomorrow? she thought, as the beginning of a smile crossed her otherwise expressionless ivory face.

Chapter 2

MSS Safe House- Bangkok

After a few short hours of rest, Major Ren reported promptly at 7:00 AM, the appointed meeting time, for the mission debriefing at yet another, but much smaller, MSS safe house located five blocks from the PRC Embassy. Contrary to instructions, he had his team set up surveillance at the location three hours earlier for added security as well as their continued operational training. For the meeting he wore grey trousers, a black t-shirt and lace-up black runners topped off with a black baseball cap. While worn to minimize surveillance, they accentuated his well muscled chest and arms.

Ren was no stranger to reviewing after action reports. Dozens of clandestine insertions over the past three years had toughened him against overly aggressive political comrades seeking power or self promotion, lazy senior officers or cadres promoting their personal agendas and hardline officers without an understanding of the complexity and nuance of special operations.

"Good morning comrades," he said, upon entering the cramped first floor room. All the surrounding rooms had been given over to highly sensitive electronic countermeasures and signal blocking equipment. The other attendees nodded in greeting but remained silent, waiting for Wang Ping to set the tone for the meeting.

"Good morning Major, please sit," he said pointing to the only unoccupied chair. "You are very casual today, I see."

Ren nodded and slid his well toned, agile body into the only remaining seat.

"Give us your assessment of the failure," Ping harshly began.

Ren's unlined face did not register surprise or irritation at the outburst. He calmly answered.

"It was not a failure or an accident that the other team arrived at that time. It was a precision operation, rehearsed and executed flawlessly. They had advance knowledge of the location and of those inside."

"Was your team not late in executing the operation?" Ping challenged.

Ren looked directly at him without blinking and said, "We were on time. There was a leak somewhere in your side of the operation, that is what I think."

Ping continued to challenge him: "Your execution was faulty, you moved too slowly, timidly."

Ren calmly repeated, "You have a leak. My team is probably at risk because of it. It must be plugged."

"Do not blame the plan, it was perfect, it was your fault and I have so reported to your headquarters," Ping smirked.

Ren leaned back in the chair and answered, "You should remember Comrade, our standard procedure on operations of this sensitivity is to use our own encrypted GoPro© cameras to transmit real-time data from the field. Time stamped video has been reviewed at our headquarters. Everything was correct, altering a report to place blame were it does not belong has no place in this discussion."

Ping stood, mouth open. "You are lying, you will be demoted, and maybe your entire team arrested as foreign agents. You have become rogues. Regardless of your family history, you will answer for your failures here," he sputtered.

Ren quietly seethed at the reference to his family but held his tongue and stared directly at him. The other MSS attendees from Ping's Station's Project FORWARD's team, looked away from the exchange.

"The one who leaked the plan is the real risk here. He needs to be located and eliminated immediately," Ren responded.

21

"Arrest him," Ping shouted to his team.

No one moved. They knew of Ren's reputation and none wanted to taste the sting of his wrath. Rumors swirled about the Ghost Shadows and their exploits on behalf of the country, their leader a solitary force.

Ren slowly stood, looked around the table of staff officers, rolled his shoulders and smiling said, "None of you want to do this."

Bodies shifted in their seats but no one made a move to stand.

"We will find the guilty party, Comrade Ping," Ren said as he backed toward the door. "You might not like what happens when we do."

Then he was gone.

Wang Ping glared at his staff. "You are useless, get out of my sight. Out!"

While he might not be able to physically hold Ren, there were other ways, maybe even better ones, to deal with him. *Ren is an outsider here, I will bend him to my will*, he thought.

He shouted after the retreating officers, "I want Major Ren and his team placed under immediate and close surveillance. Contact Internal Security! We have a major risk with this Ghost Shadows team. They are out of control. I want them sent home immediately, under guard."

The other MSS officers hesitated to comply. None wanted to risk having a broken bone or fractured skull trying to do what Ping had demanded earlier.

"Section Chief Zhou, I would like a word," Ping shouted after the departing officers. "Remain here."

*****

Doom on you Comrade Ping, Ren thought as he smoothly moved from the building and disappeared into the morning traffic on Suhkimvit Road. The MSS station

22

personnel made their way back to the Embassy except for those unlucky enough to be assigned to Ren's post-meeting surveillance. They knew blame would be theirs should he disappear.

Ren had been in the PLA long enough and had moved up through the party ranks quickly enough to understand how to use his party ties and relationships to protect himself and his team from unwarranted problems from the likes of Colonel Ping. There had been other times when party cadres had tried to blame their failures on Ren or his team. Those attempts, like the recent one in Africa, had failed and it would happen again now.

Ren's grandfather had marched from Yunnan with Chairman Mao and had fought along side him against the white army throughout the early days of purifying the party. He was a hero of the PLA. Even though the Cultural Revolution had more than somewhat tarnished his name, the family was eventually rehabilitated, if not made whole physically.

The Party allowed Ren to attend a prestigious military school and become a party member. He was now trusted with an elite PLA force to defend the motherland. *If he could not fend off the likes of a Colonel Ping, he deserved the fate being engineered. In order to do so, he would first learn more about the Colonel; then take the appropriate action.*

Ren carefully followed a lengthy SDR (*Surveillance Detection Route*) back from the meeting site, walking through shopping centers, the jumble of markets filled with counterfeit goods; even taking the Sky Train and two motorbike taxis through the heavy morning traffic on Wireless Road. Two hours later he emerged from the maze of Patpong streets and disappeared into the rear door of the condo safe house.

The team was all sitting around the living room except for Zhang Yong, *Brave,* who had been assigned counter-surveillance for Ren. A few minutes later he rushed into the room, gave thumbs up indicating no MSS surveillance, grabbed some water and slid into an easy chair near the bar.

While Brave got settled, Ren began to fill them in on the meeting with Ping.

After the debriefing, Pei finally told the group about her little run-in with the toughs the night before. There was cheering until Ren silenced them. "You need to be less provocative, don't draw attention to yourself like that."

"I did nothing, just jogging along when they attacked," she said, more forcefully than necessary. Ren's head came up sharply at the ferocity of her retort.

"Are you sure nobody saw the attack?" Ren probed.

"Very sure," she said in a more subdued voice, "and I don't think they will ever tell anyone they were beaten-up by a woman. For me, I think it was 'wrong place, wrong time'."

"No, for them!" Rocky laughed. So did everyone else, this time, including Ren.

"Major, we need to talk about a new jogging outfit, mine seems to be ruined," Pei laughed, holding up the bloodied outfit.

Everyone in the room hooted with laughter. "Those poor babies…"

"Since you're sure the attack was not mission related, my congratulations. I think last night's training effort is worth at least a replacement outfit," Ren said smiling warmly, for the first time that morning.

"All right, now, let's talk about what we know about the other situation, the one we are here to deal with," said Ren.

Turning toward his surveillance team he asked, "Was there any coverage on the meeting this morning?"

"Lot's of watchers out there boss," Rocky reported.

"Three different teams covered your meeting place. One was using video. The rest did not use very good tradecraft I would say," added Brave. "But, even with you wearing the ball cap this morning boss, they probably got some clear shots of you."

Ren shrugged, "Can't be helped."

"Since they are not trying to hide what they were doing, they must feel pretty safe. Probably the Thai security service," Pei Ming added.

"Or our local MSS team is not very careful, or deliberately sloppy," Ren commented.

"Boss, they had one guy follow you from the meeting but he couldn't find another motorbike when you did at the market. You lost him and nobody took his place." Army added, "I got a good picture of him."

Ren said, "let's have a look at it."

Army passed him the camera. Ren studied the photos, nodded and returned it.

"I believe that whatever Ping has been doing is penetrated by the Thais. Everyone at the meeting is very likely compromised. That location is no longer safe for us," Ren said. The team members nodded agreement.

"So what do we do?" Army asked.

"Were you able to follow the watchers when they departed the meeting? Ren asked.

"Come on boss, you taught us better than that," added Army, feigning hurt feelings. "Sure, we got three of the four going back to the Thai Security and Operations Command (ISOC) Headquarters."

"If ISOC knows about what Ping is doing, you can be sure that the American's know as well," Ren replied.

"Yeah, but could it be that easy? How would they know about the operation just from watching Ping or his team?" Pei asked.

"Who wants to answer that?" Ren asked, then added.

"Watching everyone and using audio penetrations does not get them into the planning that easily. What's a better way?" he coached.

"Someone on the inside," Rocky answered.

"Exactly."

Chapter 3

Making of the Ghost Shadows

The current Ghost Shadows team, now in Bangkok, had been together since the final selection testing was completed more than two years earlier. As China's 'best of the best' elite warriors they occupied a special status within both the political and military community.

Everyone who knew of their existence, wanted to bask in their successes and the special place they occupied as the 'sharp point of the spear' to protect the Chinese motherland. MSS, Party and PLA senior officers fought continually over control of any operations using them.

Being housed in a remote area of the Guangzhou Military Region Headquarters facility also set them apart from the prying eyes of the PLA General Staff. They were seldom used so while the Central Military Commission certainly knew of their existence, they did not attract much regular scrutiny.

Ren's Spec Ops (*Special Operations*) career began when he was transferred into the Guangzhou Military Region Special Force Unit, that had developed a SEAL type capability in the early 2000's. Several high visibility operations on MSS projects had solidified his role as top operator, tactician and leader.

When the PLA was looking for a commander for the new and most elite unit, he was a natural to head it. He had excelled at the PLA National Defense University; Combat training, languages and various Party and political training programs. He was being groomed for key leadership positions when first assigned to support the MSS in a daring operation in Kashmir that he carried out skillfully. After the success of that highly sensitive mission, his future was all but written as a key Spec Ops Warrior.

Before being appointed as commander of the Shadows, he insisted on taking every physical test, skill assessment and training that the other team members would be required to meet before accepting the senior position. He excelled in every phase of the testing and not unexpectedly his scores, were 'top of the pile.' Unlike many PLA officers, he was a *lead from the front* commander.

Team members were forbidden to say anything to outsiders but they all knew that several Spec Ops operators who tried out for the Shadows and failed were sent by the PLA, as a consolation prize, to the Elite Warrior Olympics in Jordan. For three years in a row, these second tier individuals bested soldiers from around the world taking the top three places in the "Best Elite Warriors in the World" competition even though they did not qualify for the Ghost Shadows.

Each of Ren's team members also brought special skills along with being a top Spec Warrior. Army, for example, could open any lock, steal any vehicle, and fly almost any aircraft. Rocky had the uncanny ability to defeat any bomb, trap or weapon system. He also was the best diver on the team. Strong was an acknowledged computer expert and communication genius. He excelled at mountain climbing and free-fall parachuting. Brave was the master of surveillance, disguise, and the medical specialist. Pei was a linguist as well as an IT and intelligence analyst and martial arts expert all wrapped into one very shapely package.

Ren often conducted group meetings to get everyone on the team to think about their tactical situation and come up with 'on the fly' solutions as a situation changed. Three years ago he would not have thought to let the team members plan their own operations. The PLA did not train its soldiers, even most Special Forces troops, that way. It was an operational trip to the USA that changed his approach dramatically.

It began when Project FRIENDSHIP, an initiative to recover stolen government funds, requested Ren for a special operation in San Francisco, California. His English was near perfect so he and two other Ghost Shadows were tasked with kidnapping the former Deputy Minister of Finance, Gao Dang, who had fled China after amassing an estimated $150 million dollars in bribes. Dang had invested the funds in American shopping centers, hotels and beachfront property. The Central Committee wanted the money returned and an example made of him for other senior Party members and cadres.

Three days after Ren arrived in California, former Minister Dang disappeared from his guarded estate in Santa Barbara and was quietly but securely brought to the upscale yacht harbor and placed on his 56-foot sailboat, *The Free Market*. Yacht Club members waved to them as the boat slipped its lines and motored out for an evening cruise. Three hours later, Dang was aboard a COSCO container ship sailing for Ningbo as it cleared U.S. coastal waters.

Ren made sure Dang's family became extremely cooperative after his sudden departure. They followed Ren's instructions; set up new bank accounts with numbers that Ren provided and began unwinding his convoluted investments. They deposited the proceeds into specific Bank of China and other foreign accounts. A local Bay area deep cover MSS Officer was assigned to insure their continued compliance and a possible eventual return to China, if they did not. Ren learned the intricacies of international finance and its controls to make sure nothing was overlooked in Dang's horde of hidden assets.

When Dang was on-board the container ship, under guard, and the family compliant, Ren flew back to China, the way he had come, on a regular commercial China Eastern Airlines flight from San Francisco International Airport.

29

While waiting for the flight to be boarded he found a book left in the gate area that changed his way of thinking about Special Warfare. At first he thought it might be a US government provocation, a trap ---leaving secret information --- for him to find. It quickly became obvious that it was just a commercial book another passenger had finished and discarded. It was the story of Richard Marcinko, a U.S Navy SEAL: *Rogue Warrior*.

He spent the entire fourteen-hour trip devouring every word of Captain "Dick" Marcinko, founder of SEAL Team 6's, story of his special brand of unconventional warfare. Even after completing similar training in China, Ren found the American's comments well reasoned. Many of the stories he told mirrored Ren's frustrations with the bureaucracy of the PLA and its use of special operations troops such as himself. Whether he could successfully use *Dickie Marcinko's* tactics and back channel connections the same way in China would remain to be seen.

The physical training he already had devised for his team sounded equal to what he read about in *Rogue Warrior*. It was how teams were used and leadership tactics that were very different. While he had studied all the major tacticians from Sun Tzu, Clausewitz, U.S. Grant, Fidel Castro, Alexander the Great, Che Guevara, General Giap, George Patton, and Thucydides to Mao Zedong: Captain Marcinko had a unique vision for the use of ultra-elite, not just special operations forces. Ren felt that the Shadows also needed to be 'shooters and looters'…very unconventional intelligence collectors and killers… but in a very focused, Chinese way.

He completed the book without eating or sleeping then vowed that he would use as many of the Rogue Warrior principles as possible to, not only bring his team up to SEAL Team 6 operational standards but, surpass them. He did not believe that decadent Western 'team building' through alcohol use and debauchery was necessary to the same extent as 'the shooters and looters' of SEAL Team 6, but tight unit cohesion, multiple skills, resourcefulness and Chinese self-reliance needed to be built-up.

Working around orders and directives to get results using personal connections would also take time to set up. Strict adherence to rules and Party discipline were not as easily circumvented as they appeared to be in the U.S. Navy. Likewise funding 'off the books' projects, equipment, travel and operational 'necessities' without having PLA funds was difficult. It was something that Ren had yet to master, although he already had ideas and taken some steps toward making things happen.

Ren disposed of Marcinko's book in the aircraft toilet just before landing. He did not wish to be associated with anything considered Western just yet. He did, however, memorize large portions of Marcinko's doctrine, and colorful language. Not that Chinese does not have 'earthiness" in it but **Rogue Warrior** oozed profanity the way a scuba diving regulator exchanges carbon dioxide for oxygen.

He believed that like SEAL Team 6, his team needed 'killers' --- men who could and would kill or pop an enemy --- 'killers' were essential to his unit being effective, so he recruited them. His Shadows also needed to be able to conduct surveillance and 'snoop' on potential or actual targets. Stealth in collecting intelligence or stealing whatever was necessary for mission success ---looting--- was the final skill. Without each of these traits plus additional skills, team members would be useless. Ren fully believed that the Ghost Shadows were now world class, having proved themselves on multiple missions.

Ren didn't blindly follow untested ideas from the book he found. He tested each idea after thoroughly thinking through how to win at all costs. The concept of "You will not Fail" and "What would Dickie do?" set the stage for remaking the Shadows into an even more lethal weapon for the Chinese Army.

Hard training to prevent "things from becoming a goat fuck" became Ren's mantra. It became his new internal signpost for planning, training and conducting operations. Ghost Shadows became better and better for it. Unlike SEAL Team 6, Ren had a responsibility to the Party as well as the army. As a Party member whatever he did was supposed to further the interests of the party first, everything else was subordinate. But, getting the PLA assigned job done, whatever it required, was all that really mattered when nano-seconds were often the difference between success and death.

Following this approach, Sun Tzu rather than Mao's political teachings were more important to follow. Perhaps some of Mao's early days of military leadership were valid but his thoughts regarding Party First clashed with Ren's spec war realities. There was not always time for class struggle or the dialectic when a knife was at your throat.

Ren also knew that even though Lieutenant Pei Ming was superbly qualified in martial arts, IT, intelligence and languages, she was nevertheless the political officer for the team and obligated to report disciplinary infractions to the Party as well as Internal Security. As far as the Party was concerned, her primary job was to observe and report deviations from Party discipline. If she did not believe his approach was *"following the correct road"* it was her duty to report it.

Pei had competed with the males on the Shadows on an equal basis and had secured her place on the team without any Party interference. Her parents watched her progress from a distance and were ever ready to shield her should she stumble in this high-risk world she had chosen. So far, she had not required their assistance.

Pei and Ren always walked a fine line between doing what was right and what was necessary. But now, in

Bangkok, the 'Dickie' in Ren would find out who was causing the problem and eliminate them quickly and very quietly. Ren's style was not 100% the Marcinko's 'Shooters and Looters' of SEAL Team 6's 'hop and pop' approach. Nevertheless, the MSS "bad guys" and Tangos (the U.S. military phonetic code "T" for terrorists") would be either in their trophy bag or dead. It was their choice.

The Same Morning, Beijing, SOC...Special Operations Command... Headquarters

"It seems that Major Ren is running afoul of our friends in the Service (MSS)," said General Zhu, head of the Special Operations Command in Beijing.

"It seems that the Service, specifically, Colonel Ping, is blaming him for the operational failure last evening," answered Colonel Li, Ren's immediate supervisor.

"Did he fail?"

"No General, he did not. Our belief is that there was a lapse at MSS that permitted the Thai and American forces to seize the terrorists before us. Ren reports that his surveillance indicates lax security and over confidence within the local embassy staff. His operational activities video also confirms his reporting."

"What do we do about Colonel Ping's demand for recall of Ghost Shadows?"

"We do nothing. I suggest that we allow Major Ren to try finding the 'leak' as he calls it while continuing to be available should additional suspect targets be identified."

"I agree," said General Zhu. "Also, send any further terrorist sightings directly to him. The MSS station in Bangkok does not need to know everything we are doing."

Colonel Li nodded smiling, "Yes General. Major Ren will not disappoint you."

Within hours of their meeting, a PLA asset just across the border in the northern Burmese casino city of Mongla, reported that preparations were being made by some rag-tag remnants of the Shan State Army to retrieve a group of hastily organized border crossers. The PLA military intelligence case officer who received the tip was provided additional information that made him believe the group in question was very likely Uyghur.

Thirty minutes later, Ren had his orders from Colonel Li. "Interdict, capture and transport the terrorists to Chinese territory."

Bangkok

Borrowing from the Marcinko's playbook, Ren announced to his team, "Let's rock and roll. Time to take down some Tangos."

They hooted until Ren calmed them as they quickly assembled in the spacious living room. "Look around one last time, because when we leave today, we won't be coming back. Our position here is compromised."

He was not worried about the audio and video surveillance in the apartment, as Strong had disabled it when they arrived. It was now the MSS watchers that had not yet been identified that needed to be neutralized.

He quickly told the team the details of Ping's earlier threats at the safe house during the after action meeting. "We need fewer people watching what we do," Ren told them.

"Okay, we pack up and head out to Alternative Site 1," Ren continued, then added, "Pei, come with me. We need to talk."

The balance of the team began packing their gear, cleaning weapons once again and preparing the apartment for their rapid departure. They wiped down all the surfaces they had touched, cleaned the drains and bagged all garbage. The litter and waste would be disposed of along the way.

Ren and Pei moved to the large balcony, faced away from the street and Ren continued. "Remember Sun Tzu's approach to a situation like this?"

She paused then responded, "The best course is to attack the enemies plans, failing that, his alliances, and beyond that, subdue him without fighting. Drive a wedge between Ping and his headquarters, disrupt his operations and attain our goal of finding those responsible for the bombing."

"I could not have said it better. Flexibility in how we move forward with these principles is our best avenue," Ren answered.

"Thank you, Major" Pei smiled.

"Wait here a few hours then take Brave and Strong and follow us to Alternative 1. We will already be gone but set it up as a secure base and await further orders from me. While we are gone your team is going to find out who is leaking this damaging information."

Then quoting *Dickie* once again, he added with a smile forming on his face, "the rest of us are going hunting."

She nodded in agreement and quietly said, "I will do what is necessary to resolve the matter."

Chapter 4

CIA Station Bangkok

"When do we tell the Chinese we have them?" asked the CIA's COS (Chief of Station).

"Later today, I think," answered his Thai ISOC (Internal Security Operations Command) counterpart.

"We should have gotten more from the three terrorists you picked up last night but time will tell when we roll up the others in their network. If we had more time, they would have been more forthcoming. As it is, we can't parade them in public just yet," answered the COS.

"In a few days, the Chinese will be pleased no matter what they look like."

"How soon before the other ones will be trying to cross the border up North?

"My BPP (Border Patrol Police) Commander says he has troops at all major crossing points in that sector now. If they attempt to flee to Burma, we will have them in short order."

"Okay if our Military Attaché, Colonel Richardson, tags-along with your guys to observe?"

"Of course, I'm sure he will find the exercise interesting."

Going North

"Why are they going North?" asked Brave. "I thought they would go South to get help from Malaysian terrorists."

"Looks like they have something else in mind. The Burmese also often fight with Thai troops; maybe they want to help each other. There are also many soldiers and police in the South fighting the Muslims, maybe they think its too hard to get through," answered Ren.

"Maybe they are just being used as cover for moving some opium or methamphetamines out of Shan State," Rocky answered.

"Right. Up there, anything is possible. But, we have our orders. We'll know when we get there...so let's go get some Tangos."

Within an hour of leaving the apartment, Ren's team was aboard a Chinese cargo flight, and soon thereafter readying their equipment for touchdown in the Northern Thai city of Chang Mai. Colonel Li's orders from Beijing had smoothed the mission preparations and coordination that the team had been working on since moving to the Alternative 1 site.

PLA intelligence assets at Bangkok's Don Mueang domestic airport had made space on the short flight for Ren's team and all their equipment without the MSS station being any the wiser. They were very careful to avoid venturing near the Royal Thai Air Force section of the sprawling facility. All communications were kept strictly within PLA channels.

The coordinates provided to Ren on the Tangos border crossing location near *Mae Sai* city were still hours north. They would need to move quickly as in this part of the world, darkness began about 6:00 PM.

Ren was told that the BPP would be in place to ambush the terrorists by the time they arrived. PLA support personnel at the Bangkok airport made sure they had nondescript transportation waiting outside the Chang Mai cargo terminal. Even though it was only a canvas backed carryall truck, they were able to load everything on it and the truck eased out into the slow moving traffic within minutes of touchdown.

On the Thai-Burma Border

The six-vehicle BPP convoy snaked its way north through the evening traffic on Highway 118 toward the border. Three kilometers from the small border city they turned west on a little used jungle trek. They would soon leave the vehicles and advance through the light jungle terrain to the coordinates crudely torn from the memory of the weakest of the three Bangkok captives.

"Right on time," Rocky whispered to Army as they watched the dull green and camo BPP 4X4's turn onto the rough red clay trail that led into the darkening double canopied gloom. They had just settled into their concealed position moments before. If it were not for the fact that the 10-man PLA Special Operation team was training in Burma's lower Shan State, the Ghost Shadows would not have been on time. The PLA Spec Ops team that infiltrated across the porous border for the link-up had provided manpower, logistics and exfiltration support for any prisoners after their hastily constructed attack.

Over the past two years, Ren's team had spent time conducting similar mock evasions, covert shadowing, ambush and counter-ambush exercises against Burmese troops. They also tested new ballistic clothing for jungle wear on these cross-border covert exercises. Ren's team was very familiar with the current terrain. Several of the PLA troops assigned to them had unsuccessfully tested for and would probably test again to join the Shadows. Their performance evaluations for tonight's operation would make a major difference for their future. Like Ren's troops, they would give their all to successfully complete any assigned mission but tonight, their sole motivation was to capture the terrorists that were trying to destroy their country.

*****

The rag-tag column of Uyghurs and Thais had followed a narrow stream through the ever darkening foliage as they skirted Highway 118, crossing under it about a kilometer south of their present position. Their hurried departure and journey upcountry from Bangkok in the covered logging truck had been brutal. Heat and lack of water had taken a toll on the untrained civilians designated as terrorists by Beijing.

"Another two kilometers," the Thai guide whispered to Yusup, the Uyghur's group leader. He nodded and passed the word to the others.

"Time to be very quiet," Yusup, added.

The trail continued to narrow as the vines and trailers began clogging the seldom-used animal trail skirting the meter-wide slow flowing waterway. The two young females in the column, Patime and Aynur, were starting to slow the group's progress in spite of their determination. Sleep depravation and insects were taking their toll. The column was stretched out over a hundred meters with Thai guides at either end when Ren's force began its attack.

The skinny rear-guard Thai never heard the PLA soldier. It was as if a magician had waved his wand and said, "now you see him…now you don't." The Thai simply vanished and was quickly tie-taped and mouth secured. Another soldier took-up his end of the column position and quickly closed up the gap with the next in line.

Four of the six in the group were taken in a similar manner by other PLA soldiers before the lead Thai guide and Yusup called a halt to wait for the now, non-existent column to catch up. While they looked around for stragglers, Ren and two camouflaged soldiers materialized out of the darkness, weapons drawn. With nowhere to run and weapons not 'at the ready' they raised their hands in submission. The Thai tried to bolt for the jungle but was cut down with a burst from Ren's silenced machine pistol. Yusup stared wide-eyed at the bullet riddled bloody aftermath, a silent scream frozen in his throat.

Ren quickly ordered the PLA troops to dispose of the body and prepare to ex-filtrate the prisoners across the border into Burma. While these preparations were in progress, Ren photographed and fingerprinted each prisoner. They were then to be force-marched to a pre-designated landing zone (LZ) four kilometers inside the Burmese border. The PLA troops had cleared the jungle for the Special Ops modified Harbin Z-19 helicopter extraction. From there, it was then a twelve-minute flight into the safety of Yunnan Military District in China.

Once the Yunnan Spec Ops troops moved out with their prisoners, Ren contacted Rocky and gave the 'go ahead' signal. Within minutes, six large trees along the BPP's jungle trail exploded. They had been carefully wrapped with an old school explosive called Prima-cord. Suddenly huge sections of decapitated trees crashed down on the parked 4X4's and blocked the narrow roadway in three locations and disoriented the rear guards at the jungle trek exit point. Without chain saws and heavy lift equipment, the BPP troopers and their Humvees were stranded. Dozens of steep limestone cliffs made skirting this simple but effective blocking technique impossible. The BPP force was out of the fight until help could be mustered from their base more than an hour south.

As soon as the prisoners were lead away into the darkened jungle, Ren sent a burst transmission to Beijing announcing his results and prisoner photographs. He also signaled for their transportation back to Chang Mai. He then walked back along the trail, obscured any lingering traces of their actions and hurried to meet the other members of his team.

The two successful Shadow groups rendezvoused ten minutes later near the highway bridge. Ren arrived first, immediately followed by the ambush duo. Their transport followed soon after.

"Hey boss, it looks like we gave them a cluster fuck," Rocky laughed.

"Better than a goat fuck for us," Ren answered with a laugh. Then added,

"Good job."

They would be back in Bangkok about the same time the prisoners were safely aboard their flight to the highly secure detention center in Sichuan Province, built especially to house Uyghur terrorists in complete isolation.

*****

Colonel Richardson, U.S. Army Attaché looked at the chaos surrounding the BPP site ambush and knew that it was the not the work of first time amateurs. Real professionals had orchestrated the attack. Maximum damage without casualties, probably cover for the real purpose of them being deployed against the Thais. What that was remained to be seen, but the Uyghurs they came to collect were nowhere to be found.

At the Same Time in Bangkok

Pei's Bangkok team had been busy moving to their new safe-house, securing their equipment, establishing surveillance on the target MSS safe-house and setting up new communications with Beijing and Major Ren. The new safe house at the rear of a ten-story apartment block gave them flexibility to come and go without arousing questions from the other transient dwellers. They would look like just five other poor Chinese trying to eke out a subsistence living on the streets of Bangkok.

"You two get some rest, I'll take first watch on the house," Pei ordered Brave and Strong. "You decide who comes to relieve me at 8:00 PM."

Pei now dressed as an old village charwoman walked slowly from the gate into the sub-soi (alley like street) near the Nana Entertainment center. She carried blue plastic bags filled with juice, rambutans and star fruit along with a model 19 Glock, a high-resolution mini-camera and a secure link radio that were concealed in the folds of her clothing. As a part of their normal equipment a six-inch gravity knife was secured in a leg holster and her personal satellite tracking device battery was newly replaced.

It was a five-block walk from the Shadow's safe house to the MSS location. Google Map® satellite view showed only two entry and egress points from the low slung wooden building. She would have to assess where she could watch both from the same place. Not an easy task when the streets were filled with hundreds of beggars, children playing, prostitutes, and mobile stalls along with organized crime thugs bleeding money from everyone for the privilege of allowing them to make a living on the streets.

Four hours later, Strong slowly ambled down the sub-soi pushing a trishaw water delivery cart. His disguise so effective Pei almost missed his arrival.

"Nice," she mouthed silently, passing him on the narrow sidewalk. "You look just like Jackie Chan."

He grinned.

"Two males still in the house. Arrived at 6:52. Take a quick look at the photos," she said as she slipped him the camera while he pretended to buy some star fruit from one of her blue plastic bags.

He moved on and she continued away from the direction of the safe house. Just then, one of the men she recognized as being from the house came into view. He had come out of a small sub-soi directly in front of her…there must have been a hidden side entrance. She followed. Darkness and overconfidence melded, making him careless and easy to monitor in the narrow streets. Fortunately, he only travelled four blocks before stopping at an old wooden gate. He quietly knocked.

A slender arm appeared through a narrow opening, encircled his neck and pulled him inside. It was into the tight, intimate embrace of a very young and attractive Thai woman. The couple caressed, as inexperienced lovers might, stumbling against each other as the gate swung closed. It blocked Pei's view. She would soon have some identification of this male, as he was in one of the photographs she sent to Beijing earlier in the surveillance. She called Brave and gave him her location.

Three hours later, the male had been identified for her by the PLA Intel Center in Beijing, as Zhou En Tao, MSS Section Chief and Station Political Officer. He was also assigned to Project FORWARD.

Pei watched as he quietly exited the gate, kissed the woman passionately one last time, replaced his black horn rimmed glasses and passed the secluded spot Pei and Strong were using. Strong continued to follow him. He walked directly to what they later learned was the residence he shared with his wife and their ten year old son, who had been born in New York City while he was assigned to the Chinese Mission to the United Nations.

Pei waited to see who else might be using the house they had been watching. Ten minutes after Zhou departed so did the woman. She had changed clothing and was now dressed in a fashionable black, two-piece suit, favored by office workers, sales girls and government clerks. She hailed a cruising motorcycle taxi and was off into the night. Brave had returned the trishaw hours before so Pei was free to take another motorcycle taxi on the corner. She hopped on and told the young tattooed driver to "Follow that taxi, that

43

woman is sleeping with my husband." The driver howled with laughter and took off like a bolt of lightening after the quickly disappearing taxi with the 'loose-woman' perched on the back.

In the late evening traffic it was difficult to keep up with her. Fortunately, within ten minutes, Pei's target got off the motorcycle in front of the ISOC headquarters, walked to a guarded parking lot, collected a small dark blue Isuzu truck, waved at the guards and took off once again. An hour of SDR later, she flashed her truck headlights at a gate in a chain linked fence that surrounded a dock area near the upper bend of the Chao Phraya River.

She pulled into a darkened adjacent parking lot and walked to a small trailer like building next to an old dock with scarred wooden pilings. Pei paid the still giggling motorcycle driver who sped away before she could even close her purse.

Not seeing any dogs, visible alarms or cameras in the yard, Pei quickly clambered over the fence and silently stole up to the building. A long-tail boat sat in the river next to the dock, unseen from the street. The driver was lounging in the bow, smoking and drinking a Singha beer while watching the barges moving down toward the sea.

The voices from inside the building were little more than a murmur. To avoid detection from the boatman or folks inside the building, she crouched next to the wall away from the door and dockside and waited. Within thirty minutes, the woman emerged along with one Western and one Thai male. Pei could hear little more than "Keep up the good work," and "take care until next time."

As she watched from her hiding place, the three unidentified subjects quickly headed out in different directions. Pei made her choice.

*****

44

A brief note acknowledging receipt of the five prisoners was waiting when Ren's team of tired men returned before first light to Alternative 1, their new safe house. Nothing else was expected to acknowledge their success at the border. They had done their job and it appeared that the Spec. Ops team did as well.

Brave greeted the team after their silent entry to the flat. Rocky, as a post mission test, had picked the lock as quickly as if he had a key to the flat. Ren grinned.

They quickly outlined the activities of the previous evening while downing beers and some food they had bought from a nearby street vendor. Pei and Strong had yet to appear.

The high-resolution tracking map on the team's Hardened Combat Computer screen showed the flashing dots for Pei and Strong in two widely separated parts of the city, no duress or emergency signals flashed, everything appeared normal.

After making sure everything at the apartment was secure, they organized a watch rotation. Power naps of thirty minutes and hot showers had Ren's team ready to continue hunting by 9:00 AM.

Still no word from Pei or Strong.

Chapter 5

The Next Day, Party Central Committee Offices, Beijing

"The Thais are again avoiding the vote for approval of the purchase," said Minister Chang. "How can you get the Admirals we control to use their influence and move the purchase along?"

The order of three Chinese submarines to be used by the Thai Navy had for the third time been pigeonholed after the bombing. Without demonstrating that the Uyghur problem had stabilized, there would be no sales of any military goods to the Thai Kingdom. Even the influence of two compromised senior naval officers did not help the situation since the Bangkok temple carnage.

The newspapers, politicians and perhaps even the Royal family were anxious about the effects of continued Uyghur tension on tourism and the overall economy. Until the current crisis could be tamped down, there was no hope of pushing through such a major sale of Chinese military hardware.

General Zhu nodded without comment; none was necessary, as everyone understood the situation completely: No peace, no tourism, no sales. There would be no deal without calm and order being restored. Now that a more direct intervention by Beijing was required, it was now his job to make sure it was effective.

"It's been five days since the bombing, how many terrorists have the Shadows captured?" Chang asked.

"As of this morning, the Ghost Shadows delivered five to Yunnan. They are now undergoing interrogation. From the pictures Ren sent, one of them appears to be Yusup. We know that the Thais have another three prisoners that they have not made public yet, and Sulalman, their ringleader, is not among them either. Our agent says they are planning to transfer the three to us in a few days. They are waiting for their injuries to heal."

Minister Chang nodded, "Their usual clumsy efforts I assume. I'm sure we will have no such problems in Yunnan."

"No Minister, we will not have any such problems."

"However, Colonel Ping continues to be a problem. He has now raised questions about Major Ren's loyalty to the Party. Internal Security has become involved," said General Zhu, of the Central Military Commission.

"How is Major Ren dealing with this situation?" asked Minister Chang.

"I'm sure he will resolve it," Zhu commented without showing any emotion.

"Let's hope he does, those contracts are important for binding the Thais closer to us. We also need to deal with these terrorists. They cannot break away a Western province to house their homeland. It has been part of our country for thousands of years. We are not to be the ones to lose it. Can Major Ren really be trusted to do what is necessary?"

"He is loyal to a fault. No need to worry about him, Minister, he will do whatever is necessary or die trying."

"I trust it will not come to that," Chang answered. As Ren's mentor, Party sponsor and cousin, Chang had a personal interest in keeping Ren shielded from unwarranted Party interference. The fact that Zhu's mother was Ren's aunt was also significant.

"But, yes, Minister, he also must find, capture or eliminate Alim Sulalman," was his only possible response. Sulalman they knew was a symbolic leader and senior tactician in the Uyghur movement. The PLA and MSS both were sure that he was the mastermind of the attack, had selected the site and provided support for the eight men directly responsible for delivering the bomb. Yusup, while only the Bangkok group leader, could nevertheless provide

47

valuable intelligence on their plans. It would only be a matter of time. Of that, Chang was certain.

Camp X, Yunnan Province

Yusup was momentarily blinded as the black hood was roughly pulled from his head. His arm ached from where an injection had been administered when he was thrown with the others, like sacks of rice, into the helicopter.

He had to urinate. If he didn't soon, he would lose control of it. It was five hours and twenty minutes since Major Ren had captured him. It had taken two hours twenty minutes for the trek to the LZ, fifteen minutes for the extraction ride, and another two hours forty-five minutes to fly to the small airbase that serviced Camp X.

The camp was a black prison compound, carved out of the forest near mountain foothills. The existence of this compound, like others used to house the Uyghurs was secret. It, like other black sites scattered around the country did not officially exist. Their number was not even counted in the 670 prisons officially known to be operated by the Chinese government.

Two hard-faced guards held him while straps around his arms and legs were secured to a stout wooden chair that was bolted to the white concrete floor. There were drains at various places in the floor and several water faucets and hoses along the walls. There were no windows in the room and only one metal door with a sliding iron curtain.

Three roll-around dull metal carts stood against a wall to his right. They were covered with gleaming steel surgical instruments. The ceiling lighting was recessed and covered with metal screening."Help me," he cried out as he strained against the straps and belts now holding him securely in the chair.

The guards laughed and slapped him across the face.

"Cao Ni de Ma...Go Fuck Yourself..." the older guard answered.

Yusup glared at him from a quickly swelling right eye.

Help would never arrive. Nobody would be there to save him or the others.

Yusup would soon learn that he was in one of several places where a variation of interrogation techniques known as "shuanggui," was practiced. Physical torture and brutal, sleep-deprived interrogations were the norm. It was not a good place to be.

His bladder released and hot urine flowed into the chair.

PRC Embassy Bangkok

"Sit down," Ping said waving at the chair facing his desk in the cramped office at the rear of the Embassy's second floor.

Section Chief Zhou En Tao sat and asked, "What can I do Sir?"

"You saw with your own eyes the insolence of Major Ren at our meeting yesterday, did you not?"

"Yes sir."

"What you do not know is that he violated orders yesterday and moved from the safe house we arranged and are paying dearly for."

"I did not know. What do you wish me to do?"

"As Station Party Political Director, I am making a formal complaint to you against the Major for failure to uphold Party discipline, failure to follow direct orders and armed rebellion against his duly authorized superiors."

Swallowing hard Zhou said, "These are most serious charges, Comrade Colonel."

"Yes they are. You must act now, decisively," Ping added.

49

"Rest assured, I will consult the Party Leadership and take all appropriate steps to insure Party harmony, Comrade Colonel."

Rising from the chair, Zhou pushed his horned-rim glasses back farther on his nose, turned and trundled from the office.

About the Same Time- Bangkok

Ren and two of his team members had just awakened when Pei burst through the door closely followed by Strong.

"You were correct," Pei hissed. "Everything we do here is known to the Americans and the Thais. That little son-of-a-running-dog needs to die," she continued. "Fuck his mother!"

Brave laughed, "I'd be happy to help. Who are we talking about?"

"Here, this one," she said holding up her camera screen. "He came out of the safe house yesterday evening. I followed him to his girlfriend's house. She works for ISOC."

Ren looked at her, then the photo. "I know him, he's MSS, one of Ping's staff."

She nodded.

"Tell me, what happened," Ren said.

When she finished, he turned to Strong who was listening attentively to her account of the evening.

He then told them his story.

"Two Western guys came out of the house within minutes of me getting in place. They stayed together, walked an SDR on the back streets and ended in a sleazy Soi Cowboy bar drinking beer and watching naked girls dance."

"That's the kind of snooping and pooping we all should do," chimed Rocky and Army. Ren gave them a cold look and they instantly stopped.

"Continue, what happened next?" Ren said.

50

"Nothing, they just drank and collected bar chits until the little red cup was full. They had a few of the really pretty girls sit on their laps until 11:00 PM. The younger of the two guys left first, the other stayed thirty minutes more and then did the same. I followed the second one. Here are their pictures."

The entire team looked closely as electronic images flashed on the small screen.

"I know the younger one," said Pei, pointing at the last photo. "He was at the riverside meeting. He lives in the American Embassy Compound. I followed him there this morning."

"I followed the older one, He lives across the street from Starbucks in a building full of Westerners on," he read from his notebook, " 1st Fl., 500 Plernjit Rd., Loompinee Patumwon Street. The building guard said it's all American embassy people who live there."

"Well, Fuck his mother," Ren said to nobody in particular.

Ren, sent-off a complete situation report to Colonel Zhu and asked the PLA officer to discretely get the details on the local MSS officers they identified. While they were waiting for a reply, Ren decided that a different kind of 'snoop and poop' was in order.

U.S. Embassy Bangkok

"Whoever conducted that operation was really good," said Colonel Richardson, the Military Attaché. "No question, they were real pros."

The CIA Chief of Station nodded. "How did they know what you were doing up there, our schedule?" he asked.

"Good question, they needed good Intel to block us in like that. Shit, it took three hours in that mud to clear those trees and get us back on the road."

"The real question is, what happened to the folks we were planning to roll up? Where did they go? Was that God Damn Yusup with em?" the Chief growled.

"Those Thais leak intel like a God damn sieve. No secrets here in Bangkok, we only have lead-time, and that's getting shorter every day. Too many in the chain of command say they need to know the details. Hell, we even use red herrings all the time to misdirect them. They still get everywhere, fucking before us."

"I've got someone from CI (*Counter Intelligence staff*) looking into it but in the meanwhile, we have a Tango to catch. Anything new that can help us?" the Chief asked.

Colonel Richardson, slowly nodded then said,"There was some PLA activity along the border about the time we were under attack but it could just be timing. We saw a lot of choppers moving around. The Burmese were probably having exercises in the area."

Pausing for a moment, he then continued, "It's also a very popular spot in Burma for the Yunnan PLA commanders to enjoy R&R after jungle exercises. No visas required, lots of cheap girls, gambling and watered down booze. Now that opium is almost all gone up there, they just have to worry about their troops getting spaced out on more speed than they normally use to keep going when they're humping forty kilo rucksacks and heavy weapons over those cliffs in Yunnan."

The COS picked up a flimsy (*Intel Report*) from his desk, glanced at it and asked. "One of our sources passed along something this morning that may have us and the Thais moving against another bunch of these guys down south. You interested in trying again with them?"

"Sure, are any of your guys going to come play with me?"

"Absolutely, can't have you playing with yourself, now can we? This is Thailand for God sakes. Here we let somebody do it for you."

52

"Why do you need to contact Lieutenant Pei? I require more details from you. She is in the field," said Colonel Li into his mobile telephone.

"She is Political Officer for her work unit, is she not, Colonel?" asked the smarmy voice of Political Director Zhou En Tao, who was now acting as the political officer for Colonel Ping's MSS work unit.

"You know that when units are deployed, they cannot be distracted. Can it not wait until they return?"

"It is mission related, Colonel."

"What is so important that it cannot wait?"

"Major Ren is to be placed in custody immediately pending a complete investigation. Serious charges have been put forward against him."

"By who? If I may ask."

"As a courtesy, I will tell you. It is Colonel Ping of the Ministry of State Security. He claims the Major is out of control, nothing short of a traitor. We are forced to take immediate action. I need her contact information now."

"Give me your contact information, I will have her contact you. She only has secure communication equipment where she is located. She will contact you as soon as possible."

"I don't have to remind you Colonel that Party discipline comes before everything, even the mission Ren's team is carrying out for you."

"Director Zhou, I am well aware of your role and my responsibilities to the Party, rest assured that I will do everything in my power to comply with your wishes. Please give me your contact information." After confirming it, a few minutes later, he provided Lieutenant Pei with Zhou's cell phone number.

CIA Station Bangkok-Later that day

"Sulalman has gone to ground in Hua Hin. Waiting for the word to break for the Malaysia border, somewhere near Sungai Golok. I'm awaiting details from our asset down south, but soon," said the CIA Chief.

"Have you told the Thais yet?" asked the FBI liaison agent.

"Nah, our CT (*Counter Terrorism*) guys want to roll him up themselves this time."

"You'll need them, won't you?"

"Sure, but we'll wait until the last minute then call them in using local troops from Hua Hin. Less chance of another leak."

*****

The FBI normally didn't participate in CIA field operations but since the Chinese agent had been recruited by the FBI in the U.S., the original Bureau case officer had been brought from the States to re-establish contact when the agent surfaced in the Chinese embassy in Bangkok.

"This guy was a bit squirrely when we first rolled him over in New York. He tried to recruit an ex-Agency guy by mistake. We recorded him and threatened to put him away forever unless he cooperated. He cried, pleaded for the safety of his family in the motherland, and generally carried on like a week-old baby until he got the picture," said the Bureau guy.

"How long ago was that?"

"Five years. He went back to the motherland three and a half ago. He's apparently been promoted and assigned party work as well as staff MSS activities in the embassy. He was pure gold for us, always high grade intel. Probably filed two hundred high-quality, actionable, reports from stuff he provided. My job here was to look him in the eye and make sure the turn-over to you guys was smooth."

"Looks like it worked."

"Time will tell. Had to convince him that he had even more to lose here than in New York if he screwed up. More to gain also, if he continued to play ball with us."

"My guy's really appreciated the help with the turn over."

"Happy to do it. What's not to like with a TDY (*Temporary Duty Assignment*) to Bangkok for thirty days?"

"Great idea of yours, sending him to the Pegasus Club last night with enough spendable cash didn't hurt his attitude either. The young ladies there are normally a bit above his pay grade. His main squeeze for the night said all he wanted to do was screw her brains out. She didn't mind. Said he was like those Japanese sex tourists, you know, not so big. She said it was an easy night, even with the two little blue pills he got somewhere."

"Didn't hurt my attitude either when your guys took me there the last night. That's quite a place. Hope he was wearing a full body condom! Most of the girl there were really something, but nothing I'd want to touch. No offense, but I don't have that much of a death wish over sex."

Ghost Shadow Safe house

The call from Colonel Li was brief and direct: "Sending Sulalman's coordinates, get him." There was no mention of the pressure that Colonel Ping and the party apparatus was mounting in both Beijing and Bangkok to recall Ren and close down his operations. No time for those distractions.

Ren closed down the encrypted link with Beijing. The mission was top priority, if he was successful, Colonel Li knew there would be time to deal with everything else later. Party discipline was being used as an excuse to hamstring his operation and everyone who mattered knew it. He hoped that those who were following orders to stop him would not be too disappointed with their negative results.

Who was profiting from these distractions? That was the real question in Li's mind.

"Saddle Up," Ren shouted to the team. He liked the wild-west sound of Dickie's SEAL Team phrase, even though he was unsure of what exactly it meant.

"What's up Boss?" Army and Rocky asked excitedly.

"Sulalman's in Hua Hin, heading for the border. We're going after him."

"Which border?" Army asked grinning.

"He's headed for Malaysia."

"What about Colonel Ping? Won't he be pissed if you disappear again? Army asked.

"Fuck his mother," Rocky said.

"No, fuck him," said Ren. "We're here to do our job. The little pleasure of dealing with him can wait."

"Are all of us going Major? asked Pei.

"Again, you stay here with Brave," said Ren. "You need to watch our six until we roll-up Sulalman. Our back needs to be covered while we keep working to find out who leaked the information on our original target. It must be someone in the Embassy. Very likely one of those MSS officers in the meeting with Colonel Ping."

She was once again disappointed, but nodded agreement.

"If you find the leak, plug it. Don't wait for us. Maintain radio silence until we return, emergency calls only."

Thirty minutes later, carrying a heavy load of equipment, they prepared to slip out of the apartment door after getting the call from Army that he had just hot wired a nice Toyota Hiace© minivan. He had changed the license plates and it was parked ten meters down the Soi from their safe house, ready to go.

"Load up and move out," said Ren as they hurried toward the door. "Good fortune Pei. Get the dirty bastard for us."

"If it's possible, it will be done," she said with a smile.

This was the answer he expected but in this case, her disappointment at being assigned what she considered a secondary mission clouded her focus. She knew that finding the source of the leak was important but it was not why they were in Thailand. Getting Sulalman and bringing him back to justice was important to the party, the Shadows and China. In that order.

What Major Ren thought about her also had begun playing a role in how she acted. While her role on the team and the party was important, his approval more so. She would do whatever necessary to find and dispose of those responsible for putting the Shadows at risk.

Chapter 6

South Thailand

Hakimi, the wizened village elder, leaned back against the side of the raised porch railing at his south Thailand home. He knew that his old friend, Naidu, and his Tamil fighters were responsible for bombing the provincial police station the night before. His grandson had told him so when he returned from acting as a lookout for whatever new Jihadi's group to which he was now professing loyalty.

I would probably do the same thing, he thought, if he were his grandson's age; the problem was selecting the right group. *There were so many now,* he thought. *It is so hard, not like when my father and grandfather fought Bangkok. Then, it was them, for Allah and Pattani against the unbelievers and the corrupt. Now it was letters, flags, and Imam's with slivers of ideas; not believers that carried weapons, bombs and swords.*

Since the Pattani Islamic Sultanate had been broken up by the Bangkok government almost sixty years prior there were just too many different groups fighting. The strongest at the moment were the Salafi Jihadists who took over from the ethnic separatists. The number of groups living in the jungle, conducting raids and planting bombs made his head hurt trying to remember what each professed. They all did agree on a few things: that the police were corrupt, the Provincial Governor worse and Bangkok a cesspool. All needed to be purified.

Perhaps one or more of these new warrior groups would be successful in promoting the word of Allah. Lastly, and more fundamental to success, was the black Al-Raya flag that now replaced the colorful secessionist flags that once had heralded the various splinter groups in southern Thailand.

With 60,000 well-armed Thai policemen, one for every thirty people, it was little wonder that over 6,000 of his brothers and sisters had been killed and 14,000 hurt fighting against the evil Bangkok government during the past seven years. This fighting had been going on since he was a child, sixty years ago. His family had survived four generations of fighting for their land and religion and they would continue until they prevailed. Corrupt politicians and police came and went. Allah's word was forever.

To have a town like Sungai Golok just across the border from Muslim Malaysia was an affront to everything he held sacred. Prostitutes, alcohol, dancing, music and foreigners, not to mention believers, crossing the river from Malaysia into Thailand to sin was more than he could bear. To have all this wickedness exist because the police looked the other way or profited from the open display of evil was an affront to all believers.

"Sungai Golok? You want to use Sungai Golok to hide him?" Mohamed Naidu asked Hakimi. "It is an evil place."

"Truly it is and it will be destroyed one day. But now, we can hide in plain sight without police interference," Hakimi answered.

"They assume we are there for sex and alcohol. For them it is money, we are not a threat as long as we act the way they expect," added Hakimi's lieutenant Ashraf, who had just returned from making final arrangements for their operations.

Hakimi nodded and added, "Truly, Allah will rejoice should our actions be successful in ridding this sinful place and those responsible for it, from the world."

On the Road to Hua Hin

Contrary to what the MSS and PLA believed, Sulalman was not thought to be a very effective terrorist by Western

59

security analysts. He was too good-looking, not quite Chinese nor Western. A blend that made him more like a movie star than a hidden warrior. Even here in Thailand, the local security service, like the PSB *(Chinese Public Security Bureau)* cameras surrounding Kashgar's People's Square had taken numerous pictures of him during his flight from Bangkok. Until then, he was successful in squeezing through their net. It was the same during his student days when he viewed the gigantic statue of Chairman Mao, the Great Helmsman, that guarded the broad expanse of concrete in the center of the city. He had to flee. That experience showed him the way of Jihad and a new life.

This was after his schooling was completed and he had witnessed the round ups of his family, friends and fellow students. He then came under the influence of an al-Qaeda affiliated Turkish Imam on-the-run from the U.S. led ISAF forces *(International Security Assistance Force)* in Afghanistan. A year of jihadi and bomb making training later, he returned to China from Baluchistan. He had two successful attacks under his belt against ISAF Coalition forces along the Afghan border.

He was now a fully trained, indoctrinated and committed adherent to violent jihad with well-honed operational skills. He found conditions under which his family and friends now lived even worse than when he departed. The Chinese had recently banned the use of traditional Uyghur names for children. Only approved names were allowed. Beards were discouraged and 'Beautification Campaigns' strongly discouraged wearing of veils by their women. Their own homeland was now a necessity worth fighting and dying for.

I will make it so, he thought. After being gone for more than a year, and crossing through the Khunjerab Pass from Pakistan back into his home province in China, his resolve to help liberate his people was rekindled. That resolve was even

60

stronger in him as he lay hidden in the rear of an old truck moving toward the South.

*****

As he lay there he remembered the final words he had spoken to the team taking the bombs he had constructed to the shrine. "Yusup, you will walk with the prophet as you deliver the device,"

"Inshallah,"... God Willing... was the only possible reply from Yusup, the local team leader, as he hefted the backpack and set off from the safe house for the crowded temple.

The operation succeeded in sending an unmistakable message to the Thais about returning the 109 Uyghur prisoners, their brothers, back to China. These brothers, who claimed to be Turkish, had been arrested and were set to be deported for planning jihadi activities in Syria. The Thais had no right to interfere with jihadi's on their way to fight against the enemies of Allah.

But, that was seven days ago and the Thais had announced the arrest of unnamed foreign suspects. Since there had been no coded messages posted to the secure website they used for communications, Sulalman believed that Yusup and his group had been taken. The support team that included his cousins, Patime and Aynur, also missed their check-in from the jihadi camp in Burma. He held little hope for them either.

Now, he was alone and on the run to the South where he had the name of a friendly brother in the fight against the government who could be relied on for help.

His training taught him to be extremely careful. Dozens of cameras in Thailand, along with the thousands placed around China that monitor airports, subways and streets, continually updated his file. Facial recognition software processed millions of images daily as the discrete

61

digital search for him continued. The false Turkish passport he carried provided some cover but avoiding cameras was key to successfully getting around Thailand and then out of the country.

Hakimi was to provide cover and safe passage for him in exchange for providing assistance in fighting the Bangkok government.

Ghost Shadows Safe House

Pei's operational phone rang several hours after Ren and his team departed. "Yes," was all she said, per mission protocol.

"Lieutenant Ming?" came the tinny voice.

"Yes, " she again answered, not recognizing the voice.

"This is Director Zhou, People's Party Disciplinary Committee."

"Please authenticate," she answered, "or this call is terminated."

"Wait, lieutenant, Colonel Li provided your contact number to me."

Pei paused then said. "Give me your contact information. I will verify your identity and call you shortly."

Colonel Li answered her call on the second ring.

Fifteen minutes later she called Zhou.

"Yes, Director Zhou, I would be pleased to discuss Major Ren with you. Where can we meet?"

"You will report to the Embassy immediately," he ordered.

"That is not possible Director Zhou. I am under operational orders to remain under cover. As you know, the Embassy is under surveillance by hostile security services. Can you select a more secure location?"

"Lieutenant, you are the political officer for your unit, I must insist that you present yourself immediately for consultations," Zhou demanded.

"In this situation, my operational orders are more important than your need for a meeting that can be conducted anywhere secure. If you insist, I will report this matter to Colonel Li and ask for his guidance."

"Very well. You will report to the following address immediately." He provided the address that turned out to be the safe house she had watched him leaving from the side door the previous evening.

"As you wish," she said and disconnected the call.

Brave had watched and listened to the entire conversation and knew what to do. "I'm leaving now to set up an OP (*Observation Post*) Let's do a radio check" They both inserted their ear-buds for the encrypted radio and adjusted the volume. After selecting a few more magazines for his mini-HK machine pistol, he was out the door loaded with his normal assortment of weapons and electronic devices.

At the MSS Safe House

"Please sit," were the only words Zhou spoke upon opening the front door and ushering her into an inner interrogation room like office. Now that Zhou was close to her, she could see the weak chin, thick glasses and unruly hair common to many MSS staff officers. She no longer wondered how he was able to have a relationship with the young Thai woman he had enjoyed the previous evening. She was not doing it for love. It was strictly business. Pei immediately decided that she would take the same approach with him.

"So Lieutenant, why do you not carry out your party responsibilities more forcefully? Are you part of Ren's disregard for discipline and following orders?"

63

Brave's voice in her ear-bud startled her. "Thermal scan indicates that he came alone, nobody but you two in the building. Acknowledge"

She keyed the transmitter twice without Zhou noticing. She then sat up and said, "Zhou En Tao, born August 7, 1962, Hubei Province, parents............." She then stopped. He had gone pale.

"Who are you, how do you know these things? You do not investigate me, I do that to you," he sputtered.

She smiled and stood, "We do indeed have much to discuss," she began.

Hua Hin, Thailand

Every night, the streets in a large section of central Hua Hin are transformed into a thriving Night Market, filled with hordes of bargain-seeking tourists and local residents alike. The crowds extend for blocks in all directions just off the main highway that snakes its way through the center of the city. The crush of bodies pushing and shoving their way through block after block of food stalls, inexpensive clothing, touristic trinkets and jewelry vendors make walking, let alone surveillance difficult. Brush contacts between someone under surveillance and an agent delivering a message can be impossible to notice.

Oversized glasses and a white "Phuket Beach Club" ball cap made Sulalman easily recognizable for his contact while he didn't stand out in the crowd. Before Sulalman had even walked two blocks, he felt the tug at his pocket. He later found the note that was slipped into it by an unseen passerby.

After another half hour of shopping, during which he purchased a kilo of rambutans and some dark T-shirts, he then slipped down a side street, glanced at the scrap of tissue paper and moved away into the dark side streets away from the crowds. An hour later he quietly entered the grounds of a two story house built only a few meters away from a huge ship like apartment building that faced the Gulf of Thailand.

"Salaam Alaikum," greeted him from the short, dark-skinned male who identified himself as Chanchai... 'skilled winner'.

Sulalman gave the required answer. They whispered for a moment then faded away into the darkness surrounding the house and moved several blocks away from the sea to a more modest teakwood dwelling.

CIA Station Bangkok

"Sulalman just surfaced last night in Hua Hin," the CIA Chief told Colonel Richardson. "We're gonna try snatching him up tonight. No Thais until the last minute. Two of my SA (*Special Activities*) guys are enroute there along with the project case officer. Ready for a little night flight?"

"Rock and Roll," Richardson said grinning.

"Yeah, well, let's save that for the after-party."

The Station Chief was not as optimistic about their chances. He knew the source but the leadership cell he reported on was unpredictable --- that's why they had lasted so long.

"Don't think that it will be a walk in the park down there. These guys are very good and deadly. That guy, Hakimi, is responsible for at least two-dozen IED's that killed ten Thai troopers and maimed many times more than that. Hell, his father and grandfather both were rebel leaders. It's like a family business for them. The Turks reaching out to him was a natural. He is trusted by them...trusted to take care of our boy."

"I'm sure between your SA guys and some of the Spec Ops team here on-loan from South Com, we'll handle him."

"Tell me about it after you roll him up."

"Why all the gloom about our chances?"

65

"Look sunshine, these guys have been hiding in the bushes for fifty years shooting at the Thais without getting caught. They're damn good and you're trying to take them down on their home turf. Don't underestimate them caus'if you do, you're gonna get your ass handed to you. Capish?"

Richardson nodded and strode from the office.

Hua Hin, Thailand

Police roadblocks did not hinder the initial part of the Shadows journey down South. Road closures and screenings would not become evident until the travellers were forty kilometers south of Hua Hin. Since the Thai King maintains his summer residence in Hua Hin, the military and navy both have a large presence to collect intelligence and keep him safe. Several warships permanently patrol the coast, undercover agents roam the streets and armed police are around almost every corner.

Before the Shadows arrived in Hua Hin, Ren warned them, "Partying and getting falling down drunk are okay. If you don't act like a tourist, they are on you like flies on monkey shit."

"Okay boss," Rocky answered, "I can do that." Ren didn't bother to reply.

They cruised to a stop in the dense tourist area near the Hilton Hotel and waited less than a minute. A young boy appeared and directed them with a wave to a side soi parking space next to a seafood restaurant.

"I hope this meets your needs," said the slightly built, grey haired Chinese parking attendant, who was wearing powder blue floral print pajama bottoms and a dirty white t-shirt.

"It's fine, thank you for your troubles," Ren answered in Thai, nodding his head. The old man pointed to a stairway leading to the upper floor.

The apartment was above one of the many seafood restaurants that crowded the ocean front. It was ideal. Lots of tourists, cars, small trucks and fishing boats were constantly in motion; easy to blend in day or night.

"Get our equipment stored Army, I'll be back in a few hours," Ren said.

"Rocky, you come with me."

"Hey boss, it's going to be tough to operate here. Too many people and police walking around," Rocky said.

Ren shook his head. "Unless he's hiding right here, we should be able to figure out a way to get to him once we ID his hiding place. Our contact should be able to help with that."

"Who's the old man in pajamas?" Army asked.

"Retired PLA sergeant from Yunnan. Married a Thai, Helps out when we ask. Been living here on the beach for ten years. Works in her family restaurant. Knows everyone and everything in town.

"Is he our source?"

"No."

They walked through the congested streets until they passed the row of tailors, tourist stores and shoe shops just in front of the Hilton Hotel. A Chinese restaurant was across the street. Ren stopped there.

"Take a table, order us some Chang beer and give me ten minutes. I'll be right back," Ren ordered. He then entered a foot massage shop next door and disappeared from view.

About the same time the beer arrived, so did Ren.

"Hey boss, that was fast. Looks like they serve up intel here faster than the beer," Rocky laughed.

Ren nodded.

"At least we know where he's staying for the next few days. We can look it over and set up an extraction plan. He's supposed to be going on an operation with the Thai jihadi's tomorrow. Call and get the rest of the team here. Time to eat.We have work to do soon," said Ren, picking up a menu. "The seafood is supposed to be excellent here."

A few minutes later Army arrived. Ren said, "Our agent gave me the address where Sulalman's staying. Rocky, time for some sneak and peek."

"On my way. Anything else I should know?"

"Get in and get out, take pictures if possible. He says it's only about a kilometer from here, near the beach." Ren handed him a small piece of paper with the address and a crude map.

"Sure thing." Rocky answered glancing at the note then tearing it up. "What if he's there? Take him or call for the team?"

"Call me. We'll figure out extraction support but don't let him get away. Oh yeah, with all the police around, be really quiet, we don't want them taking an interest in what we're doing."

Rocky patted his calf where his favorite fighting knife rested and smiled.

"Roger that," Ren said nodding, then added in Chinese..." Kai Shi ... Go."

*****

Two hours later, Rocky returned to the safe house.

"Tough place boss," he began. The entire team huddled around the computer screen while Rocky pointed to the various features showing on the Google Earth® Satellite view of the building.

"White sandy beach on one side, narrow path leading to it from the road, this ship-like building to the south and a yard overgrown with jungle to the north. Two stories, wooden construction, shuttered windows, veranda porch on two sides, and a 1.5 meter chain link fence around the whole place."

"Anyone there?" Army asked.

"Lights were on at the lower level and one room upstairs on the north east corner. Couldn't hear or see any movement. Didn't see any cameras, alarms or dogs. Nothing showed up on the thermal scanner either. Did it from all sides. Looked like a deserted old style Thai teak house, like the ones we saw up north near Chang Mai."

Everyone nodded.

"Ideas?" Ren asked.

"We need to know what's going on inside, quickly."

"Can we trust the information from our agent?" Rocky finally asked.

"Beijing trusts him enough to let him in on our operation. I don't think we have any choice for the moment. I can't go back to him and say 'Your information is shit....Cao Ni Ma...Go fuck yourself...he's not there,' can I?"

"No boss, but we can 'trust and verify' it's the right thing to do," added Rocky.

Ren looked at his watch, it was 1:30 AM, less than five hours before light. "Okay, we all go back to the house now."

*****

The white Hiace van, now with markings advertising a Chinese seafood restaurant, coasted to a stop along the side of the deserted road about a hundred and twenty meters from the Shadows target. The three, now black clad figures, silently emerged from the van and blended into the thick foliage. Rocky took the lead; thermal scanned the house once again, hopped the front fence and moved across the dirt front yard to the porch.

"Going up." He signaled and quickly shinnied up the roof-pole, swung up onto the overhang that covered the broad verandah and crept up toward the second floor windows. The others guys hung back and strung out along the street.

Rocky searched the windows for trip wires and pressure switches. Finding none he defeated the lock and slipped into the dark room. He searched it. Finding nothing and hearing nothing he slowly opened the door and entered the hallway. Three other dark rooms were unoccupied and had the dusty, musty smell of not being used for some time. He made his way down the stairway very slowly inspecting for traps, trip wires or pressure pads. Again they were clear.

As he started to move along the main hallway he stopped. The front door had been wired with a simple contact switch whose wires trailed down the hall into the kitchen. "Hey boss, we got a problem here," he whispered into his throat mike.

"This place is wired to go boom if anyone comes in any of the doors or ground floor windows. It doesn't look like this place is even being used."

Just as he finished reporting he heard, "Get out of there now" from Ren along with the pounding of feet on the dirt at the rear of the house signaling unannounced visitors. Rocky bolted for the stairs as he heard their feet approach the rear door. He was up the stairs and half way out the window when the house evaporated in a blinding white flash into the night sky. The blast knocked Ren and Army down fifty meters away.

Lights came on, people filled the street and sirens could be heard moving toward the carnage. Ren and Army brushed the dirt and debris away and moved away from the slowly building crowd. They walked past the van and continued toward the bar area. By changing their shirts, they looked like the remnants of a long night of drinking: disheveled, staggering a bit and bleary eyed. They did not have to act; the concussive wave from the blast made it easy for them to appear disoriented. Ren had seen many die in battle but none before from the Shadows.

There were no replacements in the field. Either they continued or returned to base. In this hunt Ren knew that returning, without Sulalman was not an option.

*****

Several blocks removed from the blast site, Sulalman and Chanchai came awake as the shock wave passed over their house, rattling the floor mats they used as beds. "It seems as though our little deception was successful," said Chanchai.

"It would seem so, but let's wait to hear who was trapped in it before we rejoice," answered Sulalman.

"It makes no difference, they are all corrupt, infidels or Buddhists. Any of their deaths serves our cause."

"The location of the house was known only to a few. Who chose to attack us will soon be known," Chanchai added.

"Perhaps you can stay with us longer," he continued. "We are very good at IED's, like the one we just experienced, but your type of killing can bring the battle to their cities and terror to their hearts. Killing soldiers is easy, we now need to bring the fight into their homes and families."

"I'll do what I can to assist but think we need to leave here soon. The police and army will be looking for those responsible shortly."

"You are correct, maybe once the chaos is over, we can avoid the checkpoints they will erect and move south, to our real battleground. Now, we should rest. After a moment he added, "Where we are going has already been tested.

A few years ago, the soldiers came to break up a peaceful demonstration to allow a Mosque to be built. The Army broke it up with rubber bullets, arrested 116 young men, and dumped them into trucks like tree branches.

By the time they arrived at the jail, twenty kilometers away, half were dead. Those young men had done nothing. They were not warriors, but are now martyrs for our cause. Just because we are away from Bangkok, do not think we do nothing worthwhile. You will see with your own eyes how we are prepared to act."

"I did not know about your loss."

"Few people do, Bangkok makes certain it's that way, but that does not make it any less true. Buddhists are far from peaceful in defense of their religion."

Chanchai turned off the lamp and into the darkness said, "Sleep now, we have far to travel at first light."

Chapter 7

CIA Station Bangkok

"Holy shit, all of them dead?" said the Chief of Station, Burroughs, the Counterterrorism chief, nodded grimly.

"Cratered the whole building, nothing left but a smoking hole three meters deep," he said.

"Shit, shit, shit, it's almost as bad as Camp Chapman when that little prick, Abu Mulal al-balawi killed seven of our guys in one blast," said the Chief.

"What a screw-up. Where did we get that intel?" he asked.

"That would be DB Nimrod, one of the station's key assets down there. He's been spot on since day one. He's from the south, near Hat Ya. Has a hard on for the cops down there. They roughed up his family... thought they were working with the rebels... killed a brother during questioning."

"Christ, better get on the damage assessment, it's not bad enough we lost three of our guys, but the Military Attaché and four of the locals cops...Jesus. Everyone is going to be looking up our ass with a spotlight."

"It'll take a while for the DNA work-ups to see if any of the bad guys were even in the building. Betting against it though. Seen this kind of thing in the Stan's. Lost good guys to um' before, never in cities though. Hope this is not the start of a trend there. Could be real shit storm in the works if it is."

"Any more fucking gloom you want to spread on me this morning? Get outa here and get me something hard to report. I gotta go see the Ambassador. That should be a real picnic. He's jumping up and down like a goddamn jack-in-the-box. I'm sure the White House is all over him on it."

"You got it boss."

"Oh, one more thing, I hope you're planning a come-to-Jesus with our boy Nimrod?"

Burroughs's nodded and said, "Oh yeah, that's already in the works."

Even before he went to the Station Chief's office, the emergency contact plan was set in motion for a meeting with DB Nimrod. The safe house was being prepared to receive them.

PRC Embassy Bangkok

The hastily called morning meeting with his America controller worried Zhou En Tao. He would be missed at the MSS staff meeting. The text message...offering twenty percent off soccer equipment...triggered panic; both for what the meeting might hold but also the lies he would be forced to tell Colonel Ping afterwards.

He was so tense that sleep that last night had been impossible. *Even his wife's enticements did not produce the kind of satisfaction he craved. Only the beautiful Thai, Siriporn, could provide it these days. The thought of being trapped, like a deer with broken legs in a marketplace cage, flashed through his mind. Until now two sets of barriers to being free had locked him into his current dilemma, the third, just added by this evil woman, Lieutenant Pei, made it intolerable. How can I comply? Being a spy for my country and for our main enemy was almost too much to bear. This woman is unreasonable. How can I do what she asks and keep my sanity? But, if I do not, everything in my life is gone.*

Colonel Ping is a self-serving, vile man without conscience. He should be investigated, not Major Ren and his soldiers; they had done what was ordered. The Thai security service officers had snatched the terrorists that night because of Ping's treachery. It was Ping's information that triggered their actions. I know, I heard him.

74

Zhou heard the morning news reports about the big explosion in Hua Hin. It must have been big since normally the Thais and his government hid such things when possible. But, *since it had nothing to do with him; clearly it is some other problem the Americans had that required his attention. He had to get himself calmed down, think more clearly, more focused, on the real problems at hand.*

CIA Operational Safe House

"This is about the explosion in Hua Hin, you heard about it yet, yeah?" Burroughs asked.

Zhou nodded.

"Okay, look, we need to know what information your officers have about it, what your agents are collecting. I need it fast. Today."

Relief spread through him. "Of course, I will do my best," he answered.

"Anything that you have now that I can use?"

Maybe this was an opportunity to solve two problems at once, he thought.

"Perhaps this might be helpful." He began, warming up to the task at hand. "There was a certain Major Ren at the Embassy, a Ghost Shadow…"

"Who are they? When did this happen?" asked Burroughs slowly, disguising his excitement.

An hour later, Zhou slipped out of the safe house and into the traffic clogged street. Burroughs sat there finishing his Draft FIR (*Field Information Report*) and CR (*Contact Report*) on his meeting.

"Jesus Christ, the Chinese have Spec Ops guys here looking for the bombers," said the station Chief to Burroughs, an hour later.

"Holy Christ, that's all we need, more chefs in the kitchen, It's not fucking hard enough with everyone else

75

thrashing around in the weeds down there, no, we get their, what did he call them?...Ghost Shadows... chasing after them as well?" said the Station Chief.

"Hey boss, I think that's a record for mixed metaphors, even for you. Is that what having a Ph.D. does for you?" laughed Burroughs

"Yeah, well that still doesn't answer the question on how we got bad intel about the house we hit down there, does it. What does that other source of yours, Nimrod, have to say?"

"There you go again...what does this Nimrod have to say? Really, you want to know what a Nimrod has to say?"

"Come on for Christ sake, get serious, will ya."

"I am serious, deadly serious. He says it came straight from one of his guys that's been 100 percent in his reporting for years. He's not sure what happened but is trying to find out. Okay?"

"No, it's not Okay. Get your ass down south and deal with it yourself. Langley is screaming, the White House is crawling all over this. Next thing will be the Admin pukes down stairs bitching about the equipment that got lost in the blast. Jesus, what a CF (Cluster Fuck). Get out of here, I need some answers! Now! God Damn it!"

Hua Hin

Army's ears were still ringing when they returned to their flat above the restaurant. Ren's hearing was not much better but then he was several meters further from the house when the blast wave struck. Ren tried unsuccessfully to clear the ringing in his ears but knew that it would take time. In the meantime, he silently vowed to find the agent who sent them into a trap. Rocky did not deserve to die like that.

76

Right now it was more important that they get an immediate report to Colonel Li, re-contact their local agent, and pick-up Sulalman's trail.

Ren began his call to Pei's group that was still in Bangkok with…"Rocky's dead…a bomb got him." His announcement was met with silence from the remaining team in the room.

"We need to move on. Rocky will be with us in spirit until we capture the terrorists," he paused, looked at his wristwatch and told Pei, "Choose someone and get them on a flight immediately… send them to Hat Ya on the first one available. The 6:30 AM Thai Air Asia flight would work well."

After filling her in on the mission details he asked, "What's the status of Director Zhou?"

She told him of the calls to Colonel Li, her early morning meeting with Zhou and turning him to her will.

"Excellent work! Do I have to worry about Internal Security trying to arrest me in the next few days?"

"I'm sure that when Director Zhou is finished with his report on your actions here Colonel Ping will be fortunate to escape a permanent assignment to Tibet, or worse."

"Thank you for your efforts, but please complete your work there quickly, I will need extra help here once we locate Sulalman again. He is proving to be a very resourceful man."

"I have no doubts that you will bring him to justice, Major," Pei responded as she put down the phone. With the change in plans, she realized that her work in Bangkok needed to be accelerated.

Beijing, Special Operations Command Headquarters

"So, that is what we know as of two hours ago." Colonel Li said concluding his report to General Zhu.

"It is not a good situation Colonel," General Zhu commented. "How will Major Ren resolve it?"

"He is working with our local agent to continue tracking the terrorist. Once he is located, Ren will capture him. It is only a matter of time."

"Unfortunately, we do not have the luxury of time. MSS is very upset that Major Ren was not ordered to report for questioning based on Colonel Ping's accusations."

"General, we both know that Ping's report was a fabrication. Given that it is in the hands of the Party Disciplinary Committee, we are taking radical steps to insure that it is discredited. I expect to have a favorable report on Major Ren's actions very soon."

"If we do not Colonel, it will not just be the Major who has problems retaining his position. The Minister is taking the thought of a rogue Commander of his most elite unit very seriously, especially one so closely related. I will not be able to shield him much longer. Get those responsible, then we can do something about their meddling."

MSS Safe House Bangkok

Pei put down the report Director Zhou prepared on the charges against Major Ren.

"You're writing is quite extraordinary. Major Ren should be honored at a Central Committee for his work rather than jailed if your report is to be believed."

"My work is always accurate, thorough and believed," he answered.

"When will you submit this report?"

"You were very clear about what I should do with it, I have followed your instruction, to the letter. I expect you to do the same."

"Do not worry little brother," Pei began, "I am good to my word. No harm will come to your family or girlfriend. You have done your part. Please submit the report immediately."

Zhou relaxed slightly but asked, "Are we finished? Do I still owe you anything?"

"Just submit the report, defend it and put it behind you. Do not worry about a thing so long as you continue to report to me and provide small favors from time to time."

"If I don't? Then what? What can you do to me?"

"Director Zhou, you do not seem to understand your position here."

Zhou thought. *I know my position all too well. I am already stuck with the Americans. Now she tells me to work for her in addition to working for MSS and the Americans. I think my head is going to explode.*

Pei smiled warmly at him and said, "I appreciate your honesty and willingness to be of service thus far. I must however warn you in the most graphic terms...if you fuck around with me, I will kill you, right after I kill your wife and son in front of you. Can I be any clearer with you about what you need to do?"

Zhou's bowels loosen and the foul smell filled the room. His face turned ashen, his body trembled and tears well up. They slowly began to trickle down his cheeks.

"You would not last one day in the army, Zhou. You are pathetic. Are you going to do what I ask or not?"

He slowly nodded.

"I need to hear it from you. Say it!" she demanded.

He hesitated then responded, "I'll do whatever you ask, whenever you ask for it."

She smiled. "There, that wasn't so bad was it?"

She would kill him anyway but having him send a favorable report to the Party about Ren's activities was now her first priority, right after getting out of the smelly room.

In any circumstance she would never touch his family. He would never know about this weakness.

Hua Hin

Colonel Richardson lay in the Thai Military Hospital just outside Hua Hin awaiting evacuation to Hawaii for treatment. Triage had saved his life but it was unlikely that he would have sight in one of his eyes again. The concussive force of the blast threw him like a rag doll backwards about ten meters along with a shower of debris and shrapnel from the blast.

"Hi Colonel, remember me, Burroughs, I'm from the Station?"

"Sure, how ya doing?"

"Looks like a hell of a lot better than you."

"Shit, that' wouldn't take much. We got pretty banged up back there."

"What the hell happened?"

After a few minutes, Richardson began rambling, repeating himself.

"Look Colonel," Burroughs said, "let's take a break, get some rest. I'll stop back later."

Richardson had already fallen asleep.

*****

Burroughs left the hospital and walked the two blocks over to Provincial Police Chief Sombat's office. The front of the police station was abuzz with activity in the aftermath of the bombing. He walked through the maze of parked cars and trucks to the rear door. His Embassy ID and excellent Thai got him past the guard post and into the reception area for

80

detectives. Sombat was in the middle of a scrum of uniformed officers trading information about the explosion.

"Hi Chief," Burroughs yelled, waving at him.

Sombat raised his hand in acknowledgement and waved him over to his office, then followed him in and closed the door. He looked tired and troubled after the morning's disaster.

They had worked together on several incidents over the past two years and maintained an easy professional and personal relationship. It was more than that of the obligatory drinking and massage variety. He had provided key information to help him close several major cases. Sombat had done the same for him.

"You look like shit Sombat," Burroughs quipped.

"Well, up yours too *farang (foreigner)*."

"Looks like your guys are working overtime."

"Sorry for your loss," Sombat said, turning serious.

Burroughs nodded. "Terrible situation, we need to get those bastards. My boss had to tell their families. Not a job I want to do."

"Let's hope I can help you sort out this mess."

"Let's start with what we know for sure."

An hour later Burroughs excused himself and walked out to the parking lot, took out his secure phone and called Bangkok. "Hey Chief, It's worse than we thought," he began.

Chapter 8

"We need suspects," the Commissioner General of the Thai Royal Police shouted into the telephone connected to Bangkok's Chief of Police. Then pausing, added, "It's been a week since the temple bombing and you still have nobody to show to the press." He was pacing back and forth in front of his massive teak desk covered with row upon row of tiny flags from police agencies around the world.

Across the traffic-gridlocked city, the ISOC chief, who sat listening to the call on the speakerphone across the desk from the Police Chief nodded, and whispered, "We'll have someone for you shortly. We need to make it look like we are working hard. Our Chinese friends are happy with the suspects we have collected and shipped to them. They promise to provide suitable candidates and I'm sure they will. It's in their best interests.

The Chief nodded then responded to the Commissioner, "My men are working hard, night and day, to arrest those responsible. We expect to have results in the next 24 hours."

"Can you guarantee that?" asked the Commissioner,

"Absolutely sir, there is no doubt that we will have the right parties in custody by then. If not, you can dismiss me."

"Hum, Yes, nothing like a small incentive to make things happen."

Neither would worry about dismissals as each had their own backers in the current Prime Minister's government and the Army. The illusion of power that each man displayed was more important that the reality behind their statements. Both understood this very well.

The Comissioner continued, "The Prime Minister is worried about the effect of this delay and what looks like uncertainty is having on tourism. We are still off by 28% in future hotel bookings but I'm sure if we can get the right reason for the bombing, it will come back quickly before the high travel season."

"Yes, I understand, everyone is being hurt by this situation. I will get it resolved quickly."

"Even the King himself expressed concern."

"Soon, soon we will have the guilty parties to parade for the press."

"I hope so, we all stand to lose if you are wrong," the Commissioner said as he punched the disconnect button.

The ISOC chief smiled as he heard the line go dead. Then said, "Our Chinese friends have more to loose than we do if things are not resolved quickly."

"They will make it right," whispered the Police Chief as he began making another call.

South Thailand

At six-thirty the morning after the explosion, Sulalman and Chanchai passed through the first police checkpoint with ease when leaving Hua Hin. Little chance that two shaven headed monks would be suspected as terrorists. Three more encounters much like the first gave them confidence in using this disguise. They arrived eleven traffic filled hours later, near dusk, in a small village, three kilometers from Sungai Golok.

The village headman welcomed them with the greeting of a traditional high *Wai*...A formal type of bow...as they entered the central clearing area. He led them to a small house bordering the thick jungle where a simple dinner of chicken, rice and vegetables awaited. "Tonight you eat and rest, *In Shallah* in the morning our work will begin."

83

This village had been a rebel base for over thirty years. Of the one hundred residents, sixty-five were actively engaged in armed attacks, planting bombs and helping other rebels in the area conduct raids and ambushes. Their success came from discipline and an unwavering belief that they were following the will of Allah in reclaiming the land stolen by the Bangkok government and given to Buddhists. Karma brought this shaven headed brother who would help them become better soldiers of Allah. They would put his skills to good use.

Camp X- Secret Location China

"Is he weak or a deception?" It was too easy, especially with the drugs. Breaking him should have taken longer. Was he not trained to resist interrogations?

"Is he senior leadership?" asked the chief interrogator then added to the PLA Special Operations Captain who was observing the session, "I've handled hundreds of these terrorists. With the drugs and physical stress, none reacted like him. His body is still untouched; drugs, sleep deprivation and threats only."

"What do you recommend to find out what he really is?"

"If he is not to be released, the old ways still are most reliable."

"Do what you must, but do it quickly."

The metal table with gleaming instruments was being rolled toward the interrogation chair as the Captain left the room. Yusup's initial high-pitched scream was blotted out as the metal door slammed shut.

Little information had been obtained from the other terrorists but the two females had provided some much needed recreation for the security officers. A pity they did not seem to enjoy the kind of sex practiced with metal rods and sharp tongs.

Major Ren sent the initial information from Yusup through PLA Special Operations channels to Beijing. MSS was not included in its distribution.

*****

Colonel Sombat sat quietly for a few moments thinking. His agent in the Hua Hin madrassa had just passed along a confirmation that elite PLA soldiers had been at the bombing site in Hua Hin. He picked up his telephone, called Bangkok, then his friends with the US Government.

CIA Station Bangkok

"Chinese spooks are in Hua Hin? What the fuck?" shouted the COS. "Are they sure?"

"Come on, cut me some slack, all I know is what the evidence is telling them," answered Burroughs.

"Again from the top."

"Okay, We got bits of bone fragments from four different Caucasian based DNA samples, three indo-Chinese DNA at the periphery of the blast and one with pure Chinese in a different part of the house."

"So?"

"So this, we had four of our guys and three local SWAT guys to kick down the door. None of them were Chinese."

"Yeah, but you know as well as I do that Thais can be a mix and also pure Chinese. Why are you so sure that there are Chinese in the mix now?"

"We got the shredded right hand of someone that doesn't match up to any of our guys prints or anyone in the Thai's database. It's definitely Chinese DNA."

"Still could be a local."

"Not unless it also held an encrypted and modified Huawei Ascend 6 phone."

"Ah, shit."

"Precisely."

South Thailand

Fajr…Morning prayers… seemed to come earlier than normal in the jungle. Nevertheless Sulalman's body told him that it was almost dawn and well within the prescribed time to praise Allah. He arose willingly, performed the ritual washing, prayed according to the precepts and was ready to begin his Jihad once again.

Chanchai bid goodbye to him after tea and porridge and prepared for his return to Hua Hin. Now dressed once again as a local businessman, he would travel back openly and resume work against the Bangkok government in Hua Hin.

The village chief led Sulalman to a small hut in the center of the cluster of buildings. Making sure that there were no strangers in the area, he reached down and pulled up the handle on a trap door in the floor. They climbed down a ladder through a narrow shaft, closed the door above them, and continued down about five meters below the surface into a series of rooms carved from the hard packed grey-brown clay.

Sulalman was amazed at the collection of weapons, explosives and supplies amassed there. Rooms extended in every direction…a small city of rebellion and the fight against oppression of their faith and historical ways of life. It was also a long kept secret of their ability to bring death and destruction to the soldiers of Bangkok and Buddha.

The Chief pointed to the oil paper wrapped weapons stacked in rows, claymore mines remaining from the Vietnam war and what looked to be hundreds of cases of military C-3,

C-4 and even a few cases of European made Semtex. Stacks of ammonium based fertilizer that could later be mixed with diesel fuel for IED's filled two other rooms.

The next room was a workshop in which the best bomb-makers in Afghanistan or Iraq would feel at home.

"This is our forward outpost in the fight, only three kilometers from Sungai Golok. Look around, if we lack anything for your training, let me know and it will be provided. We look forward to you helping us quickly bring the battle to this part of the country," he said to Sulalman.

"I will do my best to help while I am here. But remember, my brother, that I must return to my own fight in due course."

"Help us make Bangkok feel our wrath, our zeal, our determination before you depart."

"I truly will, you can count on it."

"So, what do we need to do to begin?"

"Bring me your technicians, I will add to their skills. Together we will give the Thais something to fear."

"Amin...so be it..." the Chief answered in Arabic.

*****

Ren realized that he had been put in the middle of a religious war between Believers and Buddhists not unlike the one plaguing Xinjiang in the western part of his country. While a Party member and not professing either of these two faiths himself, he understood power of loyalty in fighting for or against a common enemy. His loyalty to the Party, the PLA and his team was absolute. He assumed it to be so for those that he was tracking.

He also knew that those who broke ranks and informed against previous brothers, regardless of which faith they represented, could never be fully trusted again. Now he was expected to place his trust in just this type of person for putting him on the correct path to capture Sulalman.

87

What would Sun Tzu or Mao do? What should he do? What would Dickie do? He wondered.

Ren returned from meeting with the PLA's Hua Hin agent who had directed him to the site of yesterday's ambush. The retired sergeant now just told him, "Chanchai and the visitor departed early this morning going south, to Sungai Golok. They were dressed in the dark red robes of a monk."

Ren wondered, *Can I trust what he says? His information already cost Rocky's life. Is he being given disinformation to slow us down, misdirect our search or to ambush and kill us all?*

Army returned an hour later from the surveillance of the meeting. He followed the agent back to a small family compound at the north edge of the city, near the highway. "Someone else was watching him the whole time boss," Army reported. "I followed that guy back to this place in Chan Am, about ten minutes north," he said, holding up the camera. Got a few shots of him as well."

"What goes on there?"

"It's called a Madrassa, right next to a Mosque. Some kind of school."

Ren had seen several Madrassas. But unless it was coincidence that his watcher returned there, Muslims had to be involved in watching their Chinese source. He also knew that the Turkish government funded many of the schools in this part of the world to help spread their influence in the region. Was this a link to why Sulalman was in the south? Perhaps if the Turks are interested in what the Chinese are doing they know where Sulalman is going and are providing protection.

"Yes, I've seen them before, on another project in Tajikistan, " Ren answered.

"So Lo Ban, what do we do?" asked Army.

"Call Lt. Ming and have her divert whoever she sent to Hat Ya to Sungai Golok. Tell him to get three rooms for us in

88

one of the small hotels and "snoop" out the town," he said. "We'll meet him there soon."

"Okay boss." Strong said.

"In the meanwhile we have a few things to take care of for the trip down south."

*****

The bombing scene was still crawling with technicians from the Royal Thai Police, the Army and *Farang* advisors. Local vendors had already set up temporary stalls selling curry, various gai (chicken) snacks and soft drinks to the crowds that stood around watching the spectacle.

Ren and Army moved among them looking at the destruction. Their van had disappeared either from the authorities seizing it as evidence or because the keys were in it and it was stolen once again. He hoped for the latter but was sure they had left nothing of forensic value behind, except for possible stray DNA from their sweat.

There was little chance that any of their DNA signatures were as yet on file with police or intelligence services. Still, not providing a baseline for future incidents was prudent.

They watched until the crowds began to lose interest. So they would not stand out they walked past the fence line where they had narrowly missed being killed and then back toward the safe house. Within the hour they were on the highway for Sungai Golok in another small van provided by their local PLA asset.

"Remember, I do the talking," Ren reminded them. "Regardless of what happens, hear nothing, say nothing."

Minutes later, as they rounded a bend in the highway, they came to a line of traffic slowing to a crawl before reaching a Thai Army roadblock.

As their overloaded van approached the dark green 4X4 parked across the center of the road, Thai soldiers in jungle camouflage battle uniforms waved the van to a stop.

89

Seeing a Chinese driver they aggressively demanded identification and registration papers for the van. When they opened the rear their demeanor changed. They became even more solicitous when Ren emerged in saffron robes, shaven head and *Wai'd* the young soldier while offering the blessing of Buddha on him and the other soldiers who gathered around.

When Ren explained to the young soldier in Thai how the Chinese driver had offered Ren and his handicapped novitiates transportation to *make merit*, they put down their weapons and *wai'd* him as well. Ren said he was taking the Shadows, now dressed as young deaf-mute monks, on a pilgrimage to the jungle to fast and pray. He wanted to get there before the rainy season was upon them. The driver was taking them only as far at Surat Thani, about six hours away. From there they would walk into the small remote temple several kilometers off the highway.

The sergeant waved and motioned them to go through the defilade of vehicles blocking the road. Ren once again blessed the soldiers in Thai and climbed back in the rear. They zigzagged through the barriers and continue their journey toward the south.

"Wheeee boss, you should have been a movie actor," Army hooted.

"Shi Shi *(thank you)*" Ren said with a broad grin. "Anything to serve the motherland," he laughed.

Even the Chinese driver turned in his seat and gave big thumbs up in Ren's direction.

"Let's hope that they call the next roadblock so we don't have to do it again." Ren answered.

As it turned out, they were waived through the next three roadblocks each time with just a cursory look in the window and a respectful *high wai*. They stopped just outside of Surat Thani after dark, in a secure guesthouse rather than risk more roadblocks in the jungle.

They departed at first light in order to avoid elephants and other large animals on the night roadway and before all the buses and trucks started to clog the narrow roads and slow the traffic. Nevertheless, they didn't arrive in Sungai Golok until 4:30 PM. By the time they arrived they had transformed into their new identities, as Chinese businessmen on a holiday. Their reservations at the Marina Hotel awaited them.

Rather than undergo the strict security screening required to enter the hotel area, the van dropped them off at the hotel entrance and quickly disappeared into the quickly gathering darkness.

Even then, the streets were teeming with pretty, young, scantily clad girls walking to the various clubs, massage parlors and Go-Go Bars that surrounded the hotel. Brave was seated in the lobby waiting and greeted them with his cheery, "Anyone ready for a beer?"

Bangkok MSS Safe House

Lt. Ming summoned Zhou En Tau to two meetings. He failed to appear or acknowledge her requests. Director Zhou finally pushed Pei to the edge of her patience. He also kept balking at delivering the report that he had promised to forward to Beijing exonerating Major Ren against any action for breaching party discipline. He then missed another scheduled meeting where he was to bring a final copy noting receipt of his report to Beijing. This proved to be a fatal error for him.

Brave with Pei's guidance, had penetrated the computer assigned to Zhou in the embassy, stolen his password, authentication key and log-on data. For three days Zhou could not send an email or make a telephone call without Pei knowing its contents. He had not shared any of her threats either in the MSS organization or Party officials,

91

so if he chose not to cooperate voluntarily she would draft and send the report herself, with or without him.

She set a meeting with him at the atrium café of the Asia Book Plaza next to the Landmark Hotel. It was a very public place. This time, at the appointed time he appeared. No surveillance was detected starting three hours before his arrival and none came with him or was visible while he was there. Pei acted like a long lost friend, kissing him on the check when he approached her table. He seemed startled at her attention.

"So glad you decided to join me," she cooed sweetly.

"I don't think I really had any choice in the matter," he answered curtly.

"That's true, but wouldn't it be better if we at least made it not as hard as it could be?"

He didn't respond.

"Well, how shall we begin? Oh yes, how about reading your report to the Party Disciplinary Committee, I think it is very well done. You did a good job, a very thorough investigation indeed."

"I did no such thing," he sputtered.

"Certainly you did! In fact it has already been acknowledged," she said with a broad smile.

She handed him a copy of the correspondence.

"This is a fraud. I did not write this."

"But you did. It has been authenticated."

"I will repudiate it. It's a lie."

"Relax, you have nothing to worry about any more"

He blanched.

"You see Zhou En Tao, you have done a good job. Beijing thinks so, your MSS supervisors think so, why don't you?"

"This is outrageous, it will never be accepted."

"You are wrong, it already has been," she said with a broad smile.

He leapt from the table unsettling the tea service that had just been delivered and bolted for the basement parking lot. He almost made it to his embassy car before Strong intercepted him.

Sungai Golok Thailand

Military checkpoints dotted the streets and the entryways in the areas where small bars, discos and massage parlors came to life as the sun went down. Even in the short three block walk from their hotel, the team had to produce their Malaysian IC Cards (*Identity Card*) twice before the soldiers would allow them into the closely controlled recreation areas.

"Gee boss, this is almost as tight as getting into our base in Guangzhou," Brave said laughing.

"Or that young lady I saw you leave with last night?" asked Army.

"Not funny," Brave growled. Ren laughed.

"I'm glad we had complete sets of contingency ID when we left. At least the MSS guys were smart enough to think that we might end up in Malaysia," answered Army. "Having our own supply does not hurt us either," added Ren

"Well, lets not have them look at it too closely since its probably the only thing our MSS staff may have gotten right on this project," said Ren.

"I have a better idea. Let's have a few beers, maybe a massage?" suggested Army.

"You all know where the hotel is. I'm getting a few beers and something to eat. If you want to take off, see you in the morning. Just stay away from trouble," Ren advised as he peeled away from the group.

He did not follow Dickie's guidelines in these situations. If his men wanted to drink and have sex, that was up to them and nothing he wished to supervise. There were certainly enough choices within the city for them to indulge any taste, no matter how exotic.

Chapter 9

Bangkok, CIA SCIF...Sensitive Compartmented Information Facility

The station staff was huddled around the small conference table as the Station Chief howled, "What the hell are the Chinese knuckledraggers doing here?" No answers were forthcoming.

"Anything back on who the hand belonged to yet?" asked the Counter Terrorism Chief.

"Jesus, what a cluster fuck." The Counter Intelligence Chief said, expressing the sentiments of everyone in the small secure airless room.

"You, as usual, said it very well," said the Station Chief

"Yeah, but it still doesn't answer the basic question. How did he or she get there before us? We're supposed to be the ones with the source. So how is it that the Chinese were there at the same time as our guys, maybe before them?" asked the CI Chief.

"Right, that is a problem, but look, we're only a week since the bombing here and now we've got another one in Hua Hin. This time with our guys killed along with some Chinese involvement.

What does that tell us?" the Station Chief asked.

"We've got a major problem on our hands with one of the key suspects pissed off, still running around, and throwing bombs at us. Now we're pretty sure he's down south, doing God knows what; probably being helped by his 'fraternal brothers' in the cause against Bangkok" answered the CT chief.

"All right, so how do we get a handle on this thing? Langley is expecting answers, Christ; I'm expecting to have people from the IG's (*Inspector General*) Office here tomorrow to 'help out' with the investigation into what happened in Hua Hin," said the COS.

"Shit, what do we tell them?" asked the CI Chief.

"You tell them nothing! Let them try sorting it out themselves. We've got a terrorist to find. Can't waste time with them telling us what fucking time it is using our own watch," said the COS.

"What's with the source? Who did the vetting? Is he still reliable?" asked the CT Chief.

"All good questions guys, I'm sure the IG's guys will be very interested in the answers. You know how it works. They'll be looking over everything we did, everything we should have done and everything they wanted us to do until they find the smoking gun showing how we screwed up. Let's not look too bad, get out there and find some answers for me."

Beijing SOC headquarters

Colonel Li looked up with growing dismay after rereading the agent reports from Hua Hin. "How is it that Major's Ren's team was led into a trap? What happened?" he asked the project officer.

"This source has always provided excellent, actionable information. He is part of the rebel support network, trusted by senior leadership," the officer responded.

"That does not answer my question."

"Unless he was deliberately given the information about their resting for the night to lure any trackers into the trap," he responded again to the Colonel.

"That would presume our agent is known to be disloyal and they used him to provide the information, Colonel Li pressed."

"So why do they let him be part of their support network? Let him provide us with good information?"

"For exactly such a situation. They give us crumbs until we accept everything he reports then use him against us at a key moment, Li answered."

"Are they really that sophisticated in their planning?"

"Their movement has been alive and growing for fifty years. Possibly we underestimated their skills."

"What do we do about the agent? the officer asked."

"Nothing, it's not his fault. He is doing exactly what each of us expected him to do. Press him for more details, but don't rely on his information again. Three months from now we terminate his services quietly."

"In the meanwhile, what do you hear from your other sources about where Sulalman and Chanchai have gone? Li asked."

"We have a report that they departed for the far south. We know that Major Ren spoke with the contact we provided him this morning and we were told that they are enroute to Sungai Golok. He has decided to follow them there."

"Let's hope that this is not another trap. Send a message to Ren and warn him of our concerns. We do not need another potential disaster in the making," Li concluded.

Beijing, Disciplinary Committee Hearing

Chairman Yen put down Director Zhou's report and looked around the Committee's table. "There are no violations of Party discipline here, this report sounds more like a promotion assessment for Major Ren. Why are we even here dealing with such a matter?"

"Colonel Li brought the major's conduct to us at the request of Colonel Ping, a Project FORWARD Chief, who did not feel the Major was following good discipline and had gone rogue," said General Zhu."

97

"Well, unless there is some other evidence that we have not seen, he appears to be misguided in his concerns," said Chairman Yen. He paused then added, "Unless anyone has something else to offer…General Zhu, you are authorized to tell Major Ren that the investigation has been concluded. Please commend him on his actions and have him continue his duties."

"Yes Chairman Yen, Major Ren will be pleased to learn of the Committee's action."

Turning to Colonel Li, the Chairman continued, "Perhaps Colonel Ping could use a refresher course in Party disciplinary training."

Colonel Li kept his head down, nodded to him and made notes in his folio. *Perhaps it is time to move Ping once again. Tibet would be a good opportunity for him to rehabilitate himself though hard work. Should I reward Zhou for his excellent report or discipline him for not providing the kind of report that Ping wanted? I must speak with him about why I did not see the report before it was submitted to the Committee even though he does not report to MSS for these duties. He should know better.*

*****

Ping listened to the report from Colonel Li then slammed down the telephone.

"What do they mean, Major Ren acted appropriately?" Ping bellowed. "Where is that little worm Zhou? I'll cut his miserable little dick off and feed it to the ducks in the embassy pond. Find him, get him in here now!" he screamed.

His staff went to look for Zhou but learned that he had not been into the Embassy all day. He had signed out a car for a meeting in the morning but had not yet returned. No answer from his mobile telephone and his tracking device showed that he was sitting in his empty office.

"The miserable disloyal prick is frightened to face me after his treachery. Wait until he returns. He will regret the

98

day he was born. He will be chasing monks in Tibet forever." Ping yelled from his desk.

*****

Chief Burroughs also waited for Zhou to arrive. He would soon be equally concerned about Chanchai's, AKA Nimrod's, disappearance.

Lt. Ming had made sure that it would be a long time before Director Zhou turned up. Ren had listened on the secure telephone as she recounted her dealings with Director Zhou.

"That devious son of a whore tried using the party for his personal ends. Good riddance. It will be a long time before his body is discovered, if ever," Pei noted. Then added, "That is unless a body part detaches and clogs a sewer-line feeding into that covered over kalong we found our first night."

"Inspired choice, feeding him to the pigs or crocodiles would have been more poetic but your choice is more practical," Ren chuckled.

"Any chance you were observed?"

"Certainly seen but not observed in what we were doing."

"Ahh," he said smiing to himself, then quickly added, "well done."

"Thank you Major, you trained us well. We are leaving for the airport and should arrive by 9:30 tonight. Our equipment has already been collected and will arrive late tomorrow. We will be contacted when it arrives."

"Fine. We need everyone here as soon as possible as we are scouring the area for signs of our target. The local contact has no new information other than telling us that something big is in planning."

Her team had cleaned up the safe house and quickly headed for the domestic airport. PLA support assets would

99

make sure weapons and supplies were securely transferred to Sungai Golok without MSS involvement.

The Village

Sulalman's eyes burned from the bright sunlight when he emerged through the trap door. "I'll be back in thirty minutes. I expect to see your finished devices then," he said as he pushed the door back into place. The three brothers the village headman had produced were capable, practical but unsophisticated in their techniques compared to what even he had learned in Baluchistan years ago. Now, after only 24 hours, they were approaching the next level of effectiveness. He blinked back tears caused by the bright sunlight, stretched and walked outside onto the hard packed dirt outside the building.

Dressed in an old white t-shirt and faded jeans, his shaven head glistened in the growing morning heat as he did some exercises in the yard. The local tuktuk driver that serviced the surrounding villages was making his rounds while Sulalman was blinking away the effects of time underground. He made note of this stranger in the village.

Fortunately for Major Ren, the appearance of this unusual sight was reported to one of the PLA's sources responsible for monitoring the area. It was reported to Ren's team later that day.

*****

After he climbed down the ladder and walked through the underground bunkers one last time, Sulalman returned to the training room. He said, "All right brothers, let's review your work," Sulalman began as he inspected the wiring, connections and detonation devices displayed on the worktables. He began,"You have done exceedingly well."

100

Aside from one loose connection on a redundant circuit, all devices were well constructed and ready for use. Their practical final examination would be the next evening. It would indeed be a grand affair.

"Now, let's talk about site selection and detonation protocols," he continued.

CIA Station Bangkok

"What do you mean Zhou is a no show?" growled the CI Chief.

"Just that! He didn't show. Doesn't answer any of the emergency contact calls, nothing, just dropped off the screen," said the CT Chief.

"Well that's just fucking great. What does that Feebee (*FBI*) moron have to say? You asked him yet?"

"Yeah, he knows nothing about him. Says it's our problem now. He was golden working for them."

"Right, probably been a double since they recruited him. This is bad juju," answered the CI Chief.

"What do we hear from the Chinese? Any of our MSS sources have any insight?"

"First place we checked. They're looking for him too. Seems his boss is really pissed at him. Wants his scalp for getting him fucked over by the powers in Beijing about some report he wrote."

"Wonderful, sounds like this brilliant bureau asset is fucking everyone in the ass but the real question is, "Who the hell is he really working for these days?" asked the CI Chief.

"That's the question we need to answer. That's the question that the IG's people are going to zero in on so get your people on the street here and in Hua Hin and get us some answers. I don't want to get them from the Station Fuck Up's Section of some God Damn IG Damage Assessment of the Hua Hin Bombing Report," the COS shouted.

The senior management team of the Bangkok Station knew quite well that unless they figured out what happened, they would be lucky to be back at headquarters running name traces in some warehouse basement in Falls Church or worse - being assigned as an Admin Puke accounting for ops funds in Afghanistan for the rest of their careers.

Sungai Golok

Ren's team exercised, cleaned weapons and read reports at the PLA warehouse that was disguised as a trucking company. The modern metal building was located within fifty meters of the river adjacent to the Malaysian border. They had begun the task of trying to locate their target using local PLA intelligence sources. In Beijing, General Zhu made sure that the Ghost Shadows had access to real-time raw field intelligence via a secure satellite link with Beijing. A 1/25:000 wall map of the area provided a place to pin point the location of possible Sulalman sightings. The tuktuk driver was one of many reports that arrived that morning. The PLA-MID (*Military Intelligence Division*) intelligence officer assigned to Sungai Golok had few assets available to do follow-up so the Shadows split up the sightings and began to work them. Working in two man teams they divided the map area into quadrants and began their assessments. Pei and Ren drew the one from the tuktuk.

*****

The southern part of Thailand is blessed with natural beauty; waterfalls, rivers, and jungle terrain all connected to Bangkok by a well-developed road and rail system supplemented by air service. Tying it all together is an extensive series of bridges that span narrow ravines, swollen rivers and major gaps in jungle outcroppings. This man-made trail through these natural beauties provides access for the long distance trucks, buses and cars that are the life-blood of this rural area. It also connects the daily trains from Malaysia and the world famous Orient Express with the scenic route between Singapore, Kuala Lumpur and Bangkok.

Army and Brave studied area maps. "Where would you attack?" Ren had asked them before he departed for an on-the-ground review of the local area leads with Pei. "Review the maps then recon those places," Ren told the Shadows. "If we can see where to damage the Thais, these Tangos will be doing the same thing. Let's stop them before they can act."

Hours later, three probable locations had been identified. Brave took two sites close to the border and Army a bridge and tunnel about twenty-five kilometers north.

Right on time, Brave thought as he watched the slow moving passenger train come around a wide sweeping turn and enter the clearing just as the engine began crossing the narrow bridge over the fast moving river about fifty meters below. It moved past the location where he was hiding just as it emerged from the last of a series of tunnels. Then slowed down for the Sungai Golok station. The terrain shown on the map suggested two locations where the entirety of the bridge structure could be viewed. This was the least desirable of the two but less likely to be under hostile surveillance, so there he was.

He used a range-finding monocle to scan the area under the bridge, girder-by-girder, support pylon-by-pylon. Nothing...no extra wires, evidence of disturbances, attachments or tampering. What he did see was that he was correct in being cautious in his reconnaissance as there was a carefully hidden OP (*Observation Post*) one hundred meters across the ravine, just where he would have chosen to set up a protective position. He could clearly see the tiger striped pattern of the hidden Thai Special Forces trooper manning this discrete position. He chuckled to himself. *Gotch Ya!*

So far, so good. No way you are going to see me watching you. Looks like the boss was right. These Tangos do know what they are doing, or at least the military thinks they have the capability to take down this bridge. Okay, this bridge is as secure as it can be, unless the Tangos are as good as us and can outflank the Thais, set charges and not be seen. Time to move on.

Brave moved slowly away from his position, covering any evidence should any foliage have been disturbed at his vantage point.

It took two hours to extricate himself from the position and leave no trace.

The next location, just at the edge of town was well defended with regular army troops manning sandbagged revetments on both sides of the ravine. Too obvious a location. No Tango would attack such a place. So, if not there, where should they look next? Maybe Army was having more luck.

****

Army had taken a local bus through two police and military checkpoints. He had left the main highway and entered the jungle about four kilometers from where the railway bridge was located. Concern for arrest or interrogation had prevented him from taking anything but the basic equipment of a knife with built-in compass for the trip. It had taken him almost four hours to arrive at a position half a kilometer from the bridge. It was another hour to get close enough to determine that he should go no farther.

He saw the first motion detectors that were located along the main trail where it descended toward the riverbed at waist and shoulder level. They were attached to a tree trunk covered with dark brown trailing vines; very professional job. It was a well-designed trap indicating a heavily protected target that would be extremely difficult to attack. No point in

104

penetrating the defenses for this recon. He needed another six hours to safely return to the warehouse.

Their assessment so far was that the Thais were taking the threats to key infrastructure seriously and making it very hard for Tangos to mount a successful attack against these fixed positions. There certainly were no places where the Shadows could interdict them, capture their target and get away from the Thais. If time was short before the next attack, they would have to move quickly or risk more deaths but more importantly to them, Sulalman disappearing once again.

Army and Brave returned late in the afternoon, well after Ren and Pei began their follow-up travels. For all their effort, there was no conclusive evidence and that was frustrating.

Pei held tightly, probably more than necessary, to Ren while they sped down the highway on the 900 cc Suzuki motorcycle borrowed from the shipping company, The local license plate gave him good cover for driving down the back roads to scout locations for deliveries. Pei acted as his assistant should they encounter any Muslim women that would not speak to a male in the small villages scattered throughout the area. Of the four possible sightings they had been given, only this last one produced anything of substance. Two had photographs that showed indistinct images that could be anyone: one who they found working as a charcoal vendor was too old, another that they spoke to was clearly mentally retarded while the other was a *katoey (Girl-Boy transsexual)* home from Pattaya dying from AIDS. They were now on the way to the farthest village where the last sighting had been made early that morning.

The village square was deserted when they arrived. Ren shut down the motorcycle. They stretched, looked around and listened. The only sound they heard was the pinging of the exhaust pipe as it started to cool. No birds were calling, animals bleating or chickens running. In fact, there

105

were no children running around, no women tending gardens along the edges of the jungle clearing or men sitting on porches smoking and talking. It appeared to be a ghost town but one that had been very active earlier in the day. It was almost time for evening prayers but no sign of a mosque in this heavily Muslim area.

The eerie scene was in contrast with the tire tracks that crisscrossed the dirt square. Even with it being hard packed, there were deep indentations from truck tires.

"Lo Ban, look at this," Pei said softly. She pointed at the difference between the tracks that had entered the square, parked and then pulled out of the village. Very clearly the truck had departed much heavier than when it arrived.

"Hello, anybody here?" Ren shouted in Thai into the open doorway of the building where the truck had stopped. He did it again in Chinese and Bahasa with the same result. He motioned to Pei to circle around the rear of the building to see if anyone was there. Within a minute she reappeared on the other side of the building giving an all-clear signal. Carefully checking for IED's and finding nothing suspicious, Ren moved through the unlocked front door and stood motionless, eyes scanning the room, looking for clues as to what had taken place earlier in the day.

The four-meter by three-meter room looked ordinary. It had a dirt floor, table, three chairs, sleeping platform and a few shelves with cooking pots scattered along the rear wall. There were several indentations in the hard packed dirt where approximately one meter long items had been placed on top and dirt had been swept over these disturbed area near the center of the room next to the table and chairs.

Ren took out a mini-Maglite© and screwed on an infrared filter, stooped down and inspected the area more closely.

"Pei, get the saddlebag from the bike, quickly," he said. Minutes later he was able to locate the edges of a

106

wooden frame, over a meter wide, set into the floor. It was concealed under the edges of the sleeping platform. A mini electrical resistance detector and a thermal scanner indicated trace amounts of metal while the explosive residue scanner registered high levels of explosive particulates.

"Call Army! Give him our coordinates and get the team here. Also send a message to Colonel Li and tell him we have picked up Sulalman's trail."

"Are you sure Lo Ban? Pei asked.

"I'd rather be wrong than miss him again," Ren countered.

During the forty-five minute wait for Army and Brave to arrive, Ren and Pei searched the village. It was completely void of life and had been hastily deserted. Ren was now convinced that something big was in motion that involved Sulalman and the residents of this village.

Army and Brave arrived in a small Toyota© truck with a concealed compartment containing a small ground penetrating radar devise, hand tools and digging equipment. It took an hour of painstaking work to determine that wires were attached to the trap door structure in three places. Without more time and equipment it would be impossible to secure entry without the probability of an explosion.

"Looks like this was a major staging area for explosive materials." Army suggested, then added, "Without some heavy moving equipment there's no way to get into this place."

"So what we know," said Pei, "is that someone hauled away a heavy load of something that they had underground in the last eight hours or so, booby trapped their storage area and we have no idea where they are."

"It looks like the truck turned south when it left the dirt area but that's just a strong guess," said Ren looking at the edge of the roadway next to the village.

"Yeah, but we know that all the people from the entire village have disappeared as well. Why would that happen unless they all knew about the explosives being there and are worried about what will happen when they are used by the Tangos," said Pei.

"Exactly, that's the real worry. The Tangos are planning something really big and we're late getting to them," answered Ren.

"Even so Boss, we know they are on the move to deliver a big explosion. The good news is that neither the Thais nor the bad guys know we know," said Brave.

"That's fine, but so what. What do we do now?" asked Army.

"The local tangos would not use Sulalman for something small. Maybe to train their locals to do bigger things but if he was here earlier today, he is acting as an advisor or trainer for something big they had already planned," said Ren

"We're pretty sure that they are not going after any of the major fixed infrastructures in the area so that leaves hotels, schools, trains and the airport," offered Pei.

"Okay, what do you attack to make a big impact? Think about it?" Ren said. "Either there are going to be many small-scale attacks across the area or something really big. So what's it going to be with Sulalman involved?"

"Got to be big boss…Gotta be the train, that's what I'd go after. Orient Express for sure," said Army.

"It would sure make for one major 'cluster fuck' for the Thais," answered Brave.

"I think you're right," said Ren, looking at his watch. He then asked, "Who remembers the timetable for the Express? I know it comes through from Singapore and Kuala Lumpur, stops for some sightseeing then continues on north about 23:30 tonight."

"That's in about two hours," Pei said.

"Let's go get us some Tangos," Army shouted.

*****

Ren quickly called in a report on their finding and plans to Colonel Li and told Brave to standby at the village until the local PLA staff could get someone there to secure the site and exploit it for further intelligence. Its location would eventually be leaked to the Thais for their EOD (*Explosive Ordinance Disposal*) troops to dismantle. The Chinese Military Attaché in Bangkok would get some credit from the Thais for passing along the information without telling him how it came into his possession.

"As soon as they arrive join us in Sungai Golok. Call on the way and I'll direct you," Ren shouted as he fired up the motorcycle and headed for the highway.

Thirty minutes later Pei was walking on the railroad station platform looking at schedules and talking to the station attendants.

The train was slightly behind schedule and now expected to arrive at 23:45 and depart seven minutes later. Pei learned that the train was making an unscheduled pick-up of a V.I.P. passenger who had missed his connection in Kuala Lumpur. The passenger was a motion picture director who was scouting locations for a new movie in the area. He was bringing lots of camera and camping equipment that would required a small team to load everything in the baggage car attached to the historic train.

"If what Army calculated is correct, the truck had at least one thousand kilos of extra weight added while it was parked at the village," said Ren adding "Depending on what was underground there, that amount of explosives could take out the train and everything surrounding it for three hundred meters in all directions."

"Do you think they will attack at the train station?" asked Pei.

"No, if I were going to just blow up the train why go through all the trouble of setting up the stop, the movie director and all those preparation? This has been in motion for a long time. Sulalman being involved suggests that they needed his skills to made a more complex plan work properly. Fuses, timing devices or detonators are probably the best bet. If so, they want the blast timed to do the most damage possible to the chosen site and the Bangkok government," Ren answered then slowly continued, "Let's see how this sounds, 'The historic luxury train is full of wealthy visitors traveling across the exotic jungle in safe and secure Thailand... the Land of Smiles...I think their advertising says... and is blown to bits'. It's very bad publicity indeed.

If they can couple that disaster with cutting off all rail travel for months through the south part of the country that would indeed be a major blow to the economy as well. This does not even take into account all the possibilities for sabotage of the new construction that would need to be done immediately or all the troops that would be tied up with construction site security. It would be a major loss for the government, economy and a loss of face for their security services."

"Hold on Lo Ban, that's an awful lot you're rolling up into one bombing," said Army.

"So how do you see it?"

"No, what you said sounds correct but just how do we stop Sulalman and take him back home, that's what I thought we were here to do?" asked Army.

Ren paused, "You are correct, our job is not to stop the bombing but to capture Sulalman and that is what we are going to do. But to do this we need to know where he is going to be. All we think we know now is what he might be planning to do."

"Okay, so how do we catch him?"

110

"Sulalman has never been at the scene of the attacks he planned. He just plans them while others carry them out. This time it looks like he might have gone with the explosives..."

"Or still hiding underground back at the village," Army suggested.

"Exactly, that's why Brave is waiting there until our comrades arrive to take over. Should Sulalman emerge, Brave has instructions to kill or capture him on the spot."

"Anyway, Sulalman may be forced by his local brothers to demonstrate that the techniques he has been teaching them actually work. Just because he was presented to them as a trusted brother, they might not be willing to share everything with an outsider and this attack might be a good way to silence him about their operations after he has demonstrated that his techniques are good. Perhaps they trust but still like to keep their secrets closer than having their allies knowing what they do or where their hiding places might be."

"So we are doing him a favor by stealing him away from his brothers that will kill him after his usefulness is finished? Pei asked.

"Something like that. Never let a good crisis go to waste," Ren chuckled.

"So, the Tangos will make sure that Sulalman is on the train. So we need to be there also, stop the bombing, capture him and disappear in the next two hours?" Army asked, then added, "anyone have any ideas on how the fuck we are going to do it?"

Nobody answered.

Beijing SOC Headquarters

General Zhu sat back in his oversized desk chair, threw down the flash report and scowled at his aide. "It's been eight days since the Shadows were inserted into Thailand, this is all they report? He might be there, they might capture him?"

"Yes sir, Colonel Li knows no more than you at this time. Our station in Sungai Golok has staff currently guarding an underground bomb making complex the Shadows discovered but there is nothing new on their target. If he is still underground they will capture him."

"The longer this takes, the more likely our comrades in the Ministry will learn of our operation without them and cause us difficulties."

"I'll make sure Colonel Li is reminded of your concerns," said the Major.

PRC Embassy Bangkok

"Colonel Ping, how is it that Director Zhou has been absent from his assignment for the past three days without this fact being noted in our attendance reporting?" asked the MSS station chief.

"He has been experiencing some personal issues the past few weeks and has taken a few days personal time sir."

The Chief looked at him and said, "I have had three reports from your staff that he has disappeared without proper authorization and members of your team have been searching for him without making it an official inquiry. Is this true?"

"Zhou has been under strain after a Disciplinary Committee Report he prepared and I…"

"I'm aware of this disaster, Colonel. How is it that you now have two major deviations from accepted practice, both of which you have tried to conceal from me?"

"No sir, I've done no such thing. I've merely tried to bring you solutions not problems. Both of these situations are related and will be resolved when Zhou returns to work. We know his wife has not seen him and we are searching for the local Thai woman he has been visiting for the past two months. When we find her, I'm sure we will find him."

"You had better be right in this matter, Colonel. My patience is short. Your conduct has been less than acceptable. Resolve this situation or start packing your cold weather clothing."

Boarding the Train

"The stranger is under the watchful eye of Rahmin," said the headman.

"Is that enough? We cannot have him disappear at this time without proving his skill..." said Ashraf, his lieutenant.

"...his loyalty to our cause..." added Naidu.

"All your concerns will be answered," the headman replied as he continued the slow meticulous sharpening of his *Kris (ceremonial knife)*that was normally tucked into his belt. He was seated in the rear of the truck on one of the large black *Tumi* © knockoff suitcases that now contained the explosive devices developed by Sulalman.

They waited in a darkened parking area near the stall market several blocks from the railroad station. Shortly they would drive to the baggage loading area and await the train and their V.I.P. "Movie Director" brother from Malaysia.

Sulalman waited in the cab of the truck. He would supervise the final loading to make sure the bags were placed in the proper cars and locations according to the plan he had developed for the attack. It was critical that each charge be in the correct place for maximum effect.

Three minutes further behind schedule, the Express could be heard slowing as it approached the brightly lit platform. Station staff, security guards and the soldiers assigned there all began setting up for their appointed duties to handle the special passenger, his baggage and entourage. As the headlight swept across the tracks the diesel engine

113

strained to slow down without disturbing the pampered travelers as it made this unannounced stop. Just because a creative genius is joining the rolling party, it was no excuse to disturb the other guests. The rolling party was to continue without interruption.

The village headman had planned this addition to the train to coincide with the normal evening festivities in the ornate club car where the wealthy travelers on this exotic alcohol-laced adventure were congregating around the antique teak and brass piano. Their loud, off-key but cheerful songs could be heard as the train rolled to a smooth stop at the five car long platform.

CIA Station Bangkok

"Son-of-a-Bitch," Burroughs sighed under his breath, as he hit the Print and Save keys on his secure terminal. "It's not bad enough we've got the IG's troops here, now I'm officially being told I've got a God Damn, no shit bunch of Chinese bad asses on my turf."

He walked down the hall, looked in the door and seeing the COS hunched over his terminal he asked, "Hey sailor, looking for a good time?"

"I sure don't want anything you're trying to give away, that's for sure. Now what disaster are you buttering me up for this time?"

"Moi? I'm disappointed Chief, I always only bring good news, or nothing at all."

"Right, you got thirty seconds...elevator speech...or move on."

"Okay, here goes...NSA and TSD (*Technical Services*) analyzed the Huawei phone we collected. Both agree we have a top PLA SF (*Special Forces*) unit operating here. The encryption levels involved are just out of Chinese Beta testing; stuff is reserved for only the ultra elite units. At least

114

six operators in the call tree. We've got their code names, names of their control in Beijing along with contact numbers that tie to active projects in our CI (*Counter Intelligence*) and OPS (*Operational*) files. Our penetration of the MSS Bangkok Station says that they are looking for them also, seems the SF boss fucked over one of the key MSS guys here along with maybe disappearing one of his local station staff..."

"Probably only five," said the COS.

"What?"

"Only five SFers, unless you are still counting the severed hand as one of your bad asses."

"You're right as usual boss, but what do you think about the assessment?"

"I think, you have a major fucking problem on your hands. It sounds like either this team has gone off the reservation or PLA thinks MSS is fucked up and cutting them out of their operations. No way an SF unit is tracking these Tangos without ops support and if the local MSS station is not giving it, then it has to be coming from PLA or MID sources without telling MSS about it." He paused, looking up from his computer and said, "any ideas how to exploit this riff inside the opposition here?"

"I pretty much agree with your take on the situation but if we are correct, we seriously underestimated how strong the PLA network actually is here in country. If those SFers are tracking the Bangkok T's they need some heavy Intel and ops support along the way in the south. It also sounds like whoever they work for doesn't trust local MSS assets to support them."

"So, what do we do?"

Burroughs smiled. "Well, for starters, TSD says that they can get a geo-fix on one of the other telephones and sent along this...." handing the sheet of coordinates to the COS. "We have been getting strong signals from one of the last

115

numbers 'the hand' called, it is sending data right now about ten klicks from Sungai Golok."

"We own the Son-of-a Bitch," said the now grinning COS.

"Bingo!."

"You better get with the CT guys and figure out how to play this thing. I'm gonna think about how to use what we know with the IG's folks and more importantly, with the Thais and Chinese. The Thais will want to know what we found out with the phone and I'm betting the Chinese will surely want to have the remains of one of their own back for burial."

"God damn boss, you truly are one sensitive S.O.B.," said Burroughs as he walked away to get started on his planning.

The Chief waived him out the door and turned back to his computer screen.

Later at the PRC Embassy Bangkok

First Secretary Gao returned to the Bangkok Embassy after his meeting with his counterpart from the Thai Foreign Affairs Department. His assistant carried two sealed bundles they had received from the Thai Secretary along with a note of condolences on the loss of one of their nationals in the Hua Hin bombing. One package contained the severed hand, the other a barely identifiable cell phone in a clear plastic Royal Thai Police Evidence Envelope.

It took two days before word filtered to the MSS staff that this contact had been made, yet another day for the telephone to be collected and sent to Beijing for analysis.

Minister of State Security Wong read the report. He sat quietly for a few moments then picked up the phone from his otherwise empty desktop.

116

Chapter 10

Railroad Station, Sungai Golok, Thailand

The last of the oversized suitcases were piled in the Orient Express baggage car, the truck emptied of camera and lighting equipment and the porters sent on their way in record time. The train was ready to depart as the 'Director' in a white linen suit, matching wide brimmed hat and lavish yellow silk scarf, boarded and made his way to the lounge car. His entourage began taking assigned, previously vacant, seats throughout the train. Only twelve minutes behind schedule, the highly polished dark green, seven car-long train slowing began to move away from the station.

By all rights the train should not have even been crossing the border in Sungai Golok but sympathetic 'brothers in Allah' working for the Malaysian Railway diverted the train to this route. Since they effectively 'sealed the train', not allowing anyone to disembark and Thai Immigration was further down along the track, the Thai Police meeting the train were not concerned with the non-scheduled cross border visit. Thai officials closely monitored the loading and boarding of the 'Director' and his party, and watched as the train pulled out of the station moving toward the black void of the jungle. It would clear border formalities at Hat Ya, the next regularly scheduled station.

Army and Brave took the easy way onto the train. They climbed a waterspout at the rear of the train platform, quickly stepped onto the roof of the final car, laid down and held on until the train left the station. They then climbed down the rear ladder and entered the baggage car by picking the old lock.

One of the 'cameramen' from the entourage who decided to use the station toilet would eventually be found gagged and tie taped to a water pipe under a sink. Ren now had his ticket and seat assignment in his pocket along with a small tactical radio that had been in the terrorist's jacket pocket.

Pei used a more direct approach. She had changed into a traditional Chinese Cheongsam, coaxed the ticket agent with $400 USD into selling her a "seat" on the train so she could 'do some business' with the passengers before they arrived in Bangkok. The promise of splitting the profits on her return and a 'free' sample of her wares upon her return sealed the deal.

As the train left the station, Pei was patiently waiting in the lounge car watching for the arrival of the 'Director." Sulalman's seat was in the second to last car, near the rear door. He waited for the headman to appear and confirm all was in readiness.

There were now eleven minutes until the first scheduled explosion.

Into the Jungle

The engineers who planned and built the rail lines through Thailand tried to take the most direct and least expensive routes through what was once impassable jungle, rugged mountains and fast flowing streams. The line now used by the Orient Express was originally built as the Southern Thailand Line in 1903 to move agricultural products out of the country into Malaysia. It had been upgraded and re-gauged several times over the years to bring it up to modern day rail standards.

There were now two ways to enter Thailand from Malaysia by train. The Main line from Kuala Lumpur and Singapore now travelled via Hat Ya on the west branch from Malaysia. The east line crossed from Malaysia into Thailand at Sungai Golok and is used primarily for freight because the

118

Immigration Control for Thailand was consolidated at Hat Ya.

Low limestone peaks of over 1000 meters covered this part of the country. They rise perpendicular from roaring streams that make traversing them next to impossible, even on foot. They form rainforest clogged steep cliffs and valleys along their length creating a veritable border wall with neighboring Myanmar.

The Japanese Imperial Army learned the hard way about the difficulties of trying to cross this area during WWII. Thousands of troops died of disease and deprivations in these mountains. Local residents believe that this area is watched over by 'guardian spirits' that will repel outsiders.

Three helicopter crashes in 2011 and 2012 that killed dozens of military and police being just a recent example of the wrathfulness of these guardians of every crack, crevasse and mountain that form what is now a series of national parks and endangered animal preserves on both sides of the border.

The good thing about limestone is that it is very porous and easy to blast and carve. This combination made for happy engineers and accountants. Low cost construction, easy materials to work with and lots of stable fill materials from the crushed limestone aided the construction efforts. Bridges and tunnels dotted the landscape. Nature made both rail and road building a rather straightforward undertaking.

The train had crossed over the short wooden beamed Friendship Bridge spanning the Golok River on its passage from Malaysia into Thailand. There would be three other small, less than ten to twenty meter, long bridges between the station and the long trestle over the deep river canyon with the swift flowing river seventy-five meters below.

On the outward-bound leg of the trip from Bangkok the bridge is crossed during daylight so the dramatic scenery can be appreciated more completely. At night the train slows to a mere twenty kilometers per hour speed limit for safety. This fact will only be noted by the new arrivals who are just settling into the rhythm of activities on the train.

Ten minutes to detonation

Two entourage members left their end-car seats and exited the rear door of the passenger compartment, crossed the gap between the two cars and moved toward the Baggage Car door. One took out a duplicate copy of the door key, opened the lock, and entered. They locked it behind them.

At the same time, another two of the Tangos stood, collected their backpacks, and began their way two cars forward to the front of the train. They opened the locked front door just behind the two-car engine with another copy key. They held this position between the first car and engine and waited for the "go" signal. They had no choice but to breath in the heavily diesel fumed night air. The older of the two attempted to steady the nervous young man next to him. He said, "Soon my brother, soon Allah's will becomes known to the dogs in Bangkok."

Eight minutes

"There they are," said another very young looking Tango as he moved to the left side of the baggage car where three very large Tumi© wheelie suitcases sat with their pair of brightly colored Fluorescent Green PomID© baggage identifiers. Eight other suitcases and bags with equally bright, color-coded tags, waited for deployment. The older Tango checked his large wristwatch, opened the rear door and blocked it open with one of the heavy black cases. He looked around and checked his partner's progress is positioning the balance of the bags.

120

"Ei...yah, the foreigner is crazy. These bags are too heavy to do what he asked," said the younger of the two.

"Silence, it is as we practiced. It is only necessary that we lift and drop them over the trestle quickly. They will not break or split open and even if they do, the bomb will explode."

"Inshallah," he answered.

"It is our job to make sure it is so," the other Tango responded. "We must be quick, we have fifteen seconds to drop all three before we finish crossing the bridge."

"Just like before my brother, just like we practiced several times."

In the front of the train weapons were taken from backpacks, assembled, loaded and radios made ready for the short climb along the catwalk that separated the two Tangos from the engineer in the cab of the train. It was just one car ahead. They confirmed the time and began climbing.

Six minutes

From the top of the train car, Army said, "Hey boss, we got two Tangos opening the rear door in the baggage compartment," as he watched and heard the suitcases being dragged to the rear platform."

"What are they doing?" Ren asked.

"Moving big black suitcases out onto the platform. Looks like they're getting ready to dump them off the train."

Sulalman stood in the Lounge car toilet listening for the check-in's from each of his team. The first confirmed his location and Sulalman responded and waited quietly while the other two Tango's did the same.

Ren did the same in the next car behind him. He called his team and said, "We have at least four teams on board plus

121

one or two controlling them. Still not sure what they are really planning but we need to stop them."

Four minutes

"Get these Orange tagged bags ready, we'll need them next," said the young Tango.

"Okay, they go by the sliding door on the right, yes?"

"No...they go on the left you idiot. Where you sleeping during the training? The left, only the left as the train moves forward, the left. The right will kill us all."

"Yes, yes, left is what I meant," he answered with a frown on his face as he began moving four of the much smaller suitcases to the wall in front of the still locked sliding door.

The color coded tagged cases would be carried forward to the other team members when their work was completed in the baggage car, five minutes from now.

"And please, open the door now, before you forget that also."

"No worries my brother," he said easily slipping into his native Australian accent.

******

Pei worked her way to the toilet when she saw it become free. She had blatantly tried to solicit a few of the older passengers until the conductor told her to stop and go to her compartment. Instead, she had waited for Ren, with his large carry bag, to move to the toilet where she made a deliberate effort to look like she was following him there for sex.

She slipped in right after him, stripped off her dress and began getting on a form fitting one-piece ballistic cloth coverall, stripped off the caked-on makeup and put on a ball cap to cover her hair. Her knife and machine pistol were now secured in her web belt along with extra ammunition.

122

After Ren changed into his coveralls, if it were not for her breasts and long hair, it would be hard to tell them apart in the matching outfits provided by the local PLA supply depot.

Three minutes

The large suitcases were stacked on the rear platform. The two Tangos were ready to open the engine compartment while Sulalman and the headman started to walk through the gently swaying cars toward the front of the train.

Two minutes

The sliding doors to the baggage car were quietly opened and the smaller cases moved into position. The rear door propped open with the large green-tagged suitcases.

One minute

The engineer and fireman were pushed into a corner of the engine room while the younger of the Tangos took control of the train and began to slow it down. At its current speed it would take almost two thousand meters to gradually stop the train in the proper position.

"Check the time," shouted the older Tango.

"Thirty seconds," came the response from the Tango holding the throttle.

"Okay, start slowing us down," came the reply. This was followed by an almost imperceptible lurch as the brakes began to engage.

In the baggage car the three suitcases were pushed and thrown off the rear platform by the two Tangos who then quickly slammed the rear door shut. The cases hit the trestle and tracks, bounced along for a few meters then came to a

123

rest. Almost immediately they exploded into a white, yellow and red ball of flame.

Bits of timber and metal shards struck the rear of the train, smashed the window on the rear door and shook the carriage as the shock wave slammed into the train. The deafening roar that followed was magnified by metal and wooden shrapnel bouncing off the walls of the baggage car.

The Special Forces soldiers on guard next to the bridge were tossed backwards into the jungle like paper dolls from the force of the blast. They would not survive the force of the explosion. The fifty-meter wide bridge did not wobble or shake from its force, it just dropped straight down into the canyon and into the fast moving stream seventy-five meters below.

The baggage car raised up and slammed back down on the track as the shock wave violently exploded into the rear platform and door of the train. The top glass door window shattered, spraying even more deadly shards into the baggage car. The flying debris killed one and severely injured the other Tango.

Fortunately, the car remained on the track not over the ravine. The track behind them was another matter as it was twisted and torn from the falling bridge that was directly behind them. It swayed violently but the wheels bit in and successfully fought to regain forward momentum. The train bounced side-to-side but remained on the track.

Seconds later. Ren burst in from the other door and assessed the carnage. He removed the weapon from the injured man and shot him twice in the head. Since the blast almost decapitated the one near the rear door, Ren just moved past him and began taking pictures of the remaining suitcases.

Within two minutes of entering the baggage car, Ren could feel the train stopping.

"What's happening?" Ren shouted into his radio.

124

At the same time, Army and Brave, weapons at the ready, burst through the engine room door. Both T's in the compartment were stitched with three shot bursts and fell against the opposite wall. The engineer stood at the far wall from the control panel pale and shaking with fear. When the Shadows came through the door the T had released the 'dead-man switch,' the emergency brake, which also was part of the control handle for the train. The train was now rapidly stopping without anyone at the controls.

Brave checked the Ts for life. Finding none, he began searching them while Army answered the radio.

"The Tango pulled the brake before we could get to him boss," came the faint response from Brave. "Got it under control now but can't release the brake. There's some kind of fail-safe device on it. Can't do anything now until the train stops."

"Okay, secure the engine. Make sure nobody gets to it again."

"No problem," he answered.

"Just watch for more T's that might be along the tracks," Ren warned.

Just then the engine entered a tunnel.

"Hey boss, I think we have a problem up here," Ren heard before distortion and static drowned out the balance of Army's message. A minute later power to the train lighting was cut and daylight turned to pitch black as the train screeched to a stop inside a tunnel. Immediately there was a rumble while another tremor surrounded the train as dust filled the narrow tunnel.

Ren watched as someone appeared at the rear of the train walking toward the light at the tunnel entrance: an AK-47 was cradled in his arms and a large rucksack hung from his back. He was about ten meters away when Ren quietly dropped from the rear platform and hugging the tunnel wall, closed the distance rapidly. Coming up on his right side he

125

viciously struck him over the right ear with a short metal telescoping baton. The T never heard the gravel crunch under Ren's feet or cried out after he was struck. He would never hear anything else again either as the inch deep crease in his skull reflected the crushed bones and damaged brain.

Ren quickly searched him and found a detonator for what appeared to be a ten-kilogram bomb in his rucksack. Except for the detonator, tamper switch on the bomb and a radio, there were no documents or identification on him. He took a quick picture and, since he was now outside the tunnel with good satellite reception, sent it off to SOC Command along with a SitRep (*Situation Report*) on the train bombing.

GS Team on hijacked train, 5 T's down, train in tunnel, six kilometers north of Sungai Golok, nine T's, including Sulalman remain on-board. Require extraction support for team and prisoners.

As he started back to the train, shots pinged, ricocheted and knocked loose rocks off the tunnel walls around him. Diving for the cover of the rails he scampered along the center of the tracks where shots at him would be difficult. He quickly climbed back aboard the train to find Pei searching the bodies and equipment of the T's in the baggage car.

"Look at this Lo Ban," she said handing a small blood-soaked spiral notebook to him. "Looks like a floor plan of the train, sequences for firing the detonators and an escape plan through the tunnel."

As he looked through the book he asked Pei, "any word from our team?"

"No signal in here," she said ducking behind the open side door, She pulled her weapon and fired at a young man who was pushing his AK-47 into the open door. Three rapid shots and his face turned to a bloody pulp.

Holstering her weapon, she leaped to the open door to grab his weapon when she collided with another T who had started to move forward to replace his fallen comrade.

126

Grabbing his collar she continued her forward momentum jumping off the train pulling him along. She flipped out the door, pulling him over her head, slamming him against the tunnel wall. Pulling the AK away, she broke two of his fingers before he died from a three shot burst at point-blank range from his own weapon. Pei spun around scanning the immediate area before giving a thumbs-up signal to Ren who was covering her from inside the car.

"Four down," he shouted. "At least five more down the tunnel. I hope Army and Brave are doing as well."

Pei took photographs of the second one, and fingerprints of the now faceless one, searched them and very carefully took the small rucksack and carried it about ten meters down the track, and placed it on the ground outside the tunnel.

As she returned, Ren nodded. "Okay, let's go find Sulalman and get him out of here," he said, "The Thais are going to be here soon."

*****

"Are all the bombs in place?" the headman asked his son.

"All is ready, shall we start?" he asked.

"As soon as the tunnel is sealed at the rear, we begin."

"Any minute now, Abrahim and Naidu are on the way to the rear of the train."

Southern Military Army Command Center

"Sir, this message was just received," said the Army Captain handing the flimsy to his boss, General Kittikachorn.

After hastily reading it once, he did it again slowly and said, "Get Bangkok on the phone, wake up the garrison commander in Sungai-Golok, read them the message and get me a helio."

Ten minutes later he was strapping himself into the passenger seat of a just delivered Airbus EC-725 that was spooling up ready to fly him into the late night black sky above the jungle at over 200 miles per hour.

After rereading the message he thought, *Hostages in a tunnel, Eastern & Oriental Express train, blowing up bridges, I'm going to skin that useless son-of-a-whore brigade commander who let them get aboard the train.*

Western Australia, Fort Meade, Maryland and Bangkok

"Another message from the T-1 Source," reported the afternoon shift duty officer monitoring the data stream flowing through his station. "I'm sending it through to you now," he said as he punched in the routing code for the National Counterterrorism Center about twenty five miles further south in the Washington, D.C. metropolitan area. Copies were also sent to Bangkok.

Since finding the telephone at the Hua Hin explosion site, a high priority monitoring protocol was in effect. The burst transmission from Ren to Beijing had been captured from the Australia monitoring station and instantaneously relayed to NSA Headquarters in Maryland.

NSA had designated the GS phones T-1 through T-5 when they analyzed the call list on the "hand's' phone. The signal from Ren's T-1 phone was the first directed to the B-1 call tree list identified on the telephone recovered at the Hua Hin bombsite.

The earlier traffic between phones Ren and his team designated by NSA as T-1, T-3, T-5 and T-2 had previously been noted in the past two days but the algorithms for breaking the encryption had not yet yielded clear messages.

128

Early the next morning CIA Station Bangkok

"Not sure what they're up to boss, but looks like T-1, the boss of the SFer, is sending traffic to a Colonel Li in Beijing, he heads up Project FORWARD..." said the CI Chief to the COS.

"Anything back from your guys in Sungai Golok yet?" asked the COS.

"Negative, but they just started looking for them yesterday morning, using the first trace data we had from NSA's bird (*satellite*) that got a fix on the other numbers from the "hand-phone."   "Jesus, you always got to have some stupid pun or something, don't ya? You'd be better advised to push them down south, something must be happening." He paused then added, "Anything new on tracking down that Zhou guy?"

"Nothing, nada, zip. His boss really has his ass in a crack with their Ambassador over him going dark. They have half their station looking for him, hell they're even interrogating his wife and kid. But our guys tell me that the Station really still thinks he ran off to one of the provinces with some hooker he has been seeing. Since they have no idea about him working for us, I'm betting that his disappearance has something to do with the Hua Hin situation."

"Yeah, well you better damn well prove it pretty soon. Those IG wiennies are starting to snoop around those files, especially with the Bureau guys just having been here to make the turn over pitch."

"We'll find him, hell maybe he's down south with those Chinese knuckle draggers."

"For your sake, I hope so," said the COS as he walked back to his office.

"Once we know what they're doing, we've got another SA Team enroute from Afghanistan to take them down. Just a matter of time boss," he answered to the overweight bureaucrat retreating down the hallway.

Late the previous evening in Beijing

"Alert our team in Yunnan to standby. Brief them on the Shadows location, develop a mission profile for an extraction for my review by noon," shouted Col. Li into the telephone handset, then added, "Get me the Attaché in Yangon immediately, we may need him to smooth the path for us when we strike."

After putting down the phone, he walked across the hall, knocked once then entered a side door into the spacious office of SOC Commander, General Zhu.

Back in the tunnel

Dust still filled the air in the engine compartment as Army and Brave completed processing the Tangos, secured the engineer and began climbing back toward the passenger cars of the train. They tried using their radios, but like the others on the team got nothing but static, so they cautiously made their way to the first passenger car, opened the door and entered. In the dark, Brave stumbled over one of the black suitcases that was placed in the aisle, just inside the doorway.

"Yaaiyah," he muttered as he banged into the hallway wall.

"Careful, don't blow us up," laughed Army as he stopped to examine the black bag with the bright green ID tag.

*****

When he heard the initial explosion at the bridge, the headman's agent near Sungai Golok called the local Thai Police Garrison Commander. When his telephone was

130

answered at the police station the agent read the speech prepared by the Headman:

The Eastern & Oriental train is now under our control. We will blow-up the train and kill all the foreigners within twelve hours unless the 109 brothers held illegally by the Bangkok government are released from prison immediately. Do not try to attack us or we will kill everyone immediately. I will call back in six hours. Fail to comply and Allah's vengeance will rain down.

Allah Akbar

He then hung up.

The Police Commander thought for a few moments then called for an immediate mobilization of his troops and for an over-flight of the railway tracks toward Bangkok. He needed verification and a target assessment should the claim be true. He also called his Headquarters in Hat Ya and reported the call and its demands.

Even before the helicopter was being checked out for takeoff, a message was received from the area Army command that Special Forces guards at Bridge 849 reported the trestle had been destroyed immediately after the E&O train had passed their position. One guard had been killed, another seriously injured in the blast. The rear car of the train could be seen standing just inside the tunnel adjacent to gaping holes in the tracks over the ravine where the bridge once stood. Automatic weapons fire could be heard coming from the tunnel.

*****

As Sulalman, the headman, and three of the Tangos got off the train the headman whispered, "Stay close to the wall, keep moving quickly, don't become a target." They walked half the length of the train toward what appeared to be a slight crack in the south tunnel wall. One by one they slipped

131

through the narrow gash in the rock wall and disappeared. They left no trace.

Two Tangos remained on the train, one standing between cars three and four with a detonator, the other walking back and forth through the aisles shooting his AK-47 above the passengers heads and shouting for them to keep quiet.

Brave was the first of the team to hear their shouts at the passengers. Pei was rapidly leafing through the small notebook she had taken from one of the T's in the baggage car. She looked up at Ren and said, "Looks like they plan to seal the tunnel. Take everyone hostage. They have a way out"

"If they close the tunnel how do they use their radio's, negotiate? Doesn't make sense. Got to be more to their plan." The words were no more out of his mouth when the tunnel entrance near the bridge erupted with a cloud of dirt, falling rock and then, total darkness.

Chapter 11

The Chinese Response

"We must assume that they are listening to our calls," said General Zhu. He slammed down the report from Bangkok indicating that the new Huawei telephone had been returned by the Thai Police.

"Possibly they could not break our new codes?" said his aide who had delivered the message.

"Even if they don't know what we are saying, they certainly can use metadata to pinpoint where those using them are located," Zhu growled. The memorandum distribution had included MSS cadre so he was sure that they would soon be raising issues regarding Ren's carelessness in losing this sensitive technology on an unauthorized foray. *He too wondered if Ren's actions were worth the political protection he was forced to provide.*

In Bangkok, speculation swirled around the Chinese Embassy as well. *Perhaps there might be some substance to the delusions Colonel Ping raised in his criticisms of this Major Ren,* mused Colonel Li, Ren's MSS former case officer who had lost control of the operation. *Ren has stirred up a hornet's nest with the Thais and lost at least one of his team in the Hua Hin explosion. What else has he done to expose our operations? Where the hell is Zhou? He cleared Ren of the allegations from Ping. Which one of those PLA dogs has been assisting Ren? They will pay for their deviations from the right path.*

Ping on the other hand, was waiting for some decision on his next assignment, and wondered if he could still redeem himself by disrupting Ren's operation and delivering him back to Beijing or maybe having him captured by the

Americans. He needed to move quickly if there was any hope for saving his career. He picked up the telephone.

CIA Station Bangkok

"More shit hitting the fan boss," the CI Chief said as he entered the small office of the COS.

"Looks like the E&O train has been hijacked, holding the passengers for ransom against releasing prisoners. No way the Thais are going to buy that deal. We're probably in for another blood bath."

"Who claimed responsibility?" asked the COS.

"Nobody is sure yet, but it's a hell of an Op, boldest one to date. It could really fuck-up the economy for sure if anyone gets killed cleaning it up," answered the CI Chief.

"Where's that Chinese SF'er in all this? Has he turned up yet?"

"No idea but I'll bet he's around there somewhere. If our phone intercepts are correct, probably in the middle of it."

"Yeah, well, what does that do for our SA team trying to take him down? I don't want them getting into a pissing contest with the Thais."

"Right now they're doing a SITREP…assessing the situation… and will get back to us with an OPS Plan for taking him."

"I sure wish I had your confidence level in their ability. The fact that he's there tells me that if we were correct in assuming that he was sent after Sulalman, somehow he's mixed up with this train situation and this Chinese guy is there before us. In my book, I'd like to have this guy on our team, he's pretty damn good."

"What can I say? If he's on that train, trapped in a tunnel where can he go that we can't get there first? We own him."

"You damn well better be right, caus' if you're not, this entire mess is going to fall right in your fucking lap," snorted the COS as he walked away.

At the Tunnel

One squad of Thai rangers fast roped from an old Huey helicopter into the narrow dust filled clearing next to the twisted tracks and the piles of debris from the explosion while another was positioning to join them. They were to set up a perimeter on one side of the tunnel while two more squads did the same on the other side of the eight hundred meter peak that divided the two sides of the tunnel. The other two sides of the mountain were almost perpendicular drops to the old meandering riverbed below. Since it was still a few weeks from rainy season the low water levels exposed sharp limestone rocks another hundred meters below the tracks.

"The area is secured sir," reported the ranger captain. "No activity. The north tunnel entrance appears to be operational, request permission to RECON (*Conduct Reconnaissance*)"

"Stand-by."

After a hurried discussion with the local Police Commander, General Kittikachorn nodded to his Aide who gave the go ahead for a three-man team to enter the tunnel. The young ranger lieutenant clicked down his Gen3 NVG's (*night vision goggles*) and motioned them forward into the blackness, M-16A1's rifles at the ready.

*****

"They plan to let everyone die," Ren said to Pei. "Without radio contact inside the tunnel how could they even think about negotiating? It looks like they plan to let everyone die or blame the government for not saving them. Either way, the Thais lose."

135

"So, what do we do? What does their notebook tell us about their plan?"

Skimming through the notes she stopped, reread a section then raised her head and says, "There are caves, found years ago, by Malaysian workers who built the tunnels. They plan to use them, sneak out and seal the tunnel. Everyone will die, either from the explosion, falling debris or suffocation before they can be cleared."

"First, we need to stop any more explosions, then find the entrance to the caves, capture Sulalman and take him home," Ren announced.

"You make it sound so easy," Pei said. "How exactly are you going to do these things?"

"What would Dickie do?" he laughed. "Kill all the Tangos and let God sort things out."

"God?" Pei laughed, "I'm going to be obliged to report your deviation from party doctrine. Self criticism is in order."

"Fine," he chuckled, "but please wait until we get out of here and back in China for any more dialectics. But right now," Ren continued, "Let's find any remaining Tangos before they blow up the tunnel then we go after Sulalman. There is no time to lose. Go, find the cave entrance, I'll round up the rest of the team, dispose of the T's and try to send another message for extraction support."

*****

Army and Brave carried the two green tagged suitcases they had stumbled over off the train and placed them on the tracks near the tunnel exit, thirty meters away from the train. At least if they exploded, they would not kill anyone with the blast shrapnel at that distance. Concussive force and collapse were another matter beyond their control; remaining T's were not.

They quickly began a compartment-by-compartment search using their TEKNA © high-intensity, infrared mini-

136

mag lites. While moving to the second train car from the engine, a three shot burst split the wood paneling just above Brave's head. Army's answering burst, aimed at the muzzle flash, toppled one T in a pool of bright arterial blood and grey brain matter that sprayed over three huddled passengers. Army tried to comfort the passengers but merely frightened them even more.

Ren heard the gunfire and turned in that direction. He moved along the outside of the train cars toward it, Glock and light at the ready.

*****

The Thai rangers heard the gunfire and stopped just short of the suitcases laying on the tracks. They were only momentarily aware of the bright flash when the remaining Tango pushed the detonator sending the electrical impulse through twenty kilos of Semtex resting in the black Tumi bags.

Two young rangers were killed instantly, the third crushed as a large rock cleaved from the ceiling and collapsed on him. The tunnel was filled with rocks and metal shards as the blast of expanding gases and dust pushed through the stopped train and out the opening into the dark jungle. He had no sooner pushed the button then Ren dispatched the Tango with a single shot from two meters away in the dinning car passageway.

*****

Five agonizing search filled minutes later Ren linked up with Army and Brave. After learning where they had placed the suitcase bombs, Ren decided to venture toward the other entrance and see if he could send a message from his radio.

As Brave and Army went to find Pei and prepare for hunting Sulalman, Ren walked past the smoldering bomb site and found the carnage of dead Thai soldiers. He cautiously moved past the devastation toward the tunnel exit. Stepping slowly outside, he immediately encountered another ranger whom he dispatched with a blow between the eyes using the butt of the Glock. Pointing the radio to the sky he pushed the transmit button. As it began to glow red, the area around him erupted with automatic weapons fire.

He dove back into the safety of the tunnel and dashed toward the debris pile, clawed his way over it and ran back toward the safety of the train as bullets whined harmlessly overhead and ricocheted off the rock walls. Four cars back from the engine he located the entire team huddled around Pei, she had the small notebook in one hand and the other one holding on to the edge of a narrow opening in the tunnel wall. "We go this way," she said and started to squeeze through.

*****

NSA satellites noted the burst transmission from the tunnel area, sent the packets of data for analysis and tracked it to a PLA receiving station in Western China. After that it was lost in the maze of connectivity within the secure Chinese networks. Colonel General Zhu at SOG Command had the report within minutes of its arrival. The question now for him was; "What to do about it?"

Chapter 12

Into the Mountain

The entryway that Pei followed was two meters long and turned sharply right 120 degrees for another meter and a half. It then opened into a natural five-meter chamber filled with breakdown materials. Fallen rocks and boulders clogged the area with large and small debris. Once the team was all there, she stopped and asked, "Who knows anything about caves?"

All of them had been through the several months long arduous wilderness training exercises, mountain climbing and solo survival sessions but very little time had been spent crawling through drainage culverts and mud filled tunnels. Nothing in real caves was included in the training. "Not my favorite kinda place," Army answered. It was what everyone else was thinking.

Ren made a mental note to see about adding caving to some future team selection exercises but now could only say, "No".

They had no way of knowing that the passage they had just traversed was hacked out of the mountain by remnants of the old Malaysia Communist Party. They had built the tunnel complex just inside the Thai border at Khao Nam Khang during the war against the British. Their secret handiwork had only been opened to the public in the late 1990's as part of Thailand's National Park system.

The tunnel where the train now was entombed was no more than twenty-five kilometers as-the-crow-flies from the former communist strongholds. This cave system, like most around the world, was carved by water dripping through limestone.

The surrounding jungle area had not been well explored since the time when it was in former Sultanate land. Now it was only used as a royal hunting reserve. It remained isolated until the railroad engineers selected a right-of-way to pass through a corner of it for the Southern Bangkok-Sungai Golok line in June 1903. Except for imported Malaysian and upcountry workers who broke stones, leveled track beds and blasted through limestone mountains, few people ventured into this area.

In older days, its isolation was because of tigers, large crocodiles that inhabited the streams and an assortment of venomous snakes that vied for bragging rights to be the most deadly in Asia. Now fear of terrorists kept all but the occasional police or army patrol away from this remote part of the South. The true extent of the cave was yet to be explored.

None of the pitches, (*slopes and climbs*) the early adventurers had discovered were significant in this part of the cave system. There were a few squeezes...narrow areas, some tubes and several water hazards in the area near the train tunnel entry. Other than these features, the caves were alive with beautiful formations that dotted the landscape. Limestone filtered water moved freely through these labyrinths, especially during the long rainy season

The opening that the team was now inside was merely an access route from the already existing Southern Branch railroad tunnel into the vast cave complex that the communists had discovered while hiding weapons and families during the war. It lay unused until their Thai brothers needed a place to rest and evade capture in their fight against the central government. It now would serve Ren's team from the Chinese People's Army, allowing them to maintain their hold on the motherland by eliminating this active Uyghur threat.

140

The Malaysia Communists were more comfortable using their man-made tunnels rather than the natural caves that formed in the mountains and were said to-be-filled with spirits that only protected local peoples against the intrusions of outsiders. Occasionally laborers or soldiers would disappear while working on tunnels. Was their disappearance caused from falling into one of the many unmarked pits along the maze of passageways they found or the guardian spirits? None of the early explorers were sure but the caves always claimed a few trespassers that were thought to be 'payment to the gods for their right to use the sacred mountains for protection'.

Now that Hakimi, Sulalman, and the two other remnants of their team had disappeared down into the labyrinth of tunnels and caves that honeycombed the limestone hills, Ren's team would have to follow.

Just like technical mountain climbing, moving through this cave would be a challenge, especially without essential equipment. The black was absolute. Once lights were doused, disorientation easily took over. Cave noises from water, echoes and bats often drowned out even normal conversation.

While getting ready to follow into the cave network, Ren and Pei had sorted the pocket litter and documents taken from the dead Tangos. They were searching for any intelligence that could help them track those ahead of them in the cave.

"This guy has several different identification cards Lo Ban. Thai, Malaysian and a Turkish Passport," Pei said as she sifted through the contents of the evidence bag in her hands.

"Turkish?" Ren said looking up from his stack of papers. She nodded and they both continued their work.

"Hey boss," Brave asked, "what do we do about the Thais following us the way we're following these bad guys?"

"Well, if they can't get in here, there's no problem. But since we found the entrance…"

Pei cut him off, "We have the notebook. They do not."

"Correct but a thorough search of the tunnel will uncover the way we entered, I'm sure we left a trail that any good scout could follow."

"How about we do what Rocky would have done, lay down a few IED's ourselves to block our rear flank?" said Strong.

"Perfect," Ren answered. "No way they can clear the tunnel, process passengers and search for us in less than a few hours. That's plenty of time to be well away from here. Brave, make it happen."

"Hai."

Within minutes, trip wires were set just inside the entrance for the tunnel. The cache they had located was emptied, their headlamps adjusted and weapons checked. The way forward they discovered was down, through the hole in the floor.

"Okay, if we're going to go hunting in here we need light. How much to we have?" Ren asked the team.

They piled their equipment on a large flat bolder. Pei counted, "seven mini-mag lites, three glo-sticks and two packs of waterproof matches."

Each also had a sidearm, combat knife; three had automatic weapons, one with a lowlight scope, four flash-bang grenades, a few Vietnam era grenades, one medical kit and six energy bars, four telephones, and a radio. Absent was any climbing gear, D-rings, rope, batteries or water. They only had the clothing worn on the train.

Strong, their climbing expert was first to chime in. "We need rope, lights and some way to navigate through this place."

"Well, since they're not in this room with us," Brave laughed, "we better figure out how to get them."

"Yeah, maybe they have some equipment we could borrow," suggested Army.

142

"Okay," Pei laughed, "great ideas everyone so lets start 'snooping and pooping'".

With that encouragement, Strong began 'night–walking' around the small chamber and discovered an opening in the floor at one corner of the room by almost falling into it. Almost immediately after this, Army found another about shoulder height directly across from the train tunnel entry point.

"Hey boss, can I get some extra light over here?" he asked. "I think I found something that you all need to see."

"Looks like we have what we asked for boss," said Strong as he finished counting the bundles of both prusik and hard-lay rope, head lamps, ascenders and related climbing equipment cached in the shoulder high compartment. "Probably here for the others we killed on the train." he said while pulling the gear from its hiding place. "If they have all this stuff cached waiting for them, it must be a hard trail."

*****

Hakimi felt the tremor and a slight shaking of the clay beneath his knees when the blast was set off above them. *A bit early?* He questioned himself. *It was hard to measure time in this maze without losing the path. Regardless, it was now done. The Thais will never recover from this attack. He was sure that the others did not notice the vibrations, he was expecting the blast and it did not seem as strong as he anticipated.*

"Are you sure this is the right way?" grunted Naidu as he crabbed, crawled and then duck-walked along the interconnected tube-like, debris filled passageways. As second in the column, he had to hurry so he could continue to see the backlit silhouette of Hakimi who was scurrying ahead through the narrow downward sloping passage.

"Save your breath brother, we have far to go and little time. You only need to follow me. I know the way. We are

143

not returning to this place so do not worry about memorizing landmarks for a return trip."

The others behind them scrambled to keep up with their swift progress even though they could not hear or see their discussion as the ceiling height, flowstone and large breakdowns that dotted their route limited them to only seeing the person directly in front of them. They traversed a few theater like rock-strewn rooms, clambered down a few chimneys, and squeezed through several narrow areas with bedrock pillars that crimped their path to little more that the width of their bodies. Finally Hakimi called a halt.

They were exhausted after only an hour of scrambling as one by one they emerged from the narrow tube onto a broad shelf. They could feel, if not see, the grand space before them. It felt canyon like, but they could only see to where it dropped-off as the light from their headlamps bled out into the vast dark area surrounding them. A musty smelling breeze came from the void, brushed across their faces and tugged at their bodies.

"I hear water flowing brothers," said Ashraf.

"Indeed, there is much water at the next level below but it is not the water to fear, it is what lives in it that must hold your attention," said Hakimi. The group exchanged worried glances.

"What do you mean?" asked Naidu.

"In due course we will emerge from the darkness into the light brothers, God Willing," Hakimi answered. "Soon we leave these shafts and reenter our world and our brother here can go on his way."

Sulalman, who was third in the tunnel, nodded in his direction. He had once visited the caves at Tora Bora after the great one...the Sheik...Osama Bin Laden...escaped from IASF Special Forces there. The tiny spaces within them frightened him then and this tunnel did the same now, although he would never show it to these men.

The others looked around with worried expressions. Sensing their fear, Hakimi added. "This cave has been used very little in the past. It belongs to nature and her creatures. We are only visitors here and need to take care just as we would crossing the jungle. Keep to the path I follow and all will be well."

After hearing his words, what was worry now turned to fear as the group stared into the void.

"What about the train, what happens to the passengers," Sulalman asked Hakimi.

"Our brothers are to set timers and follow our path to this place. What happens to the infidels is of no consequence; it is what happens to Bangkok that really matters. They will not recover from our attack. Allah Akbar. Rest for a time. Then we move forward."

*****

"They're all dead, sir," came the report from the ranger sergeant dispatched to investigate what had happened to the Recon team.

"Proceed into the tunnel. Use extreme caution, secure the area, recover the bodies." came the response from his commander. While he waited for the balance of his men to arrive, he belly crawled over the debris. Through the dust and darkness he could see several people moving toward him in the distance. He raised his M16, spoke softly into his radio and waited.

Within minutes a ragged stream of disheveled, dirty, coughing and bloody farang (white Europeans) moved toward him following the tracks from the stalled Orient Express train. He could hear them coughing, wheezing, and moaning from their wounds before he actually saw them clearly. He lowered his weapon, called in a new report and moved forward to guide them to safety.

145

Chapter 13

Central Committee Office Complex, Beijing

"So, he is still alive?" Minister Chang asked harshly. His massive official desk was meant as a show of authority for this morning's meeting. The extraction operation was not going according to plan. He needed options.

"Yes sir," answered SOC Commander Zhu without blinking. "A message from him was received within the hour stating that the terrorist Sulalman is with local Thai bandits inside a cave complex. The Shadows are in pursuit and will require extraction support."

"This operation is taking much too long. It is much too visible, is it not Colonel?" Chang challenged.

"No sir, Sulalman has proven very elusive in the past. The Shadows have closely tracked him. He has deliberately placed many clever obstacles in their path. But, they are very close to capturing him."

"Yes, but if they cannot do so without being seen by the Thai authorities, what is the point?"

"True, but I'm confident that Major Ren's forces will be resourceful enough to fulfill the trust we all have in the Ghost Shadows abilities."

"Humm, spoken more like a Central Committee Minister than a soldier, Colonel," Chang said grimly. "But you had better be correct, there are many eyes on this operation. It will not go well for anyone should he fail."

"He will not. The extraction will be successful."

"For your sake, you had better be correct," he said then added, "Be sure to make it so."

*****

Smoke, dust and darkness combined to produce a hades like scene at the tunnel entrance. Soldiers were leading and carrying injured passengers and their comrades to hastily established medical stations. Evacuation helios buzzed overhead preparing to move the seriously injured to distant hospitals.

"Passengers are coming out of the tunnel in small groups. My men have searched and counted seventy-one so far," said the Ranger captain. "We still don't have an accurate passenger and crew headcount from the train line so we don't know for sure how many more to expect."

"Send a three man unit back along the track and continue to round-up any injured, stragglers or wounded and mark the deceased for the police. An EOD squad is enroute," ordered the General's Aide.

"Roger that," the captain answered.

Within minutes, rangers probed deeper into the tunnel, past the bomb crater and finally reached the stalled engine and train compartments. They released the tie-taped engineer, who after telling them what had happened just before the explosion, was quickly escorted out of the tunnel by one of the rangers. The smoke, smell of cordite and dust had visibility down to less than a few feet, especially in the near total darkness.

"Yes sir, that's what he says," the ranger Captain reported. "He wants to thank the Chinese guys we sent to save his life. They killed the terrorists that had taken over the train. What do I tell him?"

"Keep him separated from the rest," said the Aide, then added, "We are sending reinforcements to interview all of them. Police and more troops will be arriving shortly,"

"Yes sir, but we're going to need medical personnel immediately for the injured. Do we have that total passenger list yet, I don't want any terrorists trying to blend into the crowd."

"The medics are already in the air, should be there already. In the meanwhile, conduct a car-by-car search. The

147

entire tunnel needs to be secured as a crime-scene. There will be technicians following the medics. Don't let your men touch anything, I don't want any secondary explosions from booby-traps before EOD arrives. We'll have the passenger lists to you shortly. Just round everyone up and hold them until support arrives. "

*****

Strong disappeared down the hole with Army belaying the rope that was secured to a large block of breakdown rock on the floor of the cave. In less than a minute he signaled that the others should follow.

Ren said, "Let's get moving, we'll need all the time we can get. No telling how long it will take us to catch up to Sulalman and the others."

"How many of them should we expect, boss?" asked Brave.

"At least four, including Sulalman," Ren answered.

"How does Dickie say it? Ah yes, piece of pie."

"No, it's a piece of cake," offered Army.

"Pie, cake, makes no difference. We will kill all of them except Sulalman and get out of here," answered Pei.

"That's the spirit," said Ren as he watched the remaining GS team members drop through the hole and begin their search.

Several minutes later they had secured their gear, adjusted their makeshift headlights and were ready to head-out.

"Looks like they went this way boss," Brave said as he examined the opening to one of the several branches of tunnels that sheared off the bottom of the smooth-walled chamber at the end of their thirty-meter descent.

"Move out!" Ren ordered. The team immediately filed through the first of the narrow tunnels that radiated from the chamber just below the entry into the cave system. The height

148

forced them to duck-walk while entering the low ceilinged opening.

"*Aaiiya*, watch your heads," Army shouted after he banged into the tip of a small stalactite hanging from an edge of the narrow passageway.

"He's right," Ren answered laughing. "We should have helmets for this work, be careful. I don't want Brave, our medical expert here, to spend time treating you instead of killing Tangos."

Everyone laughed. "Yah, keep your head down," "you walk like an old lady."

"Poor baby" came from the team.

"Let's make less noise," Pei warned sternly, "we don't know how far ahead they are. No need to tell them we're coming. Even with the bats screeching and the water dripping there's no point in losing the edge of surprise."

For the better part of an hour they followed the muddy trail left by the fleeing Tangos. Stamina and nerves were tested as they squeezed through the narrow opening that required them to push their packs and weapons through before they could follow. They sloshed, slipped and otherwise got cold, wet and muddy as they closed the gap in the darkness.

Strong, who was acting as point man stopped and looked around then commented, "Hey boss, they must feel safe here. The T's left a trail a blind man could follow."

Ren nodded, "I'm sure they are not expecting anyone but their team to be following." His worry about a possible trap went unsaid. "Let's move out."

Within minutes of his comment they entered what felt like an exit from the cave, except that it was still pitch black beyond the edges of the dim illumination given off from their headlamps. Strong immediately raised a clenched fist…*Silence and hold position*…then doused his light. The team, now in single file, turned off their lights and froze in place. Two agonizing minutes later he signaled all clear by turning on his light.

They all looked around the small portion of the high ceilinged chamber that opened from the narrow tunnel. The structure and composition of the walls had changed once again during their downward march. They were now in a different type of cave. This one was big and dank. Musty smelling air flowed through it. Water flowed somewhere nearby. There were smooth rock formations that extended from ceiling to floor, narrow straw-like towers and smooth surfaces that resembled strips of bacon found in village stew. There were now vivid colors unlike anything they had seen in the narrow dust colored passageways leading down to this place.

Strong was the first into the chamber. He had seen the back of one of the Ts exiting into another passageway. He signaled for absolute quiet and pointed directly to their right. He made the sign for *...eyes on...enemy...*then holding up two fingers indicating that there were two enemy ahead.

As Ren crept out of the last tunnel he nodded in understanding, pointed to his combat knife and motioned them forward. There was no need now to tell them what to do or how to do it.

*****

The CIA CT Chief (*Counter Terrorism*) moved away from the rotor-wash as the chopper lifted off the hastily cut LZ across the river from the tunnel entrance. General Kittikachorn's briefing was disturbing but valuable. He still had no idea on how he was going to introduce the station's SA team into the area. It was going to be a problem. Police roadblocks, the military security cordon around the area and inhospitable terrain conspired to limit his opportunities for a timely insertion. He was certain that without the SA high value recovery team, the Chinese and Sulalman would once again slip through the cordon.

150

"Hey chief," he barked into his secure phone. "Looks like our Chinese friends are on the scene again. Word is they broke up the hijacking, killed a bunch of the bad guys, then disappeared."

"You got to be kidding me. Sure it's not the Lone Ranger you're talking about?" The COS answered.

"Wish it was so but they killed at least four terrorists that we know about now and probably saved most of the passengers by disrupting the planned bombing. The Thais ID'ed four more suitcase bombs still in place on the train that didn't go off. EOD isolated them. While we speak they are trying to get them defused."

"Now you're telling me we're chasing good guys around trying to kill them?"

"Nope, just that whatever they're up to, they had to take the hijackers down to do it. If we're right about Sulalman, he was on that train and not there now. Neither are any others that may have been with him."

"Then there's a way out of that tunnel that the Thais haven't found yet. I'm betting that both Sulalman and his other bad guys and those Chinese found it and are hunkered down waiting for things to cool off before they slip away."

"Your lips to God's ear," answered the CT Chief but thought, *Yeah, in a pig's ass they're hunkering down. They're probably booking down the road as fast as they can away from here. It's what I would do.*

"So what do I tell the SA guys?" he asked.

"How the hell do I know. You're on the spot there. For Christ sake, get creative. You're the one getting the big bucks to stop these little fuckers from blowing shit up around here," said the COS.

"Those IG pussies are going to have a field day with me if they find out you deployed assets from Bagram who are sitting on their asses in South Thailand drinking beer and getting laid while you're trying to figure out how to get them

151

on station to do some actual fucking work." He paused in his diatribe, took another drink of Coke, then added, "All I know is that we've got our own dead to worry about. Those fuckers in the caves are deadly and need to be put down. If you don't get with the program, someone will be doing it over your corpse. You got it?"

The chief was livid. While he was half listening for an answer he thought, *what the hell's the matter with these guys? When it's going well everyone has a plan but when it comes time to get something done, it's...well, shit boss, my source is on holiday, or it's too crowded there, I can't find a way into the place. Bullshit, bullshit, bullshit. Figure it out asshole. Get it done. We've got dead here, our asses to cover and the clock is running.*

"Roger that Chief, maybe I'll just fucking HALO those guys into the jungle near the train wreck and see what happens, how about that?"

All he heard was static. *Hmmm, maybe that just might not be a bad idea.*

Chapter 14

Water in the narrow tunnel was almost to the headman's neck as he slowly moved along the swift moving breakdown and debris filled black water. They had passed many small side passages of slow moving water that joined their currents main stream. The velocity of the main channel increased with each passing streambed.

If one knew where to look, these intersections were marked with a small cairn of three stacked rocks to the right of their line of march. It marked the correct direction to follow. Unless these markings were followed, the traveller would be lost forever in the convoluted maze of passages they were passing through.

The ceiling was now less than half a meter above his head. The frigid water level approaching their chests. Their four headlamps danced like fireflies along the ceiling and walls while reflecting off the surface of the black water as they navigated the winding passageways. They were very careful in stepping over the slippery surfaces of the stones on the river bottom. Already fully soaked and starting to shiver, the last thing they needed was another dousing from a fall into the frigid, energy sapping water.

The noise from the four Ts splashing and slipping in the swift moving water made it possible for Brave to close in less than two meters from Naidu who was now last in the line of march. He was just short of hypothermia setting in, shivering distracted by the cold and worried only about keeping his footing off the slick stones on the stream bottom.

Brave was not visible to him, even had he been more alert, having switched to an infrared light when they spotted the end of the column disappearing into the tunnel several minutes before. This 'black light' allowed them to close the gap without being seen. His stealth, coupled with the effects of the cold water preserved the element of surprise. When Naidu slowed momentarily, Brave quickly closed the gap between them.

His hand roughly closed over Naidu's mouth while his razor sharp combat knife arced down through clothing, upper chest and directly into his heart. He was dead before his brain registered he had been attacked. Brave held him until the violent death tremors subsided.

While Brave waited for the balance of the Shadows team to squeeze past his position, the column of Tangos moved further down the stream oblivious to death closing in on them.

The Shadows waited a bit before moving forward. The column of T's gave no evidence or awareness of their position so the Shadows continued to close in on them. The Ts would not see the blood that was leaking from Naidu's lifeless body in the fast moving black water.

Ren acknowledged the kill as he passed. Brave nodded then searched Naidu's clothing. He then placed everything from the dead man's pockets into a Musset bag he took off the corpse. Within minutes he was again moving back down stream closing up with Army who was now last in line. He had taken Naidu's body and shoved it up onto a small ledge just above the water line near where he had taken his last breath. It would make a natural grave with little chance for discovery.

Ren realized there was a risk in not immediately engaging the entire group in a firefight but decided that it was better to follow them to the cave exit than kill them now and risk being trapped in this uncharted maze. Quietly taking one or two of them along the way made their odds of success at the end better and if done well, like Brave's kill just now, would cause the Tangos to wonder where their men had gone without knowing for sure that they were being stalked.

*****

Immediately after Brave moved away from the corpse, the black water swirled around Naidu's body. His body slid off the narrow shelf and disappeared. Beneath the surface, it bounced, twisted and folded into grotesque shapes as it bobbed and was forced along by the swift underground current. As it reached the first cross channel it was brutally pulled at then quickly released to continue its forward trajectory.

The body quickly passed the Shadows column before they could react. It brushed by their legs, backs and arms in the ever-widening stream of black surging water. It finally snagged on a rock, twisted over and was caught in another eddy that pushed it toward the rear of the headman's column another twenty meters ahead.

"Stop pushing, if I go more quickly I might slip," said Ashraf over his shoulder but again he was nudged to go more quickly.

"There is nothing I..." he began as he turned around to confront Naidu but saw nothing but was nudged again, this time near his legs. It was then that Naidu's body was again flipped over by the current and the bloodless stump of his left arm bobbed out of the darkness and into the light from his headlamp.

Ashraf screamed.

"What is going on?" shouted the headman who had turned around and tried to force his way back against the swift current. Sulalman turned but in the watery light, could just see Ashraf pushing something away from him and thrashing in the stream.

"It's Naidu, something has attacked him...his arm is missing...he's dead." He managed to blubber.

"Arm missing? Are you mad? Are you hallucinating? Quiet down!" the headman bellowed trying to establish control over the situation.

155

Just as quickly as the body appeared it again bounced away from Ashraf and continued down stream toward Sulalman and the headman. The dead weight almost pulled Sulalman over as he grabbed at the shredded shirt that passed through his narrow beam of light. The tug was enough to force a change in direction and the body twisted toward him directly into the place where the headman stood transfixed watching the bizarre events behind him.

Seeing the body coming, the headman braced against the sidewall of the streambed and grabbed at it. He missed but saw the terrible wound, the missing arm and shuddered as it broke free of his grip and continued down stream leading their procession toward the cave exit.

*****

Strong gave the signal to stop and gather around when he heard the commotion up ahead.

"What are they yelling about up there?" Ren asked.

"Not sure boss, sounded pretty bad though," Strong answered.

"Let's give them a little more room, try to stay back a little more but we don't want to lose them."

"Roger that, this place is not healthy boss, Lots of bad joss here. I can feel it," said Army.

Pei answered, "I think he's correct, Lo Ban, nothing good takes place here."

All Ren could say was, "All right then, let's move out, get Sulalman and go home."

*****

The terrorists remained motionless waiting for the headman to act and the longer they stood motionless in the cold water, the more hypothermia began to affect them. If they did not move soon, they would be unable to continue. Sensing this problem the headman turned and started slowly

156

trudging downstream. He knew that the exit was now within minutes if they followed the right path.

*****

A HALO drop was out of the question on short notice but getting a BPP Helio was not. Getting it to drop off a few 'advisors' in an out-of-the-way place was done without question as over a third of their budget was provided with covert CIA funds. Two heavily armed and equipped SA officers fast roped into the black early morning river bottom at the base of the mountainside that contained the entombed Eastern & Orient train. With any luck, they would locate the entrance to the cave system being used by their prey before dawn broke.

The rocky-river bed was a tough slog but it bordered the base of the near vertical cliffs that extended directly to the tunnels. The top of the cliffs were now teeming with police and military activity. Carrying the extra twenty-five pounds of Ground Penetrating Radar equipment also slowed them down as would setting up the equipment and taking the required sounding every quarter mile.

Unless they were extremely lucky, it would take more than this technology to locate the opening they were seeking. Both of these officers had honed their skills in the caves of Afghanistan but these caves were different, the landscape hard, sharp and angular unlike the smooth, old looking places in the mountains where they battled the Taliban.

It would be light soon and their activities visible from the army patrols above. They would need to hurry.

*****

"We've located another exit from the tunnel in the south wall sir," reported the ranger captain whose team had already taken casualties early in the hijacking. "Request permission to enter."

157

Minutes later the Aide answered, "Extreme caution to be used, IED's anticipated, EOD personnel to lead."

Within minutes, an ABS (Advanced Bomb Suit) garbed EOD operator carefully entered the narrow twisting crevasse used by Ren and the Tango's. He advanced to the first turn but his helmet became stuck in the narrowing passage when he tried to make the 120-degree right jog. An hour later, a very shaken sweat drenched operator was extricated from the tight space.

Since a robot was not available and their fiber optic cable was not sufficiently long enough, a lone, slightly built, EOD technician slid into the opening and worked his way past the tight right turn. He spotted the multiple tripwires immediately and retreated.

Without knowing the nature of the charges set inside the cave it was not possible to safely detonate the explosives nor was it feasible to drill a new opening into the tunnel wall. They would now await a robot that was just small enough to negotiate the tight turn, the narrow opening and the height of the lowest tripwire.

*****

SOC Commander Zhu worried that Ren's next message would require response within a time he would be unable to meet unless prepositioned transport and support forces were already in place. He looked over the current training exercise deployment schedule and noted that two elements of Special Operations Forces, one from the Guangzhou Military District and another from the Southern Theater Command, were in Myanmar on Evasion Exercises. They could be tasked for a quick jump over the border to support Ren then head back across the hundred and twenty-five kilometers before the Thais would know they were there. Three helios were sufficient and easily dispatched from the Embassy in Yangon.

"Get me the attaché in Yangon," he quietly said into his office telephone.

*****

None of the sources that normally provided a flow of information about the terrorists in the south could be reached. The Bangkok MSS office was strangely silent on this part of their operations. Director Zhou En Tao's absence had the security staff conducting a damage assessment of his activities should he have been compromised by Western intelligence.

Colonel Ping was waiting reassignment and storming around the office looking for things to do without success. Nobody wanted to be associated with him for fear they would accompany him to whatever unfavorable assignment he was due to get. His attempt to sabotage Major Ren's operation fell apart as his contacts inside and outside the embassy stopped responding to his requests and orders to take certain actions he had devised.

Even Col. Wu, Ren's MSS Bangkok Case Officer, had no further contact from Major Ren or from the SOG Command in Beijing. Attempts to contact anyone on the Ghost Shadows call list through his Guangzhou Command Center were also met with silence.

Chapter 15

End of the Darkness

Now openly shivering, the ragged column of terrorists continued moving along the rapidly receding water in the stream. Fortunately it only reached their knees: much being diverted into black side channels, the balance disappearing into porous rough limestone gaps in the riverbed.

"Just a bit further. Around the next bend is the cave exit," the headman shouted over his shoulder. The others did not hear him as they were shivering and fighting not to loose their footing on the irregular rocks in the shallow water.

"Light, there is light ahead," Sulalman mumbled though chattering teeth.

"Indeed, we are safe," answered Ashraf.

The chamber they were now entering was bathed in a dim twilight, weak yellow light entering from a low horizon, little more than a pinprick of color in the blackness that still surrounded them. Light from the cave entrance was unexpected and could only signify very early daybreak.

As they moved closer, they began to smell vegetation: musty, feral and dank. It was unlike the wet, hard coldness they had traversed for the past few hours.

"We must hurry, dawn is already here. We must be away from here before the Thais begin their search for us," shouted the headman as he began climbing out of the water. He knew that daylight would bring troops swarming along the edges of the cliffs outside of the cave entrance.

This time they all heard him say "hurry…" and quickened their pace.

Even as they began to sense the end was in sight, Ashraf sensed, rather than felt the movement behind him. His headlamp swung in an arc and caught movement at the end of its beam. It was the fetid odor of death and decay that first

160

assailed his nostrils as the five-meter crocodile lunged toward him. He screamed as the gigantic prehistoric reptile separated him from the others, thrashed around to face him and lunged again.

Immersion in the cold water had slowed Ashraf's reactions and he was no match for the hunting skills of the beast. The second charge by the croc caught Ashraf's head and torso in one snout filling bite. It tore him so that his torso was cleanly cut into two pieces. The sound of the massive jaws breaking bone and tearing flesh filled the chamber. The carnage and strong odor of blood and offal sparked a wave of rustling as the other crocodiles quickly began to emerge from the darkness.

Sulalman snapped out of the shock of seeing Ashraf's dismemberment. He struggled to clamber out of the water, stumbling and running to follow the headman toward the light. Gigantic shadows moved swiftly also following them toward the light some twenty meters away.

*****

"Aiyya, boss," Army yelled in surprise. "Did you see that?" He was about fifteen meters away from Ashraf and planning his attack when the huge beast appeared from the darkness to bite the hapless terrorist in half.

"No, what happened?' asked Ren as he rushed forward to Army's position.

"You wouldn't believe it even if I told you," he said shaking his head.

The balance of the team quickly huddled together in the shallow water while Army excitedly explained. While standing there, they could make out dozens of huge shadows emerging from the edges of the chamber moving toward them in the streambed.

"Pei, Army, get the flash-bangs ready. Brave, fragmentation grenades. Everyone, lock-and-load weapons.

161

We are not going to be their lunch. Use the grenades only when they open their mouths, they must explode inside them to cause them any serious damage. I'm afraid our other weapons will just make them angry."

They quickly crept up onto the edge of the stream, spread out into a defensive line while trying to get their waterlogged, numb legs to respond. By forcing their bloodless limbs into action they crossed the blood and gore slick area where the beast had dragged the bottom half of Ashraf's body along the floor.

They avoided the awakening beasts and continued moving toward the distant glimmer of light. The coppery smell of blood and gore was heavy in the dank air. They now could see even more dark shadows moving along the walls just at the edge range of their headlamps. Several of the shadows had smelled their presence and converged toward them.

"Pei, look around, any way we can get above these animals? Any ledges, anything we can climb?" Ren shouted.

Even in the short range of the headlamp it was clear to her that ledges, stalactites, flowstones and stalagmites covered the ceiling and floor of the chamber.

"There must be a way to get us over them to the entrance but will it get us there in time to stop Sulalman from fleeing?" she answered.

"Get us away from these beasts first, we'll find a way to take him down later." Ren answered.

Pei quickly scrambled up a flowstone outcropping, secured a trailing length of rope to a limestone column and began climbing toward a ledge five meters about them. She waved for everyone who followed her path using the rope. Strong was last in line and scarcely avoided a small croc that threw itself at him as he jumped for the rope.

They quickly and silently traversed the open space on the ledges and handholds above the floor that was now crawling with large crocodiles. They finally reached a point above the entrance to the cave. Even in the dim light, Army could see the two remaining terrorists who had avoided the beasts below and were on another ledge just above the cave opening across the chamber. They did not seem to be aware that Ren's forces were there and within striking range.

Now that their eyes had become accustomed to the dim light near the cave entrance, Ren's team could see that dozens of large and small crocodiles infested the ground below. They were thrashing about, looking up at both them and the terrorists as future nourishment; their red and yellow eyes gleaming in the half-light.

The GS team was high enough up the cave wall that the terrorists could not easily see them unless they made an effort to do so or heard some noise from the other direction. Aside from being able to see that their quarry was still there the Shadows task at the moment was to find a way to take them down without getting themselves eaten in the process.

"What do we do now boss, we can't stay here forever," said Brave.

"We wait. A solution will appear," Ren said.

"Wow boss, you still sound like Yoda, that little green guy from Star Wars. 'Do or do not, there is no try'."

They all quietly laughed.

*****

"Looks like we got something through there," said the younger of the two SA officers taking off the headphones from the radar receiver and pointing toward the cliff across from them. They were on the edge of a small streamed that fed into the river they were following just below the railway tunnel. "Looks big on the scope. We need to get closer. Get in there and take a look," he finally groaned, "All right, Let's do this."

They stowed the radar unit in their backpack, put it into the lower limbs of a kapok tree just outside the cave entry, hefted their M-16A1's and moved closer toward the cliff wall. Ten minutes of poking through vines and more kapok and dead tree leaves they became even more skittish as they dodged several deadly Malaysian pit vipers that infested the area.

"What the hell is it with this place," the younger one said.

"Yeah, it seems like this entire jungle is trying to kill us today. These little suckers are worse than the three steppers...snakes that kill within three steps..." said the other. They both knew other officers who had not been as fortunate with snakes and they were taking no chances today.

In the end, it was the strong stream of cool, but foul smelling air that brought them to the vine covered, two meter opening in the limestone cliff wall through which a stream of water flowed. *Maybe this was the place we're looking for*, thought the older of the two; *time would tell.*

"Looks like we ID'ed a possible cave, looks big on the radar, roughly three hundred meters north, up river, of the blown up trestle. We're going in to check it out," reported the older SA officer.

"Roger that, good hunting, be quick. Out." was the terse answer from the CT Chief.

"Okay, rock & roll time," said the younger officer as he ducked down and bear-walked through the opening into the gloom, M-16 up and ready. His partner, another former Delta operator, followed.

Once inside they stood and looked into the darkness for a few moments to get their night vision then switched on their mag-lites. The large chamber was dark, rank smelling and had signs of life from scratches on the muddy floor, bits of branches, bones and bat droppings.

They slowly moved forward toward the large pool of dark water that flowed from the stream toward the opening they had just used to enter the chamber. They crossed along a narrow ledge next to the water and continued about thirty meters toward the rear of the large gloomy space.

"Doesn't look like this goes anywhere, let's get out of here," said the older one.

"Roger that, this place is giving me the creeps," his partner said. But, just as they turned, a three-meter crocodile burst from the pool and blocked their path.

"God Damn, I hate it when you're right," quipped the younger one as they began firing their M-16's. When they did, several more crocs began emerging from the pool and closed toward them. Between the muzzle flashes and light reflected in the reptilian eyes, the cavern pulsated with an otherworldly glow.

*****

"That sounds like automatic weapons fire nearby," said the headman. "Look, the animals are leaving us and going into the water."

"Wait until they are all gone," warned Sulalman.

"They are distracted, let's go now," shouted the headman as he began scrambling down toward the exit.

Pei saw the old man bolt and without hesitation, leaped down on the fleeing man. She landed directly on him and they both tumbled to the wet, rocky floor. She immediately bounced up. The old man did not move after cushioning Pei's fall but Sulalman drew an automatic and began firing at her from his perch above the floor. With no place to hide, Pei sprang for the opening and threw herself through the cave exit, tearing her uniform in several places, blood staining her trousers and shirt. Seeing an opportunity, Sulalman began scrambling down toward the cave exit. Ren and the others charged after him.

165

Brave was the first to reach him with a tackle that sent both of them back against the smooth flowstone wall of the cave. Sulalman weakly tried to kick at him but a punch to the throat stopped it in mid-swing. He collapsed, gagging, into a heap that Army and Ren dragged outside the cave. Once he was secured with tie-tapes, Army returned to the cave to retrieve the headman only to find a meter and a half long croc dragging him away by his right leg.

Army opened fire with his handgun and merely seemed to annoy the animal. It thrashed around, dragging the now bloodied body toward the pool. The shots did, however, manage to momentarily slow his escape with the headman. The croc opened his snout, dropped his prey and gave a loud roar. It was just long enough for Army to toss a fragmentation grenade into the open mouth then dive over the headman's body to shield him from the concussive force of the blast.

At the sound of the explosion, Ren and Brave burst back into the cave to find croc blood and body parts all over. Army was covered in croc blood as well as that from the shredded leg of the headman. As the trio dragged the headman toward the cave opening, Brave pulled out his medical kit.

Once they found a well-concealed defensive position along the cliff wall, he performed first aid. He applied a tourniquet on the headman's torn leg and quickly added some Combat Quick-Clot © to stanch the flow of blood from his massive wound. A Syrette of morphine completed his field treatment. Shaking his head with concern, Army said, "He needs a hospital boss, or he's not going to make it,"

"Let's see what we can do about that," Ren commented as he headed back for the cave. "Get him ready so we can get moving. Let's hope the Thais didn't hear the grenade or shooting or they'll be over this place like ants on a honey pot."

"You're right boss, but maybe that other automatic weapons fire we keep hearing is keeping them busy. We must have missed some of those guys on the train. The Thais sound like they are having their hands full," said Army.

Ren nodded. He then prepared and sent an extraction message, then set about formulating a contingency plan should he not hear from Beijing before the Thais forced him to move the team into the jungle.

Only minutes later, SOG Commander Chen's aide said, "Sir, Priority incoming message for you from Major Ren."

*****

The thrashing continued in the adjacent cave for thirty minutes as the feeding frenzy continued. The crocs that were bullet riddled by the two SA officers gunfire were also attacked and eaten by the uninjured ravenous predators from the cave the team had just vacated. When they finished their feast, some made their way to other adjacent caves while most returned to their main resting places recently vacated by the Shadows. They found some added treats in the form of body parts from one of their own that Army had pulverized. They fought over and devoured them as well.

Chapter 16

Who Were Those Bad Guys?

The last of the passengers on the ill-fated Orient Express train had been airlifted to Hat Ya for medical evaluations, more thorough police debriefings and repatriation to Singapore or Bangkok. They would be held away from the press until the entire incident was fully analyzed. What was abundantly clear from initial statements, was that a major disaster had been averted by a group of Chinese anti-terrorist agents who acted to thwart the potential kidnappings and bombing of the train.

"What does ISOC, the Police or anybody here know about these men?" asked General Kittikachorn. "They seem to be better informed and tactically superior to any of our specialized units. Who are they?" he demanded of his staff.

"We don't know sir but we will find them, they are operating without any authority. It cannot be tolerated," answered the Southern Area Commander.

"Authority or not, they saved this train and all the passengers know it. How do you propose we deal with this reality once they start talking about what happened on that train?" he demanded. The officers stared blankly at him but said nothing.

"Get out of here, all of you, and get me some answers. We need to report to Bangkok within the hour."

*****

"Kittikachorn is giving his staff hell," began the CT Chief. "They have no idea who these masked-men are, where they came from or why they were there to break up the plot. Yeah, he's telling his troops to come up with a good cover story ASAP."

"Okay, what can we give him to help?" asked the Bangkok COS.

"I haven't heard from my SA guys yet but I know they found a cave below the train site that they were entering about an hour ago. I'll give you more as soon as I get it. Anything else I should know?"

"Just that everything seems very quiet with the MSS spooks these days. From what we're being told, their station is in lockdown since Zhou disappeared and Ping was discredited. Damn, if we could have something like this every week, working against them would be a walk in the park. They would never have time to recruit anyone."

"You wish," answered the CT Chief.

*****

Huddled against the vine-covered jungle cliffs in the watery early morning sunlight, Army completed searching both prisoners who were then tie-taped, gagged and blindfolded. While he completed his work, Pei and Ren poured over all the letters, notebooks and documents they collected from the Tangos on the train and the items discovered after Brave had photographed and fingerprinted everyone they had killed.

The pile of documents included twelve passports, ID cards from Malaysia, Thailand, Singapore, Turkey and a stray one from Myanmar. Pei had coded each one to the dead Tangos.

"Looks like most of the dead T's on the train were carrying Thai or Malaysian documents," she commented. "The last three from the cave were the most interesting; the old guy with the bitten up leg had Malaysia, Thai and Singapore; Sulalman had Malaysian, Thai and Turkish and the one Brave took-down had Turkish and Thai."

169

While looking through the materials Ren received a message congratulating him on the capture and the details for their extraction.

"All right everyone, twenty minutes to clean weapons, eat and get ready to move out," Ren ordered.

The Shadows used the time to wash off the cave dirt and blood, refill their water bottles, bury their trash and prepare the prisoners to walk out to the extraction site. While this clean up went on around him, Ren composed and sent an intelligence update on what they had collected. They then waited for their marching orders. It was not long coming.

Minutes later Ren ordered, "Gather round, everyone. Looks like we now have too much daylight for air extraction, and much too much time in Thai airspace to plausibly deny the incursion. We are walking out."

"Lo Ban, the old guy won't make a walk," said Army.

"We leave the injured one here. Arrangements are underway for the Thais to collect him within the hour. We take Sulalman and disappear. Brave will see to wiping our trail clean. We must be long gone before they arrive. We've been here too long all ready. Saddle up. Time to go."

"Strong, you take point and head south toward the South China Sea. We will follow the river for now until we gain some space from here. After that, let's see what the future holds."

The team hoisted their equipment, secured suppressors to their weapons, chambered rounds and began scanning the nearby jungle. Strong silently moved downstream to lead the team following the edge of the bolder strewn flowing water. He remained just inside the tree line. Twenty meters out, he stopped and signaled the all clear. The team slowly began moving forward, a two-meter length of rope secured Sulalman. The blindfold was removed but, for the time being, the gag remained firmly in place.

170

"Before we go, I need to prepare our prisoner to be collected by the Thais," Ren said as he secured the stacks of materials in his small backpack then tied the inert body of the village chief to the kapok tree. Ren turned on one of the telephones taken from the Tango's and placed it in his pocket. Reaching into the backpack again he took out some of the identification documents that had been taken from the village headman earlier and stuffed them into the prisoners pockets.

Ren waited until Pei disappeared into the jungle, looked around once more to check the area and followed the team into the jungle. Brave, watched him go, then re-checked the prisoner's wounds, the bindings that secured him in place and then did one final pass to sanitize the area. It was in making this final circle around their rest stop that he noticed the bundle hidden in a tree less than ten meters upstream from where they left the prisoner.

"Hey boss," Brave harshly whispered while waiving his arms in the air, catching Ren's attention. "You need to see this."

Ren signaled the team to halt in place. He returned to where Brave stood just inside the upstream side of the clearing that they had just left.

Brave pointed to the backpack and said. "Don't think we should touch it boss, could be wired."

Ren nodded and said with a chuckle, "Let's move the old man under that tree. It will give the Thais something else to sort out."

"Good thinking boss, it'll slow em' down a bit more. We need all the time we can steal."

Ren laughed.

Two hours later, Ren called a halt to the forced march as the Shadows team had traversed almost seven kilometers along the river. They had stopped hearing helios and any sign of pursuit long ago. "Rest, ten minutes, defensive perimeter," he ordered. The team melded into the jungle.

"So, Major Ren has captured Sulalman? We have proof?" demanded Chairman Chang.

"Yes sir, facial recognition software confirms it, they have him. Getting them out is, however, proving to be more complex that anticipated," said General Zhu.

"We will have an extraction plan shortly. In the meanwhile, they are secure in the jungle far away from the train-wreck site. I will have a strategy for dealing with the Thais and their allies for your review later today. The disinformation staff is working on it now."

Chang merely nodded. *He knew that whatever they recommended, final approval and responsibility would be his. What to do with the prisoner once safely here, was another matter.*

"Someone is there, by the rocks," whispered the Thai ranger scout into his throat-mike as he crept slowing toward the cliff.

"Hold position," came the quick response from the squad leader. Moments later he appeared with field glasses and after scanning the site, signaled the team to move slowly forward.

The river bottom was not wide enough for a medical evacuation helio so rangers secured him to a field stretcher, administered tubes for plasma and saline in his arms and carried the seriously injured headman out.. Thirty minutes of forced march brought them to the riverbed explosion site where emergency equipment littered the tracks and right-of-way above them. They used an available heavy crane to lift the stretcher to a waiting helio for transport to Hat Ya for treatment. He was to be isolated there under the tightest security.

*****

"Looks like the information we received from the PRC Military Attaché was accurate," said the General Kittikachorn.

"Yes sir," answered his aide, "Makes one wonder how he received such timely information, does it not?

"Indeed," responded the general. "Did we find anything of interest on his body?"

"A few curious things so far on him, but the backpack found with him is waiting for EOD examination before it can be moved," answered the aide. "He had several sets of identification, including some from Turkey even though he appears to be Thai."

"Let me know immediately what G-2 (*military intelligence*) has to say about him."

"Yes sir. And one more thing."

"What is it?"

"This prisoner would not be here if some very sophisticated medical attention had not been provided to him. He was just short of losing a leg. Surviving as long as he did required excellent care. How is it that this was possible? Our troops do not have this capability."

"Let's ask these terrorists, when you catch them," answered the General sourly.

Chapter 17

Beijing

Colonel General Zhu rubbed the sleep from his eyes as the incessant ringing of his telephone roused him from a fitful power nap at his desk. The blotter on his large desk bore the imprint of his uniform sleeve and a slight oily mark from his forehead.

"Zhu here," he mumbled into the handset.

"Minister Chang asks you to report to his office immediately, sir," said his aide.

"Call my driver, on my way," he answered, buttoned his tunic collar and smoothed down his often unruly hair. Now fully awake, he opened the office door, the sleep mark-crease on his head rapidly fading.

Across two ring roads fighting Beijing's notorious late afternoon traffic and forty minutes later, he presented himself as ordered. When the door opened he found himself in the midst of a meeting room filled with a dozen senior officers and party political leadership.

"General, thank you for coming on such short notice," Minister Chang began by glancing around the room and nodding to each person at the large meeting table.

"I'm sure you know many of those present," as he began the round of formal introductions.

"These are representatives of the State Council Secretariat, Central Military Commission, Branch Services, of course, General Zhu. All will have a role in this operation," he continued. "Shall we begin?"

Two hours later, consensus had been reached and Zhu had his orders, coordination contacts for the extraction operation, and protocols for handling the prisoner. *About half way through the meeting its real purpose became clear to him. If the extraction goes wrong, everyone here is now holding on to the horses tail together*, he thought. *None can let go without falling off. Very clever of Minister Chang but if he was sure of the operation he would not have used this ploy to cushion his risk of failure or dilute his success. What does he know that I do not about what's happening in Thailand, with Ren, or the prisoner?*

U.S. Embassy Bangkok

"The Thai government media guys are going bat shit trying to keep the real stories on the train disaster out of the press. The Bangkok Post already has dozens of interviews with passengers to the effect that the police are trying to suppress as national security matters," said the CI Chief.

"Yeah well, what's new? They've been keeping the brakes on any bad news reporting from the South for years, this is just more of the same," added the CT Chief.

"Well that may be but this one is different. Way too high profile to keep the lid on it for long. They have to come up with something to deflect attention from the problem down there. They need something big, maybe outside the country, to point at as a villain behind it," added the COS.

"Look guys, we're up to our ass in alligators on this thing. I've got two SA guys missing, the Thais have some of our equipment that they say belongs to the bad guy they're holding in Hat Ya, who, by the way, is still in critical condition and we don't know where the PLA knuckle draggers are. Does that about sum up where we are?" asked the CT Chief.

"Not quite," said the COS. "The IG's people are starting on their third day of trying to separate pepper from fly shit on the Hua Hin bombing. Remember that little problem, guys? I know it happened a few days ago, but we haven't even cleaned out the desks of our dead guys yet,

175

okay? Those folks from DC are still trying to find fault with what we did. Now you're telling me that we have another potential flap in the making? I mean, what the hell?"

"Look Chief, to borrow a phrase from an old Paul Newman movie... 'What we have here, is a failure to communicate'...or maybe to mix even a few more metaphors, perhaps the quote should be 'God help me!' Tom Cruise asking Jack Nicholson in *A Few Good Men*... 'I want the truth' and Nicholson answering, 'You can't handle the truth...' These IG pukes don't want the truth; they want their version of the truth. Big fucking difference."

"Makes no difference how you say it, but, really, you're quoting Tom fucking Cruise, Mr. Scientology, as an authority on dealing with the IG? Give me a break."

"Look," he continued, "Unless we figure out what the hell is going on with the Chinese, you might start by telling your wives, Thai whores, and significant others that they should start packing their bags, caus' we're for sure all going home. With any luck we might save our jobs but certainly not our careers. We'll be lucky if they don't strip the buttons from our uniforms and drum us out of the corps. Our lives as we know them are over unless we figure out how to manage the rest of this situation."

"Don't get so dramatic boss, this isn't some post Civil War frontier army post for Christ sake, and you don't wear a uniform any more, remember? What do you guys have? Early onset Alzheimer's or something? Get off your asses, stop feeling sorry for yourselves and get this problem solved. You're smart guys, certainly better than those knuckle draggers out there somewhere in the boonies. Get it figured out and get these IG pukes back into their cages in Langley."

"Great pep talk boss, but you're right, we do need to focus. The Thais need a scapegoat they can sell to the public; maybe the hospital guy is the one. Remember its always better to blame things on an almost dead guy than someone

176

that needs to be on a very public trial. Maybe he'll keel over soon and save everyone lots of problems. Give me a corpse and I'll give you a solution."

"If this whole things turns to shit, you can bet I'll be quoting you on the After Action Report," answered the COS as he ended the meeting

Hat Ya, Thailand

"You can have two minutes with him," the white-coated doctor warned. "He's in very critical condition."

"Only a minute doctor," said the Thai police inspector with a soft smile.

He was grudgingly waived past the military guards outside the hospital room door and into the IC unit room. Leaning over the sleeping body in the bed, he brushed against some of the tubes and multicolored wires that were protruding from under the covers. "You may die soon," he began in a very soothing voice. "Where can we contact your family to be with you? I'm sure you would find comfort in their presence?"

The headman's eyes opened slightly. He struggled to get the words out. His mouth tasted like it was filled with dry rice but finally whispered, "Yet Mung...Liar...Allah Akbar...Get Out."

The inspector, changing his demeanor, stepped away from the bed and answered, "Listen old man your days are numbered, your friends are all dead, you gain nothing from your actions. We know everything."

"You know nothing," he whispered and fell back to sleep.

"Well, I know that you will never plant another bomb or kidnap anyone ever again," he answered to a now silent room.

177

*****

While the abortive interview was happening in Hat Ya, the analysis of the materials taken from the old man was underway in Bangkok. Mounds of weapons, clothing, documents and bodies were spread out in three tents at the ambush site and in Hat Ya. A dozen forensic investigators hurried to understand what it meant.

"Turk indeed, he was the headman of the tiny village near Sungai Golok. We are positive from the facial recognition software. He's been on a watch-list for years. His whole family are rebels, always have been. We just couldn't prove it till now," said the Police Detective coordinating the forensic investigation.

"What about the other materials that were seized. How does he fit in with it?" asked the detectives working on the train bombing.

"Look we have five bodies from the train and thirteen passports, a dozen ID and Malaysian IC cards, weapons, as well as suitcases and backpacks filled with explosives. We're trying to sort it all out as quickly as we can. What I can tell you is that the pictures and personal data on our ID and Malaysian IC cards and those in the Thai, Malaysian and Turkish passports match the guy in the hospital. We're still working on the ones for the dead terrorists."

"Anything else you can tell us now?"

"Yes, whoever killed the five are professionals. The shot groups were too well executed for amateurs and the physical trauma on the others was vicious but very focused for maximum damage."

"One more thing. We found two explosive detonators on the ground near the train; one was next to the hand of one of the dead. He had been shot in the head twice, at close range. My guess is that someone tried to stop him from blowing up the tunnel."

Line of March

The mosquitoes swarmed over the Shadows as they pushed on at a punishing pace through the rough terrain, over, between, and down the limestone cliffs that dotted their path toward the South China Sea. It was still more than fifty kilometers and another long day and a half away. Much to the surprise of the team, Sulalman trudged along without complaint even though he chaffed under his bindings and the rope tether. The years of privations and jihad had hardened his body like those of his captors. Ren was sure that given the opportunity, Sulalman would try for an escape as soon as possible. It is what anyone on his team would do if the circumstances were reversed. *There was no way he would allow that to happen.*

Chinese Embassy, Bangkok

"Yes, Uncle," Gao, the Bangkok PLA Attaché said softly into his secure telephone. "I am quite sure. The Admirals still have funds ready to proceed with the orders, they merely require the right atmosphere within the government."

"It will be forthcoming. Please assure them of this as a fact. Do they suggest the proper timing?" Minister Chang inquired. "We are able to proceed within forty-eight hours. Since you will be the one to give them the recovery details, you decide on when, I will tell you where."

"As you wish, Uncle," he answered.

"One more thing, have they accepted our other terms and conditions?

"Why would they not? They received equally as much, if not more, for approving the purchase."

"Of course the two percent, per your request, will be deposited in the UBS Geneva account; half on signing, the balance on delivery."

"As always, your diligence will be rewarded," said the minister.

"Thank you, Uncle, I await your instructions." *I also await*, he thought, *my one percent from the Thais as well as another $500,000 USD from you.*

"One more thing," Chang continued, "I want you to contact the Americans. We need a diversion, let me explain what you are to do…"

CIA Station

"Our day just got a whole lot worse boss," said the CT Chief as he walked up to the COS inside the secure conference room.

"Now what?"

"Our guys in the BPP just got word from the rangers who brought the old guy in that while they were searching the area they found a cave nearby with some weapons, boots and scraps of bloody clothing. They also secured a backpack with our GPR gear in it."

"Shit, double shit, what about our guys?"

"Nothing. The tracking device on their phones went dark right after they told me they were going into the cave; there is still no signal. BPP has a guard outside to secure the cave. We should be getting a call through liaison shortly asking what we want to do?"

"Do? Do you need a four-color glossy picture? Get your ass down there and find out what happened and where they are before anyone else around here starts asking questions. Do it now!" he shouted.

Three hours later the CT Chief was back near Sungai Golok walking along the riverbed and approaching the guard at the cave entrance. The guard stood and saluted the Chief and the BPP Captain who accompanied him. "All quiet sir, nothing to report," the guard shouted. "Stand easy corporal, we're going to inspect the cave. Please remain here," said the captain.

They hunched down, turned on their mag-lites and quietly entered the fetid smelling darkness. Immediately upon entering they swept their lights over the dark pool of water. Littering the muddy floor were small, scattered piles of cloth, rubber boot soles and half of a boot with some bits of bone matter spilling out. There were several large mounds of spent brass shell casings from M-16's along one side of the pool while one rifle lay broken at the receiver stock on a rocky outcropping.

"What the hell happened here?" the Chief asked. "Looks like a major fire-fight and an explosion of some type."

While he was examining the weapon, and getting DNA samples, the captain walked near the pool and shone his light into the water. Almost immediately, a large crocodile surfaced ten meters away and began swimming toward his location.

"Let's get out of here!" he screamed and bolted for the cave entrance with the Chief directly behind him.

They exited the cave and yelled to the guard, "Crocodiles! Lock and load your weapons". Fortunately, the Chief had collected enough samples of bone and blood for DNA matches just before the chaos erupted. They were safely in his small Musset bag. Once outside the CT Chief placed a call back to Bangkok. Four hours later, he was back at the Station completing his report to the COS.

"Son-of-a-bitch," said the COS, "crocodiles? Jesus what a way to go."

He then smiled sadly and said, "Reminds me of a story that went around Langley during the early days of Vietnam.

Back then, young officers had weekend duty chores reading station cable traffic from Saigon and preparing daily summaries for all those in the executive offices on the 7th floor ---DCI (*Director of Central Intelligence*)and DDP (*Deputy Director Plans, AKA Clandestine Services Chief*), you know the top brass. Anyway, one night a cable came in with the summaries that read: 9 KIA (*Killed In Action*) 2 MIA (*Missing In Action*) but there was an additional category on the report that he had never seen before: 1 EIA. He searched and searched and finally sent a cable to the Saigon station and asked for clarification. A few hours later a note comes back to him with the following explanation:

Pfc. Johnson, 1st Marines assigned near Danang went to use the latrine at night a short distance from the company area in dense jungle. He was eaten by a tiger, hence the EIA…Eaten In Action. Sorry, it's the best description we could think up.

Many hilarious skits were produced by young clandestine service officers during dozens of Operations Training Courses to recreate delivering the bad news to Pvt. Johnson's family about his cause of death."

He paused and said, "If we're sure it's them, do you want to give it a try with some crocs?"

"No thanks, I'll let Bagram Base take care of the notifications once we confirm the DNA and blood matches. However, I just can't wait to see what you're going to tell Langley," he laughed sourly and walked out of the COS's office.

MSS Station, Bangkok

"So Major Ren has captured the terrorist after all," said Director Li to his MSS staff in Bangkok. "I just received orders for us to assist with the operation directly from

182

General Zhu at 1st Directorate. It was followed by a personal call from Minister Chang's aide on the sensitivity of this matter."

"What are we to do sir?" asked Wang Ping, who still awaited reassignment.

"I'll have specific operational orders shortly but this project is to take top priority for the station until further notice," Li answered.

The MSS station surveillance team had been quick to set up for the morning's cold pitch...not pre-planned meeting...between the Attaché and the American CIA officer at that decadent coffee shop that almost nobody at the embassy could afford unless they had operational funds allocated.

CIA Station

"Excuse me Chief, but we need to talk," said the CI Chief excitedly breaking into a conversation the COS was having with another case officer.

"I'm really busy here, can't it wait?" he answered.

"Wish it could, really urgent," he responded.

"Look, let's finish up later," he said to the young woman sitting across from his desk. She gave both of them an annoying look as she huffed out of the tiny office.

"Now you've done it, I'm probably going to get another lecture from the HR weenies about sensitivity in handling our new gender free workplace environment. How I'm not showing proper levels of sensitivity to our female staff. Anyway, what's so important that my ass is going to get chewed on again?"

"I just came back from Starbucks..." he began.

"How nice, you want to talk about coffee? What, some new blend? Special pricing for spooks? What?"

"No, I just got approached there by the PLA Attaché and was given some serious Intel."

"You got to be shitting me," he said, now sitting upright in his chair.

"Wish that was true but he wants to cooperate with us on the bombing situation. Says he knows where the knuckle draggers are. Wants us to help get the planning mastermind back for the Thais'."

"That makes no sense at all, what's he up to?"

"Beats the hell out of me, but he wants another meeting to discuss details and quid pro quo's."

"Any bona fides from the meet today or just 'I can give you something for free'?" the COS asked.

"He passed along their radio frequency," he said smiling. "I've already sent it to NSA for verification against what we already have. Hopefully a location for them as well."

"Okay, for this I can justify being labeled an HR dinosaur," he laughed. "Keep me in the loop."

The CI Chief called his BPP contact, sent follow-up's to NSA to get current coordinates on traffic from Ren's radio and laid-on the meeting plan for the Attaché's next visit.

"Look, we're going to need your SWAT guys for some support sometime in the next few days. Get them on stand-by status ready to move on thirty minutes notice," he told the BPP Commander.

Central Committee Office Building, Beijing

"Why do we need to involve them?" asked General Zhu. "All we can expect is more of what they did last time. Even that good-for-nothing Ping is still wandering the halls looking for a place to make our life more difficult."

"Be careful who you share these thoughts with, General," answered Minister Chang.

"But you know it is the truth."

184

"Enough, you know full well that truth is never a justification for making yourself vulnerable to their spies and deceit."

"So the plan really is to let the Thais take our prisoner? I don't trust the MSS to either do it properly, take credit for it, or blame us should there be a problem."

"Chang smiled slightly and answered, "All is not as it seems General. We give them the illusion of participation but when the times comes, they will experience difficulties in carrying out their orders."

"Ah, my apologies Minister, my view was of the front of the plan, not its inner workings."

"All in good time, General, all in good time. Several others on our team have assignments that may exceed their grasp as well. Remember our goal? That is still the most important portion of the operation."

"My officers are ready to serve your plan," Zhu said, saluted and departed for his office at Special Operations Command Headquarters.

Chang again picked up his secure telephone to begin the real work of the operation. Colonel Li's forces would very shortly begin their part of the shadow play that was now being orchestrated.

Police Headquarters, Bangkok

The Bangkok Police Chief and the Director General of the Royal Thai National Police sparred regularly about everything possible but mostly about making sure that the correct apportionment of monies flowed to their offshore accounts. In the old days, promotions were purchased and while not exactly done the same way now, additional funds were considered a side benefit of each and every level in the police bureaucracy: from patrolman or traffic cop to city chief and on up the line to the very top of the pile like a multi-level

185

marketing scam. Everyone got some and gave some up the line.

Those at the top were always afraid that those below them were skimming, so tensions always existed. In a high visibility matter like the Erawan bombing, old grudges and animosities bubbled to the surface along with day-to-day finance.

"My friends at ISOC tell me that we may soon finally have the one responsible for planning the Erawan bombing in custody," the Director General said to Bangkok's Chief.

"I hear it a bit differently. It's that the army has him in custody in Hat Ya, only that he is responsible for both Erawan and the train," said Bangkok's Chief.

"If there are two different terrorists, not one, we need to have the facts clearly spelled out. The press is clamoring for details. Hotel bookings have dropped another 12 percent. The Tourism Minister is jumping up and down, the hotels are screaming and even the whores in Soi Cowboy are restive. We need closure as soon as possible," said the Director General.

"ISOC and the Army are convinced that the old man they are holding in the hospital is a long time terrorist who planned and took part in the train bombing. He may have been involved in Erawan but there is no physical evidence yet to support it," answered the Bangkok Chief. "My detectives are down in Hat Ya now, trying to interview him, but the Army has refused, saying that he is too ill."

"ISOC tells me that he is a major link in the terrorist networks in the South. His arrest or death would be a major blow against the rebels," he said.

"If that's true, we might be able to suggest that he had a role. It would temporally take off some pressure from tourist hotel bookings and airline ticket purchases," offered the Chief.

"Humm, but what happens if and when we catch the real bomber?" asked the Director General

"We charge him also, no problem," the Chief quickly answered.

Line of March

It was 1830 and full darkness covered the jungle. "The GPS says we've covered fourteen kilometers since we left the cave at 0720," said Brave.

"Rest," called Ren. "Defensive positions, I'll take first one hour watch, everyone eat and sleep. We depart in four hours. Go."

The Shadows were tired but this forced march was well within their performance envelope. Dragging the prisoner along was slowing their progress but they were far from the train and had not seen any police or army patrols in the past three hours. They had evaded several patrols early in the morning and again just after their rest stop four kilometers back along their trail.

Brave, Strong, Army and Lt. Pei were all in good spirits. Sulalman fell asleep sitting against a tree the minute they stopped.

Ren took his radio, composed a situation report, prepared the burst transmission and sent it on the SOG Command. Before he woke his replacement for guard duty, he had received a response.

Evacuation within next 24-48 hours, Proceed on current azimuth...compass direction... reading until further notice. Extractions details to follow.

"Rock and Roll everyone," Ren called out to the Shadows. "Time to get back on the trail," he continued as they cleaned up their resting places and erased any traces of their stay.

187

"Pei, stay back for a moment, " he whispered as the team silently moved forward into the early morning darkness.

"You will be leaving us for a special assignment in a few hours. We will rendezvous with some MSS operatives four hours down range from here. You will accompany them with the evidence we have collected from the Tangos we encountered and bring it to the PLA Attaché in Bangkok. When you complete your work with him, you will return directly to base. We will meet you there in three days."

"That's unfair," she stammered at a loss for words. "I'm always given the easy assignments just because I'm a woman"

"Lieutenant," Ren began. "This assignment is not because you are a woman but because you have the skills that our other two team members lack, namely tact and brains. Yes, it also does not hurt that you are a beautiful woman as well." He continued with a slight coloring of his cheeks.

She looked at him and slightly smiled at his embarrassment. While still angry that she would shortly leave the team, she understood his problem. It was not good tactics to split forces...sending her on a side mission...but it was essential given the orders he had just received.

"There is no one I would rather have at my side than you," Ren finally continued, "but there is no other way to complete the mission. Your job from now until we meet again is to help convince anyone and everyone that our one legged old man was responsible for the temple bombing. That Sulalman does not exist. Nothing else. Can you do that?" he paused for effect.

She nodded.

"I need to hear you say it," he said.

"I'm a Ghost Shadow," she said. "I can do anything! It will be done as you ordered."

They both smiled, he touched her face gently and they followed the team into the jungle.

"Hey Boss, looks like NIMROD is finally paying off. He tells us that his MSS handlers have asked him to organize transport for six of their staff to head down south for some 'meetings' tomorrow morning," said the CT Chief to the COS.

"Did he have the coordinates for this meeting? asked the COS.

"Exactomente, Señor," he said. "Precise map coordinates put them about four klicks north of the highway and twenty klicks south of the only village in the area. Basically right in the middle of nowhere."

"Your basic black hole," the COS offered.

"Dark, quiet and lots of soft earth that makes digging holes fast and easy."

"Just make sure we get the right folks in the holes this time," the COS added.

"Roger that boss, my BPP SWAT guys are the best at what they do."

"Well they had better be caus' those Chinese troopers have been kicking some serious ass in some pretty tough places recently."

"They won't know what hit em' boss, guaranteed."

"Yeah, well, tell me about it with some body count."

"We have them enroute to the ambush site while we speak. Their snipers will be set up within the hour. No one will get out of that place alive unless we want them to," said the CT Chief.

"You're sure we can trust NIMROD on this one?" asked the COS.

"Listen boss, we're sure that what he's telling us is kosher this time. We know the spooks are scrambling to help get those bad asses out of the country and NSA continues to get coordinates on them that track almost a straight line to

189

where NIMROD tells us they are headed this evening. Sounds pretty convincing to me."

The COS nodded and headed back to his small office.

Chinese Embassy Bangkok

Colonel Ming Ping sat bolt upright in the hard chair in front of his superior's desk.

"Ping, I've decided to give you an opportunity to redeem yourself," said Colonel Li.

"If Personnel had moved more rapidly you would have already been reassigned away from me to some place in the far reaches of Tibet. But since you are still here and under my command, I must find something useful to do with you."

"Sir, I will do anything you ask..." Ping began.

"Do not interrupt me Ping, I don't want to hear your whining voice during this meeting except to say 'yes,' do you understand?"

Ping was silent.

"Well?"

"Yes, sir."

"Good, now then," he continued, "You will be part of a six person team that has been assigned to recover, secure and return a hostage currently being held by Major Ren and his team of Ghost Shadows to the Embassy in Bangkok. Do you understand the assignment Colonel?"

"Yes sir."

"Your training file indicates you are fully proficient with the weapons being assigned to team members. I expect you to familiarize yourself with those being assigned to you. Should it become necessary, I do not want any of you killing each other by accident. Is that clear?"

"Yes, sir."

"The mission profile is now on your desk. Read it, memorize it and be ready for departure by 1800 hrs."

Ping started to rise from his chair.

"Didn't you forget something Ping?"

Ping paused and looked confused.

"Sir?" Then it dawned on him.

"Yes sir."

Colonel Li glared at him and said, "Now get out of here and don't come back without the hostage."

Ping began to mouth "Ye.." when Li, with a disgusted look on his face, waved him out of the room.

Chapter 18

Line of March

As he broke into the clearing, Strong signaled 'halt' and waited for the cacophony of birds and animals to continue their sounds and songs, signaling a safe passage ahead.

"Five hundred meters to go boss," announced Strong as he tilted his head and looked up at the limestone wall that marked another steep climb up the thirty meter brush and vine covered cliff face. Rivulets of water dripped from the rock face making it slippery. Mist filled the air. Large ferns and trailers dangled from trees and the limestone rock face itself.

"Okay, let's rest here for fifteen then I want you and Brave to recon the meeting site before we move the prisoner any closer. But, let's move back from the cliff and set up a perimeter inside the jungle" Ren said.

"Sure thing boss, don't want anyone throwing rocks or grenades down on us while we're waiting," said Brave.

Ren nodded in agreement adding, "Listen, it's better to have them above us right now than to have to jump off if we need to back up"

"Sounds right to me," said Strong. "Let's rest and get moving. We need to get the site under control before we move the prisoner."

"Sounds like you don't trust our orders either," said Brave.

"It's going to be light in about four hours and our meeting is set for 0700 tomorrow. I want us to absolutely control that space before anyone else gets there. Everyone copy that?" Ren asked.

The entire team vigorously nodded assent and settled down for brief combat naps while Ren again sent a SITREP (*Situation Report*) and asked for mission updates.

Before Ren could close his eyes the red light on his secure radio was rapidly blinking indicating an incoming message.

Hold at current location. Site security being provided by Bangkok Assets. Proceed as scheduled for 0700 prisoner transfer. GS transportation confirmed.

Ren consulted his crude map of the area and then waited for the team to awaken from their brief rest.

"Okay, everyone. We have a problem," he began. After reading them the message he did not have long to wait for their reactions.

"That's bullshit, Are they kidding? We aren't going to do that are we boss?" erupted from the team.

Ren laughed bitterly. "Not a chance we're not even going to hold in this position now. We move in two minutes. We will provide our own site security for this meeting. We're certainly not going to use anyone from Bangkok to cover us with any kind of weapon," Ren snarled.

Minutes later they moved further down stream from the cliff and pushed south, away from the established rendezvous site.

What the hell are they thinking? Ren wondered.

Prearranged Meeting Site

Three rough, yet discernable animal trails converged near a small stream that fed the main river that would eventually empty into the South China Sea another ten kilometers further south. A nearby highway carried occasional sugar cane related traffic during the harvesting season yet some months away.

Currently it was seldom used save for the odd Tuktuk type farm vehicle or farang bicycle backpacker tourist seeking a country style Thai holiday experience. The last vehicle to pass within a few klicks of the spot was two days ago.

The BPP and SWAT (*Special Weapon and Tactics*) Teams followed the advice of local farmers. They 'fast-roped' into a jungle clearing three kilometers northwest of the site and walked in to avoid disturbing its tranquility. Two Ghillie suited sniper teams and two three-man blocking and assault forces took their time approaching, assessing and setting up their positions on the site. Interlocking fields of fire, excellent high ground positions for the snipers and spotters were established that would prevent the escape of anyone entering the meeting location coordinates. There were three hours of daylight left when they completed preparations for spending the night normalizing the wildlife and foliage to camouflage their presence.

"Sure twelve hours is enough?" The CT Chief asked the BPP Captain who had organized the ambush.

"Certainly enough, no problem. Nobody will know we are here until it is time to strike," he answered.

The two officers sat in a portable nylon camouflaged hunting blind command post about twenty five meters south of the coordinates. The BPP Captain thought: *what's wrong with this guy, nobody uses a tent to keep the mosquitoes away. He should be making merit by not killing them and honoring the Lord Buddha all night. Crazy farang.*

The CT Chief, sent a secure message to the Bangkok Station: ***Teams in place, site secure, awaiting 0700.***

*****

The six MSS tactical team officers left their minivan on the roadway one kilometer from the trail leading to the meeting coordinates at 2100 hrs.

194

"You have picked positions for covering fire?" Ping asked the team leader.

"Yes sir, four locations have been identified. My men will secure those places and wait for your command to commence firing at the traitors," he answered briskly.

"Good, good, the two of us will wait at the meeting site for them to arrive. They need to see that we are here at the appointed time. Get your men in position while I select a place for us," Ping commented.

*****

"We have company coming," said the CT Chief into his tactical radio as he saw the first of the MSS column pass within five meters of his position.

"Roger that," came the Captain's response. "I see them, any orders?"

"Stand fast, let's see what they are doing before we do anything. Pretty poor tactical skills, I thought these were their best of the best."

"Very strange indeed. Everyone is on hold till your command," answered the Captain.

The entire BPP contingent watched in disbelief as the Chinese column dispersed into the jungle, except for the two men who walked directly into the center of the kill zone and began preparing to light a small campfire.

*****

"This should be close enough to show Major Ren that we are here waiting for him to arrive," Ping announced.

"Definitely sir, there should be no doubt in his mind that we are here, unarmed and waiting for him," answered the team leader.

"Now," Ping said, "we wait."

"Perhaps some tea?"

The computer mapping system the MSS planners had used chose this particular location as it was an escarpment marking the end of the more mountainous jungle covered terrain and the beginning of the agricultural coastal plains. Several natural knolls were to be used by Ping's force to provide sweeping fields of fire over the coordinates. The center of the zone was rocky in places with bare dirt in others.

"Collect some wood, the smoke should keep the insects at bay," Ping told the team leader. "I'll get the site prepared."

There were many rock piles, tree limbs, stumps and piles of brush nearby that suggested recent land clearing and more sugar cane planting soon. *Strange,* Ping thought, *this area was supposed to be unused...secluded ...how is it that this recent activity was overlooked in the mission planning? Well, too late to worry about it now, we need to take charge of the prisoner, complete our assignment and leave before whoever has been working here returns.*

"Three of our security detail have checked in from their assigned positions, the fourth is having radio issues but from checking his personal locator on the tactical network computer, he appears to be in correct position," reported the MSS team commander.

"Excellent, now we just wait, perhaps you would like to rest while I keep watch?" suggested Ping.

"Yes, that would be good, the team will also be awake watching with you," he commented. "Two hours, then I will exchange with you. It will make the night move more quickly."

The night had already been moving quickly for Ping's team making their way to the assigned positions scattered throughout the surrounding jungle. Tactical planners work from a similar template when laying out an ambush site. There are normally several options that work best for a given set of terrain, objectives and manpower. The BPP and MSS planners had both analyzed this site with remarkable

196

precision and similarity. Since the BPP troopers had the advantage of arriving on station while there was still daylight, they were able to tweak their positions for more optimal effect than those of the much later arriving MSS.

The late arriving MSS officers had the misfortune of setting up their positions either adjacent to or in front of those already established by the BPP. In three of these locations the BPP shooters were several meters away and merely noted their positions and awaited instructions on what to do about these new neighbors.

In the fourth location, however, the hapless MSS officer stepped on the back of a Ghillie-suited sniper and was immediately silenced with a knife. His tactical radio remained on but manipulated to feign transmission difficulties. His body was left where it had fallen.

Now, none of the MSS contingent could effectively move without being instantly cut down by point blank fire.

*****

After receiving a report of the takedown over the encrypted radio network, the BPP Captain shook his head and muttered, "Never have I seen such ineptness," to the CT Chief.

"Indeed Captain, a dazzling display, textbook quality even," laughed the Chief. "But, the night is still young, who knows what other lessons we might learn before we finish this operation. We can take turns monitoring their actions with our NVG's, no telling when they will give us even more to marvel at."

The Captain nodded his head, clicked down his goggles and grinned.

*****

The embers in the campfire had burned down as Colonel Ping stretched and reached over to gently shake the team leader awake. "It's 0100," he said to awaken him.

Two hours had elapsed and the tea induced fullness of Ping's bladder cried out for relief. The light from the coals produced almost nothing that could be used for vision. Light in the jungle at night is virtually non-existent. It is black sky unless one is not under the double or triple canopy cover of trees. Tonight, clouds and threatening rain made it difficult to see a meter away without artificial means.

"I'll return in a few moments, nature calls," he joked as he placed a few more twigs and branches on the fire causing it to smoke and briefly flare as the coals fought for oxygen. The team leader grunted acknowledgement. As he stretched, Ping took some toilet paper from his small musket-bag and headed toward the edge of the light being thrown off by the fire. The jungle was only a scant two meters distant where he could find an isolated place to relieve himself.

There was a small bush that Ping located with the help of his mini-LED flashlight. He removed his pistol belt, slung it over a low branch near at hand, and dropped his trousers and underwear. He hunkered and tried to relax with the mosquitoes circling and buzzing his exposed bottom. In moments he was finished and reaching for the scraps of paper to finish his toilet.

It was then that he sensed, rather than felt movement from behind, but because he was squatting, it was difficult to turn his head and located the source of his discomfort. But instantaneously what was a vague sense of unease became a blinding, searing flashing pain in his groin. It was so strong that it forced him into an instantly upright position with his legs locked at the knee, his buttocks tight together and his head raised toward the heavens with his mouth wide open to scream…but nothing would come out. The pain was so intense that he was unable to utter a word.

What he did notice was that the length of his penis seemed to expand. It now seemed to extend to his ankles, it also was moving, twisting and turned against his thighs and knees as though it had a life of his own.

After the first waves of pain subsided, Ping reached down to see what had happened only to have another intense pain shoot through his hand. As he bent his knees he felt his penis fall off as another stabbing pain seared his left ankle. He looked down where his flashlight illuminated a narrow circle on the ground and he could see the tail of a snake rapidly moving away from him and back into the darkness.

His scream of "AAIYYEE..........." could be heard all over the site as he stumbled, tripping over his trousers and underwear, falling back toward the campfire.

"My dick is on fire," he screeched, "Something bit me. Help!" he sobbed, collapsing to the ground.

"Let me see," said the team leader, inspecting Ping's hand, ankle and rapidly dis-coloring penis. Puncture marks were very visible in all three locations that were oozing blood, and a clear fluid covered the torn edges of the blackening skin.

"Did you see the snake? What kind, what color?" He asked the blubbering Ping.

"Nothing, just felt it, just the tail, green I think, so fast, happened so fast." Ping moaned.

"Unless we can get the poison out of your system, there is nothing we can do for you," said the team leader. "It sounds and looks like a pit viper of some kind. Even if we get the venom out..." he continued as Ping began to roll around on the ground, moaning even louder "help me, help me..."

*****

"What the hell is going on down there? Why is that guy screaming? Can you see anything?" asked the Chief.

"It appears that one of their leaders has been bitten by a snake," he said without humor.

199

*****

"Pull back," Ren ordered briskly. Army lay across the clearing from where Ping was now writhing in agony. "Okay boss, did you see what that guy was just doing?" Army responded.

"Just do it now, talk later," Ren instructed.

They too had watched as both teams moved into their current positions surrounding the meeting coordinates. *What are they thinking back in Beijing? These people are a disgrace to the country, they deserve to be killed. They are too ignorant to breed let alone defend our country. These are the people they sent to protect me? But the other troops that arrived, they are well trained, a worthy opponent and dangerous.*

Two hours later, Ren and Army re-entered the Ghost Shadow campsite and gathered the team for a briefing.

"…and this guy from Beijing that has been trying to discredit us, went to take a shit and got bit in his balls by a snake. It actually hung-on while he was dancing around trying to figure out what had happened," Army reported as the tears of humor rolled down his face. "Can you believe it?" he continued until Ren raised his hand to silence him.

"It's true, Colonel Ping was bitten several times, I think, by a snake, I assume to be poisonous," Ren continued.

"Hey boss, think anyone of the MSS guys is going to try sucking the poison out of his balls?" Strong asked, convulsing with laughter.

"I'm sure they would not even try. If it was a pit viper, it would be poisonous to them as well."

"He is probably already dead and one less problem for us to concern ourselves with," interjected Pei who merely rolled her eyes at the gallows humor of the team. "More importantly Major, how does his death impact what I'm supposed to do in Bangkok?"

200

"That depends on what we do about the two ambush teams covering the meeting place," Ren answered, then continued, "Remember our assignment: get the prisoner back safely and get the information we have on Hakimi to the Attaché, and that is exactly what we are going to do."

"We have four hours until we are supposed to walk into that clearing with this guy," Army said pointing to the sleeping figure lying next to the small fire.

"Whatever we do, it has to begin pretty quickly," Strong added.

SOG Command Beijing

Ren's situation report was quickly routed directly to General Zhu moments after its arrival. Zhu threw it on his otherwise spotless desk and stormed around his office glaring at his ADC who had brought in the flimsy.

"It seems that our Ministry comrades once again have failed in carrying out a simple directive," shouted General Zhu. He then continued in a more controlled voice, "Major Ren's assignment has just become more perilous for all of us. Without assistance from the Ministry in getting Lieutenant Pei back to Bangkok, we have a dilemma. Who do we provide as the suspect so the Thais are satisfied with our results. We need Sulalman here and they need a ringleader there. Our former plan allowed for both to happen, now, we must once again choose."

"Perhaps the answer is in front of us already," answered his ADC.

"You mean?" asked the general.

"Allow Major Ren to decide. If he is successful in choosing the right path, all will be well. If he fails, we can rightly blame the Ministry for the failure. In either event, blame is deflected and success assured," the ADC answered.

Chapter 19

The Ambush

Birds are normally the first creatures to react to the coming dawn. Their calls start getting louder and closer together as they awaken and shake off the slumber of the dark night perched in the safety of their protective foliage.

Once awake their daily ritual of mating calls and searching for prey or food begins. Larger animals also commence scurrying around the jungle floor, moving toward sources of water or food to get them started on another day of survival. Insects do the same as they try to avoid being a meal for something larger while they stalk and devour their sustenance.

MSS officer Wen Ji had the misfortune of being assigned to the northern quadrant of the ambush site on a slight knoll that overlooked the site of Colonel Ping's demise during the night. While he could not see what had happened, he heard muffled screams and knew that there had been a serious problem.

I need to move. My legs are getting numb from lying still all-night, I itch all over. Aiyee, I know why my father never wanted me to be a regular soldier, and arranged for a Ministry position instead after basic training.

I'm on fire. I have to move. The Colonel says we cannot but....now I am itching and on fire, what's wrong with me? He thought, *I need to move, get up and run and scream.*

Not being able to control the pain and discomfort any longer, he jumped to his feet. As he did, a powerful grip closed over his mouth as he was forcefully pulled back into a seated position and his neck broken at the C-2 vertebrae with a single twist. He died instantly as his brain stem was severed. The fire ant hill that the hapless officer had been laying next to was now awake and would soon begin working to transfer as much of the hapless officer into their nest as possible before it once again became too dark to work.

Before the BPP sergeant who had dispatched Officer Wu was able to regain his camouflaged position, Strong pulled him roughly backwards and squeezed three silenced subsonic rounds of 9.0 mm ordinance into his back. The rounds disintegrated inside his chest cavity as copper shards shredded his heart and lungs. He died silently in Strong's arms.

The motion from these three combined actions made little more than a ripple in the early morning sound effects of the wakening jungle. Even the continual scanning done by the BPP Commander from the tent witnessed no discernible movement from that sector of the ambush site.

A peaceful looking jungle was the last thing he ever saw. An under-hand pitched fragmentation grenade cut through the thin nylon tent while the still sleeping CT Chief was on his back. He was thrown two meters away from his position. He had no time to react, shout a warning or pray to Buddha. His life ended in a blinding flash and sharp explosive report.

Three more simultaneous explosions rocked the site where body parts and foliage flew through the brightening dawn. The thup...thup...thup of silenced weapons followed as the Shadows finished wiping out the injured among the already dead Thai troopers and MSS officers scattered throughout the nearby area. There would be no prisoners.

In a little more than two minutes, the Shadows had reduced both ambush forces to only one badly shaken MSS commander who was cowering behind the now rigid body of Colonel Ping. While weapons were collected, personal identification stripped from bodies and photographs taken, Major Ren and Lieutenant Pei roughly searched the MSS officer and moved him away from the carnage.

"What were your orders?" Pei demanded.

"I don't understand…" he began.

Pei slapped him roughly across the face. "Answer me," she yelled at him.

Again he stood mute, staring at the bodies.

"Your orders, what were your orders?" Pei shouted directly into his face.

"Search him," Ren told Pei.

She patted his pockets, turned out his trousers, upended his backpack and tried to unlock his telephone. "What is the code?" She demanded.

Still nothing.

"Pull down his trousers," Ren barked.

Instantly, Pei cut his belt with her knife and tugged them down revealing some lime green boxers.

"Now the underwear," Ren continued.

As Pei reached for them his trance seemed to evaporate and he tried to push her away. For his efforts Pei rewarded him with a quick strike to the scrotum with a balled fist and a hip toss to the jungle floor. As he lay there, her knee was quickly on his stomach and her knife cutting through the slick lime green nylon.

"I'll bet the ladies are going to miss your charms after we finish here, such as this miserable little dick of yours might provide," she hissed.

He struggled but gained no ground as Ren turned his head away from the spectacle and chuckled as Pei gave a superb theatrical performance as a crazed terrorist.

"No," he wailed, "No,"

Pei grabbed his scrotum and brought the knife tip to the now shriveled flesh. "Tell me or prepare to die a slow and painful death," she laughed as if thoroughly demented.

"Easy now Lieutenant," Ren shouted.

"Fuck his mother, sir, this worthless scum needs to learn a lesson in honesty."

Then turning back to him, she squeezed his balls tighter and pushed the knife into the spongy flesh until blood began to ooze at the point where the knife was entering.

His eyes began to roll around and his moaning became embarrassing to witness.

"Go easy on him Lieutenant," Ren smirked.

"Hold him for me sir, I'll find another of those snakes that killed his Colonel. Perhaps he would prefer getting bitten by one of them?"

As she released him and began to rise he started to thrash around causing her to punch him not so gently between the eyes. "Don't move again if you wish to see full daylight this morning," she warned.

"Sir, if you would please watch him until I return?"

"Certainly, Lieutenant."

As she strode off into the jungle Ren leaned over and whispered to him, "Listen, I don't know how long I can control her, when it gets to be that time of the month she gets really nasty. I suggest that you answer her questions as none of us can control her when she gets like this."

The commander blanched and rolled his head back and forth.

In what seemed like moments she was back holding a two-foot long black and green striped snake by its head. Its body twisted and squirmed around her arm as she moved quickly to kneel next to the commander.

"I found this one, near a blast site, it's a bit dazed but it is coming back to life very quickly. It is not happy about being tossed around by the explosion."

She lowered the snake slowly toward his groin.

"ZXP947"

"What are you babbling about?" Pei snarled.

"The code, it's the code," he whimpered, "ZXP947"

Pei continued to hold the twisting viper inches from his balls while Ren entered the code into the encrypted

205

telephone. Immediately, he began scrolling through the last twenty-four hours of messages.

Ren finally looked up and motioned to Pei that he had what they were looking for. The interrogation was finished.

"Move one finger, and I swear by Mao's balls that I will cut off your dick and feed it to the ducks. Shake your head if you understand what I just said?" she whispered to him.

Very slowly he nodded. She lifted her knee off his stomach and backed away to the edge of the jungle and threw the snake as far away as she could from the campsite. It snapped and bit viciously at the air as it sailed over the open ground and landed with a thud in the foliage.

"Roll over," she commanded when she returned to the scared and shaking officer. He did not respond quickly so she repeated,

"Roll over now or I will cut you in several places and stake you out for the ants as the Japanese did during the war in these jungles. Not at all a pleasant way to die. It might take days," she giggled.

The fear that shone in his eyes was primordial. *This crazy bitch will do it,* he thought as he rolled over to await his fate. Zip tape handcuffs quickly cut into his wrists.

Ren marveled at her performance. She winked discretely at him as she turned away from her prisoner.

Pei had taken Dickie's 'good cop, bad cop' interrogation routines to a whole new level.

Central Committee Office of Minister Chang

"How did a simple operation get so confused, so quickly?" asked Minister Chang. "Ren should have delivered the terrorist days ago, instead he is still in the jungle, dozens more deaths follow in his wake and we still have no closure with the Thai Navy."

206

General Zhu stood before him, grim faced. "Ren sent along evidence that the Bangkok MSS command team had orders to interdict and kill Ren and his team, recover the prisoner and return him to Bangkok to gain favor with the Thai government." He paused then added, "Ren was forced to eliminate a large force of Thai police as well as a senior American intelligence officer who was there advising the Thai troops."

"So we have an even worse situation," the Minister added "and I can not even recall him at this point without truly losing control of the situation."

"Perhaps, the Major can still prevail in his mission sir," said Zhu. "I have already confirmed his plans sir, should he fail, it is my responsibility."

"Yes General, you can be sure that you will get the reward that is due to you after this affair is concluded," agreed the Minister.

Chapter 20

Police Headquarters Bangkok

The gridlocked traffic he looked down on from his office seemed to reflect the anxiety and lack of movement that now permeated the government and foreign business community. Dark noxious emissions caused his traffic officers to wear masks and respirators to work the streets.

His officers in the south had to patrol in groups and his top brass was taking sides preparing for the up-coming political battle over who's version of reality they would be forced to adopt.

Tourism even in this city of twenty million people was reaching its lowest point in memory regardless of reductions in hotel room rates, airfare and local services. Even the girls in Soi Nana and Soi Cowboy were talking about giving *farang* free samples to get business.

"We cannot wait much longer to make an announcement," shouted the Director General of Police into the speakerphone that was perched on the corner of his gigantic desk. "The press, the Prime Minister and even the King are beginning to doubt our capabilities and our resolve in bringing these bandits to justice."

"As I told you three days ago, we are almost there," answered the Bangkok Chief of Police, then continued as if he heard nothing from his boss. "The train bombing intervened but as it turned out, it took the pressure off the temple bombing while we continued to make progress on that front as well. We are 100% sure that this Hakimi fellow is responsible for the train attack and very sure that he was instrumental in planning the temple bombing as well. We lack the final evidence to make the public believe we have solved the case and can be able to withstand judicial and

208

press scrutiny." Still hearing nothing he finished with… "We expect to have the information to link them together by this time tomorrow."

The line hissed until he heard, "Either I have a suspect charged for the bombing by this time tomorrow or I expect your resignation on my desk. You are out of time."

As the telephone line went silent, the Bangkok Chief punched in another number. When it answered he said, "Tomorrow morning we name Hakimi as the mastermind of both events. No discussion."

He listened for a few moments then answered. "I'm told we will have all the proof we need to put him in front of a firing squad for both attacks. I don't care what the passengers are saying about the Chinese saving them, tell them that it was your troops that just look more Chinese than Thai. Farangs think we all look alike anyway, who's going to believe them. Just get on with it. Do as I order!"

Chinese Embassy Bangkok

The Attaché's encrypted desk telephone quietly rang. He smoothly picked it up on the first ring and gave his customary "Wei…yes" into the shielded mouthpiece.

"Listen carefully," the caller began. "Plans have changed, you will no longer be transferring…."

*****

Fifteen minutes later, the Chinese Military Attaché sat at his desk trying to formulate a new script for dealing with his Thai government contact and those delivering the information.

"Do not allow this difficulty to weaken the terms of our agreement with them," the Minister had warned. "It is imperative that they recognize the simplicity of what we

209

provide to them. The threat they had is now completely neutralized. You must make them understand this reality."

The information required by the Thai Minister would be delivered to him in Bangkok within twelve hours. "You will have the meeting arrangements shortly," his uncle, the Minister had promised.

The Attaché made the required call.

"I will have everything by the end of the day," he assured his Thai contact. "You will have everything to resolve your problem once and for all."

At the ambush site

Sulalman and the MSS officer had been secured to stout trees some distance away while the Shadows finalized their plans.

"Lieutenant Pei and I are leaving you here," Ren told the remaining Shadows. "A five man detachment is now aboard the type U032 submarine that will meet you at the coordinates on this sheet," he said handing the scrap of paper to Strong.

"We'll take the bus the MSS thoughtfully brought for our prisoner back to Bangkok," Pei said with a smile.

"I think you have everything we sorted out from the guys back at the tunnel," Army commented. Ren scanned through the piles of papers, passports and identification materials then nodded with a grin.

"These papers could prove that Mao himself came back from the dead to stage these attacks."

Strong's head bobbed up and down then said, "Looks like enough if the old guy is dead. If he is alive, it might be more difficult to prove if he protests." Sulalman and the MSS officer sagged against their tree while watching the meeting intently.

"That's not our worry," said Ren pointing toward the two prisoners, "our boss want's Sulalman in Beijing, so that's where he's going with you two," he said, then pointed to Strong and Army. "You both will be having a hot meal on the submarine before Pei and I even get near to Bangkok. Consider yourselves lucky to be baby-sitters," he laughed.

"Sure we have to return this traitor boss, sure would be lot's easier to just lose him along the trail," Strong answered. "Remember, he tried to kill us."

"He was just doing what he was ordered by his commander. Let our boss handle it. I don't want to hear that he died while trying to escape," Ren ordered.

"Don't worry boss, he'll get there," Strong answered.

"All right then, make this place look like a battle took place here before you leave. It must look like 'our friends' from the south did it," Ren ordered as he and Pei moved away from the ambush site. They followed the path to the hidden mini-van that their attacker had identified during the interrogation Pei had done.

As soon as Pei and Ren departed, the Shadows began staging the ambush site to look like a battlefield. While they were sanitizing the area to eliminate any evidence of their involvement, Strong had located a small deep pond 150 meters back in the jungle that had been hidden from view. The weapons collected from the seventeen dead were taken there and thrown into the scum-covered water. They would never be found.

"We need to make sure that one of these Muslim terrorist units becomes responsible for the attack and takes credit for the weapon theft from the dead" Strong said to Army.

Pocket litter, scraps of notes and a few of the weapons taken at the tunnel were scattered around the corpses and in obvious places where they would be found.

Within an hour, Strong led the column of four as they disappeared into the dense jungle enroute to a rendezvous point some ten kilometers away. The coordinates were within half a kilometer of the coast.

"Six hours till dark," he quietly announced, as he shouldered his pack and weapon and walked into the brush. "We need to be there just before then."

The prisoners trudged sullenly onward in between the two shadows as the foliage closed in on their small column. Birds and animals slowly moved back into the now abandoned ambush site.

*****

On the Coast

The Qing-class submarine cruised at 10 knots below the crystal blue waters off the coast of Thailand. It moved below the gentle swells well under its rated maximum submerged 14. 5-knot speed. It came to a full stop at a point three kilometers off the coast. When in its prescribed position it gently descended to the sandy bottom of the Gulf, 100 meters from the surface.

There were two hours before astronomical twilight when the five-man Spec Ops recovery team was to be launched. The vessel would surface, launch and dive within a seven-minute window of time. There it would wait for the recovery of the team and the high priority passengers they were accompanying back to the boat.

"Surface, Surface, Surface" the order sounded throughout the boat as the submarine rapidly rose, hatches popped open and five nimble camouflage clad, darkened faced operators untoggled the ridged boat lockers, launched and then started the silenced outboard engines on the two, twelve foot long boats. Within three minutes the boats were launched, engines started and teams loaded. Another minute and they were away from the already sinking sub. As it returned to the bottom to wait, the rigid boats sped toward shore in the gathering darkness.

It took less than ten minutes for the boats to reach a point 500 meters from the sandy shore where the team leader scanned the beach and surrounding areas once more with NVG's looking for signs of unwanted observers, fisherman or tourists. Seeing none, they sped for shore, dragged their boats into the tree line and covered them with netting they brought specifically for this purpose. One operator remained with the boats while the others immediately moved off on the azimuth setting they were provided.

Twenty minutes later, the team spread out and waited in ambush positions along the narrow trail they had followed to the meeting site. They settled in to wait.

Ten minutes after they arrived, Army slowly crept up to the team leader from his rear and tapped him gently on the shoulder and whispered, "Looking for us?"

Strong had to wrestle him to the ground and hold him until he realized that Strong was one of the 'passengers' they were to receive.

Once the team was recognized, Army walked the prisoners into the meeting coordinates area after the all-clear signal had been given by Strong.

"Okay, let's get out of here and back to the boat," the team leader commanded. They all headed for the beach. The new team double-checked the bindings on the prisoners, gave them some water, and securely re-taped their mouths to prevent them from shouting or making any unusual noise for the remainder of the journey.

A half-hour later, they were securely aboard the O32 and underway. They would rendezvous in eight hours with a helio from the one aircraft carrier that had been cruising near the Philippines. Once aboard they would transfer to a fixed wing transport for a six-hour flight to a small military airfield near the fourth ring road in Beijing. From there they would turn over their prisoners and the Shadows would return to their base in Guangdong Province.

Chapter 21

Road to Bangkok

"Nothing about this assignment has been according to plan from the start," said Pei as Ren drove steadily though the slow moving traffic. He nodded.

"I'm sorry that you must choose between what is right and what is necessary for the team."

"What do you mean?" she said.

"You are the Political Officer and must make sure that what is done measures up to party standards for discipline and good order. We have bent, broken and eliminated those rules many times over the last few days. It must give you problems as to what to report."

Pei reached over and placed her hand on his thigh, patted it gently and said, "The Shadows come first, before party discipline, we are brothers and sisters, maybe more..." as she put her head down and turned away from him and the windscreen. Her eyes began to flood with pent-up emotion.

Ren placed his hand on top of her's, gave it a gentle squeeze and said, " Thank you."

They sat in silence for a few kilometers without moving their hands.

When the spell broke, Pei said, "We need to have the location for the meeting,"

Ren nodded and said. "It is still 120 kilometers to Bangkok. If we have no call within the hour, I'll send another message. Try to rest, he will call, I'll awaken you." He squeezed her hand gently and resumed peering out the now rain splashed windscreen.

As they approached Bangkok late afternoon traffic slowed traffic to a crawl. They may as well have been walking as the afternoon rains really began to deluge the roadway. Torrents of water poured from a sky that had turned black with streaks of lightening that forced trucks to pull off the road, cars stalled at intersections and farmers with plastic bags over their heads tried to keep some water off their hair.

As lightening again flashed near to them, Ren's telephone rang.

"Yes," was his non-committal answer. He listened nodding to himself as he made mental notes then hung up.

"Well?" said Pei. "What are we to do?"

"He says the streets are badly flooded, we need to meet along the Sky Train route. He will pick a location when he is sure that trains are still operating. In the meanwhile we are to get to one of the stations so we can take a train, if they are moving."

"You're kidding? That's his plan?" Pei said.

"That's what he just said," Ren answered.

"What kind of agent is this guy? Wait for a subway? By Buddha, the man is an idiot."

"Yes, but it also puts us at a serious disadvantage. How are we going to set up surveillance for the meeting ahead of time?"

"How are you going to prevent him from trying to kill us after we turn over the materials?" Pei asked.

"No, I really think he has no idea what he's doing," answered Ren. "Maybe it is to our advantage as he will not have adequate time to set a trap for us either."

Pei nodded in agreement adding, "I guess you just keep driving, we still have a long way to go before we get close to a Sky Train route."

Ren smiled as he swerved to avoid a stalled truck stuck in the middle of the road.

"Just don't stop or slow down. If you do, we're going to get stuck like the rest of these cars." she continued.

Ren slowly answered, "He'll call back as soon as he gets something organized. It sounds like he is on a very tight

216

schedule himself. Whatever he plans to do with what we give him, it needs to be done very soon after we see him."

The Meeting

Ren saw the man who fit the description of their contact standing near the entry turnstile as he came down the long escalator from the city bound train. Something about him triggered an old memory. As he got closer, he remembered where he had seen him before.

Seven years earlier, Lieutenant Ren was struggling through combat training exercises in the far reaches of Chengdu Province. A group of senior cadre was being shown the camp on an inspection visit. The contact waiting for him had been the aide to a Party Secretary, who had made several derogatory comments about the state of troop training and preparations for defending the motherland.

His comments, mouthed by the Secretary, made life exceedingly more difficult for all the troops at the camp for months to come. If they had been valid, rather than the arrogant observations of one who had never crawled through mud, slept in ditches or ate insects, they might have been accepted. His were for gaining face, demeaning those in lesser positions and to make himself look more important to his boss.

Since this was the same person, Ren wondered, *what does he gain from whatever will be done with the materials we hand over to him? More importantly, can he be trusted to do what he says?*

Reaching the bottom of the escalator, Ren walked up to him and said, "Good evening Comrade." He paused then added; "Now that we are together, tell me, where are we going so I can securely provide you with the materials?"

"What, where are they? Why didn't you follow orders and bring them with you?"

217

Ren nodded affably while he was speaking then answered, "Your instructions to me were for us to meet and then make arrangements to transfer the documents. We are now meeting. Please tell me where we can conclude the transfer later?"

"This is not acceptable Major, you are deliberately endangering our negotiations," the Attaché said.

"I was not aware that there were negotiations, this is merely the transfer of evidence that terrorists were involved."

"You have no need to know about any of this. Your job is to fetch what you are ordered and bring it to your superiors. He paused then added, We think, you do."

Ren nodded again and smiled, "Still, my question stands, where do we go for the transfer? I'm sure your training is better than this idea of meeting on a subway platform and exchanging sensitive documents about terrorists out in the open."

The Attaché's face turned livid at the rebuke. "You will turn over the documents to me immediately or face the consequences."

"I've now asked you three times for a secure meeting place away from the prying eyes of the surveillance you've brought with you. Are you sure you wish to pursue this approach?"

The Attaché looked furtively around but did not spot the Thai Security Service watchers strategically placed around the station to supplement the ubiquitous CCTV cameras that monitored everything, around the clock.

"So far you have compromised this meeting, gotten my face into their facial recognition database and Buddha knows what other damage you may have caused to our relations with this country," Ren softly hissed while continuing to smile for the cameras.

Ren had seen Pei pass through the station twice while they were talking. She quickly signaled that there were additional watchers outside the station.

"This site is not secure for you to receive the materials. Are you positive that the roads are impassable to conduct this business at the Embassy or another secure location in the city?"

"No, it's not possible to conduct this business at the Embassy. It's too sensitive."

"Too sensitive for MSS, the PLA, the Ambassador? Just who knows about what you are doing here in Bangkok?"

"That is none of your concern. You were ordered to deliver the materials to me. Do it!" hissed the Attaché.

"My job is to make sure that whatever I have is delivered to you securely. That is what I am attempting to do. It does no good for my men to be killed or injured to obtain something that you are willing to compromise because you are not taking even the most basic security precautions."

"Major, you forget your position. Those killed were not your men, they belong to the party. The party decides who lives or dies, is sacrificed or honored. As the representative of the party here, it is my decision to make, not yours." He looked down at his wristwatch and said, "I have exactly three hours to transfer whatever it is you have. You will turn them over to me immediately."

"With all respect for the party, either you take seriously your responsibility to safeguard what we will provide to you or it will go with me to Beijing in due course. Your choice."

Ren made a decision. He turned away from Wen and said, "You have my number. Call me when you come to your senses."

Then, before the watchers could react, Ren ran for the escalator and the train that he could hear entering the upper level station. He raced across the platform and into the train as the doors were closing. Pei moved along side of him briefly in the aisle then walked away down the car as the train sped toward the end of the line near the Shangri-La hotel at the Chao Prya River.

Wen was near panic. Especially when he noticed several people who had been standing around the station running up the stairs after Ren while two others stayed in their positions, pulled out their smartphones and began talking excitedly. *What to do?* he thought. *I must have those materials within the next ninety minutes otherwise there will not be enough time to get them to my contact.*

After bolting from the train at the end of the line minutes later, Ren and Pei made their way down a shabby side soi until they came upon a small No-Tell hotel that rented rooms by the hour for prostitutes, lovers and others who wished a few hours of privacy. If Ren noticed the very thin shabbily dressed Thai who followed after them from the Sky Train terminal, he appeared to take no notice.

When they arrived soaking wet and put the required 500 Bhat on the counter, a room key and small towel appeared through the opening.

The uninterested clerk said "Hey, don't get water all over the floor, Who's going to clean it up? You? Ha!" He snorted and went back to his newspaper.

Ren and Pei quietly climbed the three flights of narrow stairs to the assigned room. Even before the hotel entry door had closed, the follower pulled a plastic bag with an encrypted smartphone from his pocket and hurriedly reported his location.

As Ren was inspecting the dank room, his phone rang. The number belonged to the Attaché. Without waiting for him to speak, Ren crisply gave him instructions for a meeting time and location. "Confirm it to me," he ordered. When Wen did so, he added, "Be there in the next thirty minutes," and hung up.

Border Patrol Police Headquarters

"From the air, it looked like there had been a major firefight, sir," said the BPP Captain in the helio who was sent to find the overdue SWAT Team. "I sent two men down to scout the site and confirm what happened and to secure the site. We found no survivors."

A team of medics and security personnel were inserted. More details were still unavailable as darkness and rain hampered flight operations. The mood, regardless of the details, however, was somber in Bangkok.

Incense burned in the sand filled urns placed in front of the golden Buddha that adorned the entryway to the SWAT Command Center on the Border Patrol Police Compound.

The air was heavy with grief as a line of slow moving officers filed past the quickly set up black draped pictures of the ten officers who perished at the ambush site. Ten open lockers filled with their personalized equipment stood mute while senior officers conducted a damage assessment as to what went wrong with what was supposed to be a simple support operation.

Parents, spouses, children, monks and well wishers all gathered at the elaborate shrine in the Compound. The Chief Monk would soon be conducting a special commerative ceremony to pray for those lost in the tragedy.

Once blame could be determined, retribution would be swift and merciless for those involved. If, as preliminary assessment seemed to point out it was Southern Muslims, there would be a bloodbath of epic proportions.

MSS Office Beijing

"I hear that Colonel Li is in army custody," said General Zhu to his ADC. "He is to be returned here to Beijing shortly for interrogation. You will not allow this to continue."

"If he is in Central Command custody it will be impossible to prevent him from sharing his knowledge," said the Colonel. "They are skilled at loosening tongues."

"You are a senior intelligence officer, use your brain, your resources, and make it happen. He is not to talk about his orders to anyone."

"What if he has already done so?"

"Nobody, understand me, nobody, is to have access to what is in his brain. Is that clear enough? Do whatever it takes even if you have to sink a submarine, do it."

"But general..." he stammered, but he was already talking to an empty room.

*****

In the Bangkok MSS Station the mood was funeral-like. Since radio contact with the extraction team was lost, it was through Beijing that they learned that Colonel Li had been taken into custody by PLA elements.

The fate of their dead comrades was not mentioned. Station personnel were certain that there would soon be repercussions that would permanently change careers, maybe even result in prison or worse for those thought to have a role in this disaster.

CIA Station Bangkok

"I understand completely Ambassador," said the COS as he backed out of the window lined, tropical motif office. His eyes kept wandering over the lush gardens of the Embassy compound as the anger, frustration and recriminations were heaped on his head by the political 'big donor' appointee who currently occupied America's top job in Thailand.

"Fix this problem or start packing your bags. The Thais are angry about losing their men who were supporting your operation," was the last thing he heard from this appointee who spent about $1.5 million in political contributions to get this Ambassadorship. He closed the double doors leading onto the wide first floor hallway and hurried back to the second floor secure area where the Agency offices were located.

What the hell happened out there? he thought. As he walked by the open doors of his key staff he waved at them to follow him to the secure conference room. He motioned to the CI Chief, who was the last person entering the room, to close and lock the door.

"Has anyone heard from Jackson?" he quietly asked.

Heads nodded negatively as they looked around. "He's supposed to be back later today," offered the CI Chief, "We're supposed to have a beer later today."

The COS nodded and said, "I think you can cancel that drink. Our CT Chief's position is now open. It seems as though he, along with the entire BPP SWAT Team, have gotten themselves killed in a firefight down South. The Thais think it was separatists. Can anybody here tell me different?"

Stunned silence held the room.

"Look guys, we are all going to miss Jackson but we've got to know what really happened down there. I thought he had solid information that Sulalman was going to be transferred there from the knuckle draggers to the local MSS team."

"Don't know boss," answered another case officer, "he held his deals pretty tight."

"Okay," he continued, "I want you...pointing to the CI Chief...to comb through his contact reports, case files, everything and come up with some timelines, plans and whatever you can find to give us some clarity on what the hell went wrong out there. We're losing more people here than in the Stans. The IG folks are going to be turning around and coming right back here to chase us some more if we don't get to the bottom of what happened immediately."

Everyone in the room just sat there trying to make sense of what they had just heard.

"Come on, let's get moving," the COS said softly, "We've got lots to do, move it."

They filed slowly out of the office and began the tedious process of conducting yet another damage assessment and preparing an after action report; this time on a very much loved and respected member of their station team.

Chapter 22

Bayi Building, PLA General Staff HQ

"The Shadows have delivered the MSS renegade, Sir," announced the obsequious Colonel who served as the ADC (*Aide de Camp*) to General Zhu. Then he continued, "They arrived thirty minutes ago and have already transferred him to the custody of Central Command security officers."

"And the Terrorist Sulalman? What of him?"

"As requested, sir, he was taken into custody by elements from the Central Military Commission. He is to be detained at one of their special camps."

"Excellent, make sure the Shadows are commended for their fine work and transferred back to their base as soon as possible," Zhu responded.

"Well, not all of them are here sir," the Colonel added.

"Yes, yes, I know about their casualties," he replied.

"No, Major Ren and Lieutenant Pei are not with them. They are in Bangkok, dealing with an unexpected development. They are to be returning directly to their base within the next 24 hours."

"I was unaware of this change, who authorized it?" he said scowling.

"New information was developed in the field by Major Ren and he has proceeded without headquarters authorization."

"Has he indeed, well there had better be a good reason. He is not irreplaceable. Keep me informed"

"Yes sir," said the Colonel with an evil smile forming.

Border Patrol Police Headquarters Bangkok

"Ten good men dead," the chief hollered at his top staff. "They were our best, how did untrained, village-grown,

225

terrorists kill all of them with no casualties of their own that we could find? No blood trails, no graves, nothing?" he paused for breath then added, "Where are the weapons our men carried? There were plenty of shell casings, shrapnel and scorched grass but nothing else. I thought this was a simple 'snatch and grab' support operation. Talk to me, what happened?"

"When nothing was heard from the team, we sent a helio down to investigate and saw the bodies from the air," said a BPP colonel. "We called in a support team who then secured the area and searched out to 500 meters from the site of the fighting."

He turned to a major who continued. "A bit of background first sir," he began. "The American CIA man told us that they needed a support team to take possession of a prisoner captured by the Chinese soldiers who had interdicted the terrorists. I believe they were the ones that attacked the train near Sungai Golok. It was supposed to be a simple security operation. The turn over was to be friendly."

"Yes, I know all that, get to it," said the chief.

"When we arrived there were bodies and body parts scattered over a fifty meter area. Ten were ours, one American and three Chinese. Forensics confirmed what we believed. Claymore mines, automatic weapons, knives and handguns were all used in the fighting. Two definitely were killed with knives. Appeared to be from ambush. One suffered only a broken neck. We're still trying to sort out the details but its unlikely it was only the work of Southern terrorists. They may have been there but to surprise our SWAT Team…I really don't think so."

"So what are we doing about it? Are we looking for trails, suspects, what's the current status?"

"We set up a twenty kilometer cordon around the site and have two hundred troopers on the ground looking for trails, suspects, anything that can help us find out what happened. No army support yet, we didn't want to talk about our problems with outsiders yet. We're also waiting for CIA to tell us more about what they might have found but again, nothing."

"So what you are telling me is that I have ten dead with no one responsible, no suspects and no leads. Is that correct?"

Embarrassment flooded the room as the chief summed up where they were. "Yes sir, unfortunately that's about where we are at the moment. As soon as we know more…"

The chief waved them off and turned away from the group as they filed out of his office.

What did they see during their last moments? What was the American trying to do? Was he fooled by someone into thinking the meeting was something that it was not? Questions and more questions, but no answers. More importantly, could he trust the Americans after this disaster? Where was their liaison officer? He should have been here already.

No Tell Hotel, Bangkok

Ren finished the call. They looked around the tiny room for an exit. He whispered to Pei that they were leaving immediately as he checked out the small bathroom window hoping for a possible escape route to the roof. It was nailed shut. They dumped the towel on the bed, tossed the covers and pillow around and then quietly opened the room door and went back into the hallway and continued up toward the top floor.

The dimly lit hallway had no exit signs but one door did not have a number. Ren turned the knob and pushed. It was what they were looking for. The ladder up to the roof hatch took less than a minute to scale. They immediately broke open the cheap hasp lock and climbed out into the driving rain.

227

After three minutes of crossing a series of rooftops, they were a block away dropping down from a low parapet to a flooded street that ended at the Chao Prya River near the Sky train terminus and boat landing. They had made a full circle of the neighborhood. Now all that remained was hijacking a boat before the Attaché arrived. Pei moved off into the darkness to get one.

Ren conducted a reconnaissance of the meeting site. It was one he had selected on their way to the down-at-the-heels hotel having seen it on his last SDR in Bangkok. He then moved into a darkened place in a vacant market stall along the river, slipped into the shadows, and waited. The rain increased in intensity.

Ten minutes elapsed, then fifteen, then twenty before he saw the Attaché moving slowly along in the now knee high water filled soi toward the meeting site. He waited and watched until he passed, anticipating the surveillance team that he knew would be behind him. He was not disappointed.

There were two of them, one twenty meters away, the other thirty, across the soi. He waited until the first one rounded the last corner before the meeting site, then struck the lead man in the head with the butt of the Glock he had taken from the dead American. He pulled the limp body into a doorway. He quickly gagged and tie taped his hands to the pull-up metal screen covering the store window.

As he waited for the second in line, he pulled out the man's cell phone and hit the power button. No password needed. He hit the last number call button.

The phone he called buzzed quietly. Ren mumbled in Thai, "Quick, cross the street, he's going inside a building over here." Ren hung up and waited. In less than a minute the second man, now running as quickly as the knee-deep water would permit, was in front of him. Minutes later Ren was on his way to the meeting with both cell phones, plus one more

Glock 19 and a Browning Hi Power weighing down his pockets.

Colonel Wen was waiting at the meeting site and did not see Ren approach until he was right next to him.

"You're late," Wen began. "Playing all these spy games will get you nowhere when I make my report to Beijing, I have ninety minutes remaining to deliver what you are supposed to have or the consequences will be dire for everyone." he continued.

Ren continued to look at him without any comment as one of his phones buzzed. He looked at the number; punch answered and listened then held up his hand for Wen to be silent. He quietly answered in Thai and turned it off once again.

"I told the head of the ISOC surveillance team that you were waiting in a door way several blocks from here and that your contacts had not yet arrived. We need to move immediately," Ren said.

Wen stared blankly. "Do you understand Chinese?" Ren asked him. "We need to move now or the rest of the surveillance you brought to the meeting will be here. Do you understand me? If the phones I took from the agents have tracking devices, we have even less time."

"You're lying," Wen said. The rain now began to come down in sheets.

Ren quickly grabbed him and shoved the Glock into his face and said, "I just took this gun and another one plus two cell phones from the team that was right behind you. These agents are now tied to a building around the corner. We are walking to the river right now. The rain will cover our trip. Let's go." He pushed Wen forward out into the deluge for the twenty-meter walk to the dock.

Pei had been successful and waited at the controls of a typical Klong long-tail boat with an old V-8 engine roughly idling. The plastic sheeting strung from the roof around the open passenger area kept some water off the passengers and stopped some of the rain from completely flooding the boat. Whoever owned the boat would not miss it until first light.

They clambered aboard and Pei cast off, turned up river and opened the throttle. They quickly disappeared into the night. The purloined cell phones had been bundled into a plastic bag they had found in the trash. Ren hid them beneath some discarded skin and husks from durian and jackfruit that had been lying in a pile next to the bridge abutment. ISOC would have difficulty extracting them from the rats that infested the shoreline trash piles.

Ten minutes later they were moored in a klong across the river under a small dock used during the day for off loading cargo. It was dry, dark and quiet.

"We have little more than one hour to get you to your meeting with the materials Lieutenant Pei has in her Musset bag. You need to look them over now and understand what we are giving you. Lieutenant Pei, will brief you," Ren ordered.

"Yes sir," she answered crisply then began a 'show and tell' using a Maglite that took ten minutes. Wen nodded and looked over the documentation she removed from her bag.

"Are these real?" he asked incredulously.

"Of course they are, I collected them myself from the terrorists. That's their blood still on some of them," she answered. "I put it there."

Wen swallowed and nodded as she folded everything back into the plastic waterproof evidence bags and then into a tightly closed Musset bag.

"Give me your cell phone," Pei said to Wen.

"What?"

"Your cell phone please," she said again.

"I will not."

Ren reached over and snatched it from his pocket before he could react and handed it to Pei. She immediately began scrolling through messages and emails.

Wen looked on in anger then finally said, "You have sealed your death warrants, both of you. This is treason. You will both be shot, your families destroyed. Nothing you can do from now on can save you. Your fates are sealed."

Ren nodded, smiled grimly and moved closer to Wen as Pei continued to type feverishly on the smartphone.

Ren looked at Wen, then in a conversational tone began, "My team was sent here to find the bombers of the temple. We did so. We were tasked to return them to the motherland, we did so. We were tasked to provide you with information to satisfy the Thai government, we are now doing so. What we did not anticipate were those from our own government impeding our efforts, sending foreign agents on our trail, lying about our work and enriching themselves while my team was subjected to unnecessary risk and death. You, Colonel, are a prime example of what is wrong with the Party, not the Shadows."

Just then Pei cut in, "Got it," she said smiling brightly.

Wen turned, with a questioning look and faced her, "You have nothing," he snarled, grabbing for the phone.

Ren swatted Wen's hand away from Pei and glared at him.

Ren then said, "Tell me." She did.

Wen looked on it stony silence.

"Options?" Ren asked her.

"We could send all his correspondence with the Thais to his uncle, he might be interested to learn that his nephew is making more money than both Ministers from these sales, or we could send everything to General Chang, Central Military Command. I'm sure he would be interested in the details or we could work out an arrangement with the Colonel here that would be in everyone's best interests. What do you think Major?

"Why don't we ask the Colonel?" Ren answered. Then repeated, "Colonel?"

"You are bandits, you know nothing of government relations. These arrangements are normal, the minister knows about these arrangements."

"Even the UBS bank transfer arrangements for your account in Zurich?" Pei asked sweetly.

"What? How did you?"?

"How about the balance you already have? What is it, $9,476,598 Euro? I'm sure you are holding it for them as well."

He blanched.

"Amazing what you can glean from a smartphone, especially one without proper safeguards or encryption. But then, I guess you have nothing to worry about and your uncle knows about everything, correct? So those things are unimportant to share with him."

"All right," said Ren, "we have no more time. Lieutenant, let's just send the files to both the Minister and General Chang. The Colonel here is correct, we just do not have the understanding to make the correct decision about these affairs. They are way above, how to they say it? Oh yes, above our pay grade."

"Yes sir, one minute I should be ready."

Wen was looking around furtively then said, "Wait please, we need to discuss this matter in more detail."

"Lieutenant, are you ready to send the files?"

"Yes sir."

"Don't," Wen shouted.

"Don't what?" Ren answered.

"Do not send the files."

"We don't have time to negotiate with you," Ren said. "Either we come to an agreement immediately or the

232

Lieutenant sends the files and we leave you to do what ever you wish with the materials we provided. Our work here is finished. What happens, happens."

"What do you want?" Wen whispered.

"Half. We want half of what you have in the account and half of what you will get from this assignment. I want it transferred tomorrow to an account that I will send you later this evening." He paused and held Wen's stare before adding, "Do not think that you can betray me. Should anyone ever learn of our arrangement, you and every member of your family will die, very slowly and painfully. Do you understand?"

Wen nodded in agreement.

"Say it," Pei interjected.

He turned to look at her but nodded again and softly said, "I agree, it will remain between us until I die."

"Let's all trust that it never comes to that," said Pei as she solemnly nodded in agreement.

"Good," Ren added. "Now, let us conclude our business and get you to your meeting on time, the Thais need a terrorist bombing ringleader. Let's give them one."

Ren was at the controls of the boat as they crossed back to drop Wen near the Sky Train station. The rain continued to pound on the narrow boat as it crossed the choppy water of the river now at full flood stage. Ren eased the boat to the weather beaten dock near the Oriental Hotel and watched as Pei helped steady Colonel Wen as he began to clamber off clutching the Musset bag and its invaluable contents. Pei had continued to manipulate the smartphone while crossing the Klong and handed it back to Wen just as he departed.

"Remember, we'll be watching you until the money transfer is complete," Ren shouted over the noise of the wind driven rain. Wen nodded, slipped over the side onto the dock and jogged into the maze of alleys and sois that crisscrossed the area.

"Colonel," Pei shouted, "one more thing. Assume that everything you say or do will be watched. Do not use another phone or lose this one. If you do...well just remember our conversation."

Central Command Interrogation Center

Colonel Li sat shackled to a table in the small interrogation room. He had seen many like it over the years. This was just one more, except that he was now waiting on the other side of the table and expected to give information rather than extract it.

They must be under orders not to injure me. No rough treatment from the first moments after the ambush went wrong. Very professional, no opportunities for escape or talking to them. Blindfold, food, water, no contact with anyone. Maybe one or two days since the fighting, for sure we were on a submarine, helio and transport aircraft. Could be anywhere but probably somewhere near Beijing...If I hold out long enough someone will get me removed from custody... just hold on.

Someone entering the room and tearing off the blindfold broke his reverie. The bright light pierced his eyes temporarily blinding him.

"So the traitorous dog is awake," a rough voice shouted.

"Confess your guilt and things will go easy for you. Tell us who sent you to damage our operations," said another.

A rough slap knocked Li back in his chair pulling the chain to the end of its tether. He slipped sideways across the table. Strong hands pulled him upright once again.

"Do I have your attention Colonel?" asked the second voice.

234

Li nodded and swept his tongue across his lips to remove some of the blood that trickled from his mouth.

"What were your orders Colonel, who gave them?" the rough voice asked.

"My orders were to observe the prisoner hand-over, act as liaison officer, nothing more. Why am I being detained, interrogated? This is madness. Someone will pay for this outrage," Li thundered.

"Oh dear, it's all a mistake," the rough voice croaked as he mimicked a famous actor. "Let's release him shall we, prepare dinner, some flowers maybe," he said as he slapped him once again with even more force.

This time, Li fell from the chair to the floor. He was efficiently pulled upright once again.

"Call my office, this is all wrong, you will be punished for your actions," he moaned through now blood-covered teeth.

"Call my office, they will tell you..." he again muttered and passed out.

"Check him, is he faking?"

"No, he is unconscious," the second voice answered as he checked his pulse and heart.

"All right, report what he told us and see what they want us to do. He's not going anywhere," he said. They pulled him from the chair then each kicked him sharply in the groin. They laughed, let him slide to the floor his arms still tethered to the table and departed.

No sooner had they walked down the hallway than the door reopened and another slightly built PLA officer wearing a fitted green uniform entered the room. He quickly moved to the prostrate body, took a small syringe from an inner pocket of his tunic and carefully inserted it into Colonel Li's neck just above his heart. He quickly stood, looked around, replaced the empty cylinder into his pocket and exited the room. The tight line of an evil smile that was his trademark never left his face.

Ten minutes later the interrogators reentered the room and began shouting at Li. His lifeless body did not respond. Their attempts to revive him were unsuccessful.

It was later determined that the CCTV camera system monitoring the room had developed a brief malfunction for two minutes. Upon restarting, the unmoving body still lay where it was when the interrogators exited the room. Everything in the room appeared just as it was when they departed.

Chao Prya River, Bangkok

After Colonel Wen disappeared, Pei waved to signal she was ready. Ren then gunned the big V-8 engine and spun the long tail boat across the fast moving current. They once again moved up the choppy broad brown water of the swollen river. Twenty minutes later they had navigated around two bends in the river and approached the Memorial Bridge where they turned onto a much smaller klong. Ren guided the boat to an old dock, switched off the engine and moved to the center of the boat as Pei tied it loosely to a rotted piling. They waited as the rain began to slacken.

The motor launch materialized almost immediately out of the darkness of the klong and pulled along side of the long boat. Ren grabbed and held fast to the line tossed to him while Pei quickly boarded: he released the tether holding the long boat to the pier and followed her aboard the boat as it quietly turned up river. Even before they entered the main shipping lane they could see the long boat bobbing, listing and broaching in the fast moving current, it was rapidly taking on water.

Thoroughly soaked and dripping water, they went below into the spacious cabin where they were warmly greeted by another retired PLA sergeant, the former commander of their old Hua Hin restaurant owner contact.

"Welcome back to Bangkok, Major. Sergeant Ma sends his greetings," he said then continued. "Tell me what you require and I will try my best."

"A place to wait, some Internet and dry clothing would be a good start,' Ren answered.

"Go forward, everything you require is already on board. But now, let us move away from this place, should your route to this place not have been as effective as it appeared to be."

Pei nodded and climbed down the stairs into the spacious saloon that disguised a floating computer center, armory and sleeping quarters. A hot meal waited. Fresh dry clothing hung neatly in the built-in teak wardrobes. Pei began stripping off the wet mismatched remnants of clothing she had taken from those unlucky souls at the ambush site.

Chapter 23

Thai First Army Headquarters, Bangkok

"Funded by the Turks? We're supposed to believe the Turks are behind these two attacks?" thundered the Thai Army Major General who received the report at the hastily arranged 0200 meeting.

"Yes sir," answered the Attaché's contact. "The source is impeccable, the documents authentic and corroborates the statements, evidence and reports from our sources, those of the ISOC and the Police."

"How can this be? Except for some paper you are waving in front of me, the old man the police are holding in Hat Ya, does not seem capable of planning, let along mounting, such precision attacks."

"Just because the police or ISOC never identified him before does not mean that he could not be the one following the orders of a foreign intelligence service rather than merely a home-grown terrorist, Sir"

"If we are to believe what this source of yours provided, we have a much more difficult problem than we imagined. How can we admit that an outside government is fomenting violence and stirring up our religious extremists?"

"Sir, how different is this new information than what we originally believed to be the situation with the Chinese Uyghurs? We blamed China for the Erawan bombing but they managed to prove that they had nothing to do with that particular violence, rather the Turks took advantage of the confusion to cover their tracks."

"Humm, I see your point. But, how can we trust that it really is still not the Uyghurs pushing the blame on yet another government?"

"Why would they blame the Turks when it is Turkey that has been providing support for their separatist actions in both China and here? Perhaps it has been Turkey all along using the Uyghurs to put pressure on the Beijing government, here and in Western China."

"Are they really that clever?"

"Both China and Turkey are extremely adept at deception, diversion and manipulation but only China has sent assistance to try resolving the incident. Remember, if it were not for the Chinese soldiers, there would be no tourism left in the country right now."

The general nodded, "That's true enough," he muttered, "continue."

"So, if we assume that it is the Turks behind both incidents, using Thai terrorists as their surrogates, will it not make all of us...ISOC and the police...look foolish?"

"With what we have been given, I think we can place blame with the ISOC and the police. We will gain *face* by solving the puzzle that our two other security services could not."

"Remind me, what did we have to promise the Chinese to provide us with this information?"

"The Chinese have been eager to build us three new submarines."

"Yes, now I remember, Admiral Pornchuk and the other procurement staff were to release the contract should their efforts to identify the bombers be successful."

"Correct sir."

"It seems as though they upheld their side of the bargain. You should contact the admiral and confirm their compliance with him. We will then need to work with the Foreign Ministry to forge out a response to our Turkish friends, along with a strategy with the police, ISOC and the press."

"Yes sir, perhaps now that we know the true source of the violence we can use it to our advantage."

He then continued, "We need to improve our image and keep control of the situation. Up to now, the police were promising an arrest. We need to take that away from them. These documents give us the real criminal for all the world to see."

Nodding his head in agreement the General said, "Ah, little wonder you are handling these duties Colonel, you always think three steps ahead."

"Thank you sir, I will speak to the Admiral immediately and then the police. Time will now be of the essence. Perhaps you would prefer to speak with ISOC?"

"Excellent idea, first thing in the morning. Please ask their commander to visit at 1000 hrs."

The Colonel strode from the room to complete his assignment as the General picked up the telephone once again.

Hat Ya Public Health Hospital

Hakimi looked up at the clock as he heard what sounded like thunder but was, in fact, a scrum of police and army officers as they stormed past the guards at his door. They pushed through the narrow opening as reporters, TV anchors and photographers jostled to capture his arrest for the morning news.

"What's going on? What's happening at 3:00AM to cause all this commotion?" asked Hakimi.

"You are under arrest for murder, terrorism and kidnaping old man. We finally have the evidence against you," shouted a police colonel. "We now have the evidence to make sure you will be executed."

Without any emotion showing, the village chief quietly said, "I have done nothing, whatever you have is lies…propaganda against my people."

"Put handcuffs on him immediately," said the Colonel pointing to a Sergeant who stepped forward, unlocked the single restraint that held Hakimi to the bed and roughly pulled him to a standing position. Other officers grabbed plastic tubes and suspended bags with clear solutions.

"Let's go," he snarled while clamping the handcuffs on the compliant, hospital gowned old man as TV klieg lights and digital cameras captured the arrest. The injured leg collapsed under Hakimi's weight and he crashed to the floor.

Hakimi screamed.

"Get him up, support him."

The reporters shouted, "Why did you do it? Who paid you? How did you stay hidden so long? Who helped you," while he was half dragged, half pushed by the police and army escort. The Sergeant forced the way through the crowd in the hospital hallway, into a waiting elevator and down three floors to the front entrance. The press, who were alerted to the pending arrest, had set up even more cameras and microphones for an impromptu outdoor press conference.

An Army Major General took the podium and read a prepared statement.

"After days of intensive investigation by police and army units, the Armed Forces of Thailand were successful, in cooperation with the Royal Thai Police, in apprehending the leader of the terrorist group that planned and carried out the two worst attacks ever against the people of Thailand. Tonight, Hakimi was taken into custody and formally charged with masterminding these despicable events that cost the lives of so many of our brothers and sisters. Those still at large who assisted, financed and along with Mr. Hakimi, directed these criminal acts, will also be hunted down and brought to justice…. Thank you."

With that he turned and walked back into the hospital as the reporters began a loud high-pitched string of questions.

The Bangkok Post's reporters, who had been at the scene of the train hijacking, had interviewed dozens of foreign passengers. All gave lengthy stories about a group of soldiers who had prevented the terrorists from blowing up the train. All told of almost superhuman acts of courage and skill by both the male and female operatives involved and wanted to thank them for saving their lives.

Neither the Army nor the Police would comment on the unit that they were from, why they were on the train and if there was strong intelligence, why didn't the train get stopped before it was inside the tunnel? Lots of questions were only met with absolute silence from the normally quite willing press officers who always tried to make the police and military look good.

"Look, we've been through this before. There is a blackout on any reporting about this group," said the Police Press Officer. "This is still a sensitive matter."

"Yeah, but seeing how the ringleader of the group has been arrested this morning, why should anyone care about telling a positive story about something that happened almost a week ago?" answered the lead Post reporter.

"Until the others in the terrorist network are captured, there is nothing more to say. Nothing regarding incident details from the train attack will be made public. You have the official script. Follow it!"

The reporters grumbled but they knew that if anything was leaked…well, they didn't want to even think about the personal and professional repercussions that would crash down on their heads.

No further questions were asked. None were answered.

ISOC Headquarters, Bangkok

Reports of losing contact with two surveillance teams assigned to the PLA Attaché reached ISOC headquarters within minutes of the event being reported from the rain soaked street. Several back-up teams were dispatched. Embarrassed agents were cut free from shop house doorways but no trace could be found of either the two foreign agents who's photos were captured earlier on the Sky Train CCTV cameras. More significantly, the Attaché had dropped from sight. Facial recognition algorithms suggested there was an 85% probability that one of the two suspects at the Sky Train Station was the same person observed at an MSS Bangkok safe house eight days earlier.

Later in the morning the ISOC Commander returned from his meeting with the Army Major General in a very foul mood. "How did those idiots in the army manage to get what we could not?" he asked his ADC. Then adding, "We were tracking these terrorists and there were no indications that they had anything to do with the bombing here in Bangkok. Could we really have missed what they were doing? Was there any indication that outside support was coming into Thailand to fund these people?"

"I don't see how it's possible, Sir. We had people inside all the dissident groups reporting to us. If money or direction were coming from outside the country we would have known about it. Either we underestimated their skills and we missed something, which is unlikely or the Army is trying to write a new history for the attacks.

The general paced for a few moments then added, "Go back through all the reports, get our sources checking all their contacts once again. We need to know if, as the General says, 'we now have proof that both these attacks were fomented by the MIT (*Turkish Intelligence Organization*) in reprisal for not being more lenient with the Uyghurs. They thought they

243

had covered their tracks but the proof the Army has looks quite convincing."

The ADC, turned to leave and answered, "Immediately sir." He stopped as he heard a last comment.

"Listen to me, I want absolute proof one way or the other. If the Turks really are involved, our troubles in the South are going to get worse, but if they are being scapegoated it might just cause them to really get involved. You know they are active all around us in Central Asia with that damn mosque-madrassa building initiative for every village. All we need are more viper nests being set up around the country!"

Chapter 24

Central Committee Offices, Beijing

"It is done Uncle," Wen said over his secure telephone. "The transaction is approved and the transfers are complete. Just as planned. Please check to make sure everything in your account is in order."

"Excellent, excellent! I will. You have done well," answered the Minister, smiling broadly then adding, "I trust you will make sure that everything goes smoothly as work progresses?"

"Yes Uncle, the first inspection delegation of Thai naval officers will depart for our Hainan Island facilities rather than the Wuhan factory in ten days time. They insist on firsthand viewing of the construction progress although I suspect they are more interested in the new Sanya Casino and other diversions. The heat, smog and congestion in Wuhan...the furnace of China...holds little attraction for them. I will, of course, accompany them."

"Good, perhaps we can enjoy a meal during your visit?"

"At your pleasure."

"Anything else we need to discuss?"

Wen paused then blurted, "Except for an insolent PLA Major who almost cost us the goodwill of the Thai government, there were no problems."

"What Major caused problems?"

"A certain Major Ren who was tasked to bring me the required materials was insubordinate, late and almost caused the arrangement to fall apart. Fortunately I was able to get everything back on course in time. He needs to be disciplined."

"Give me his full name and I will take care of this troublemaker."

"Immediately."

*****

Pei looked up from her monitoring station and signaled for Ren to listen to the tape she had just made of the call.

"It looks like the Colonel could not leave well enough alone," she said.

Ren smiled and said, "What would Dickie do in this situation?"

"I believe it would be something like, 'Burn them all down'," Pei answered and laughed.

"Close enough, close enough but I'll need a little assistance, Lieutenant," Ren answered smiling as he moved closer to the computer making room for Pei to join him. The SS7 tracking software Pei had installed on Colonel Wen's phone along with the related penetration features made it simple to monitor his every action.

CIA Station Bangkok

"Got a minute Chief," asked the case officer assigned to monitor the deceased head of Counter-terrorism's projects. The COS nodded for him to follow him into the SCIF (*Sensitive Compartmented Information Facility*) conference room. "Talk to me, elevator speech," he said.

The case office nodded in agreement, took a deep breath.

"Four things you need to know right now," he began. "First, BPP is really pissed at us for getting their guys killed. They want to know what happened on our end. Second, the five dead Chinese guys that were found at the ambush site were from the MSS Station here in Bangkok."

The COS looked up at this revelation "Five?"

246

The case officer continued, "Five! They just charged the old guy...Hakimi... with the Erawan bombing and lastly, they're going to blame the Turks for inciting all the violence." He paused then added, "looks like our Chinese friends made nice with the locals, maybe because of those knuckle draggers that cleaned up their mess down south but whatever the reason, I hear that the deal for the subs is going through very soon."

"Whoa there, slow down, how do we know about the Turks? That's going to be a game changer if that goes public."

"Seems as though they got documents, passports, and correspondence from guys they are now claiming to be Turk spies. We're trying to get the ID's from them for name checks so we can see what we have on them, but our source says they are convinced that the documents are real."

"Shit, I hope we didn't miss something along the way, all we need is another screw-up to go along with everything else that's been turning to shit around here."

"Don't think so. Looks like it was directed from out-of-country, least from what our source knows now."

"Okay, good job, thanks for the heads up," he then added, "Get a cable written up on the finding to date. ASAP. I'll want to add to it before you hit the send button."

"Roger that," he answered opening the door and moving down the hallway to his cubicle.

*****

Thai army rangers, BPP troopers and police conducted sweeps through the jungle for twenty-five kilometers around the ambush site. They found nothing of value. Forensics was limited and crime scene analysis inconclusive because of the heavy rain and continual police personnel in and out of the area. What became known as the "Circle of Death" in the Bangkok Post reporting was so contaminated that it had

247

virtually no forensic value remaining. After the initial visits by the troops hunting for the terrorists responsible for the carnage not even snakes could be found. There was just too much contamination and foot traffic. Even half hearted attempts to checkout the small pond contributed to rendering the 'crime scene' unusable for forensic purposes.

Much the same held true for the train-hijacking site as tracks were cleared and rail service restored on the main rail line to Bangkok. Four days without trains running was straining the tourism economy and public opinion about the safety and reliability of the tourism industry in Thailand.

Within ten days the entrance to the tunnel used by the terrorists was unsealed, debris cleared, bridge trestles repaired and trains rolling again, albeit with visible guards posted at sensitive points for security. Nobody would venture into the caves beneath the tunnel, as the army EOD technicians had not cleared the entryway into the cave system yet.

Police and military checkpoints along both main and secondary roads were increased as were roving checkpoints and more controlled access to hotels, restaurants and public buildings throughout Southern Thailand. Keeping the terrorists on their back foot was thought to be a low-key, low casualty method of pacification in areas that were not critical to promoting tourism.

Chapter 25

Special Operations Headquarters Beijing

"Please sit Major. I have followed your progress and read your After Action report with great interest," said General Zhu.

Ren nodded and said, "We were fortunate for good support along the way or else the outcome may have been different."

"You are too modest Major. Your team performed well and accomplished every task assigned," he paused then added. "It seems though, that you may have overstepped your mission guidelines. The Central Committee member responsible for the Thailand project says you were not responsive to their requirements and caused grave risk to the success of the project. How do you respond? The Minister wants you jailed for what amounts to treason against the Party."

Ren smiled and said, "I believe that inaccurate information may have been transmitted from the Attaché that caused him to raise these concerns. I have an addendum to my official report that you may wish to view," as he handed a thumb drive across the desk. Zhu put it into his computer and it whirled to life. He silently read for several minutes, turned back to Ren and said, "There is much here to think about, Major."

"Yes sir, there is."

"Do you have any recommendations on how this situation might be resolved?"

"Questions like these are only addressed by those with higher rank than me, sir."

"Ah, of course you are correct. But, humor me, what might be done to resolve this problem?"

"I'm a soldier, unless ordered otherwise, I don't take prisoners. Since I'm positive that the information in front of you is accurate, I think it should be used to eliminate the source of the problem being raised."

"Eliminate? You suggest killing the Minister?"

Ren smiled at the thought but answered, "Certainly not sir. There are many ways to overcome an enemy. If the objective is either to take them off the battlefield or neutralize them, many options exist for each unique threat. Perhaps, sharing information with the enemy of your enemy would be appropriate. Other times, simply eliminating the source of the threat works best."

The General sat quietly for a few moments. He then added, "You have given me much to think about, I will call you. You are dismissed for now, return to your base and give my congratulations to your team for a job well done."

"Yes sir, the Team will be traveling to attend the funeral of Sergeant Tang Lei killed on this deployment. Will this be a problem?"

"Of course not Major, please express our sorrow to his family at his loss."

"Yes sir."

Before the door had completely closed on Ren, General Zhu reached for the secure telephone. When his contact came on the line he said, "We need to meet immediately, I think we have the answer to many of our problems."

He listened then said "thirty minutes, usual place." He pulled the thumb drive from the computer put it in his pocket and quickly strode from the office.

Rocky's Funeral

Rocky was the first under Ren's command to be killed in an operation. One comrad had died and another had been injured on a night HALO parachute exercise earlier in his career but he did not have to visit the family or attend the funeral. This was his first. Having the entire Team with him did nothing to ease the discomfort with that role. Because of the secret nature of their assignments, his family would never know Rocky's true military service.

The SOG Headquarters provided a letter of condolence to his family from a fictitious company for whom Rocky and the rest of the Shadows allegedly worked. It told of his exemplary contribution and leadership and his tragic death in an automobile accident outside of Wuhan. Army and Strong had taken turns carrying the urn containing Rocky's ashes along with the extra weight added to the remains of his hand during the trip from their base to this coastal city.

At the traditional Buddhist cemetery the Shadows found Rocky's father and mother talking quietly with a group of what appeared to be neighbors from their small village near Foshan. The whole area was being absorbed by industrial blight.

"We were friends of your son, we were in his work group," Ren began, "He was a good man."

As Mr. Tang nodded a greeting to them he had tears in the corner of his eyes. His wife was openly crying. Not at all what custom would dictate but from their hearts and from concern about what would happen to them now that their only son had been taken from them so suddenly. "How did it happen?" Mr. Tang muttered softly.

Ren had never spoken with Rocky about his family or what his parents did but it was clear that they were eking out a living, not having made the transition to the privileged class in the modern China.

"Your son was very brave," Ren began. "A young boy crossing the street did not see the truck coming so fast around a corner. Your son was walking with us, saw what would happen and pushed the boy out of the truck's path. There was no escape for him. He was killed instantly. There was nothing

251

anyone could do. The driver was drunk, reckless and now in jail. Your son will be honored forever by the boy's family."

"Yes, he was a good son, always sent money, and came home when he could for holidays. His mother and I will miss him very much."

After the ceremony, Ren and the team filed past the grieving parents and again gave their condolences but did not stay for the luncheon to mark the end of the burial. Instead, Ren and Pei asked to speak with the father in private.

In a quiet part of the cemetery, behind some mausoleums dating from the early 19th century, Ren handed Mr. Tang an envelope containing a letter and renminbi. He asked him to open and read the letter. As he finished, tears again welled. "I did not know he was so wealthy, how did this happen, he never talked about his work. You're not criminals are you?"

"No, we are not criminals, Mr. Tang. Why would you even think such a thing?"

"Our son never was interested in money, only serving the country. You can't get rich here if you are poor without being a criminal, that's why."

For the first time, Ren and all the Shadows laughed. "No Mr. Tang, you son was not a criminal. Just a very good person who served his country the best way he could. He saved his money and invested it wisely. Please count the money in the envelope."

He did.

"How much is there?"

"$200,000 RMB"

"That's correct. If you follow the instructions in the letter, you will have an additional $25,000 RMB each month for as long as you and your wife are alive. The one condition is that you tell nobody the source of your good fortune. Spend quietly; possibly move to a new village where you are not known so well. Your son would have wanted you to enjoy your life otherwise he would not have provided so well for you."

Tang was speechless as they walked back to his wife and the other mourners.

Ren stopped him and finally said, "Your son was all that is good in China. Do what he asks of you."

Mr. Tang gripped his wife's arm tightly nodded to Ren and the Shadows as they walked past him and out of the cemetery.

"Did he understand what to do?" Pei asked.

"In the end, yes. It is the least each of us can do for Rocky's sacrifice."

Ghost Shadow Base of Operations

The Shadows had just returned to their Guanzhou base when there was another call summoning Ren back to Beijing. When Ren arrived at the military airfield in Beijing near the fourth ring road, a car took him to a nondescript office block near the Forbidden City and Chang Am Avenue. Ren wondered if having the meeting near Eternal Peace Street had any particular significance for what was going to happen.

As the car cruised to a stop, the driver turned and said, "Straight ahead, Room 340."

Ren walked up three flights of stairs and entered to find General Zhu and another, vaguely familiar looking man, waiting for him.

"Please sit, Major, we have lot's to discuss and little time.

General Zhu deferred to the other man, who without introduction began.

"Major, do you know me?"

"Sir?"

"Do you know who I am? What I do?"

"No sir, I do not."

253

"Well, I know you, Very well in fact. I had the pleasure of reading the report on the allegations put forward by Colonel Ping."

Ren and General Zhu both looked up at this revelation. "In fact, I thought that it read more like a recommendation for promotion than an investigation of poor conduct."

"If I might," Ren began but a raised hand silenced him.

"I now understand why it portrayed you as it did. You have a real talent for getting to the bottom of problems and making them disappear. The Party needs talent like yours. I was just thanking General Zhu for bringing another example of your work to my attention.

Ren began to speak but a look from General Zhu silenced him.

"I reviewed your report, Major. Excellent work," he then added, "Who has had access to its contents?"

"Myself and Lieutenant Pei Ming."

"Keep it that way," he ordered.

"As you wish sir."

He nodded, "Have you had time to think about how this information might be used?"

"I have. Two targets, two different approaches sir. Neither solution related to the other. No attribution, repercussions to the Party, the Army or anyone."

"Timing?"

"As you command. But probably better sooner than later."

"Agreed."

"Do it."

"Sir?"

"You are to, as you put it, '*Take them off the playing field',* using whatever means you think appropriate. Just the two of you. The entire Shadows Team is not to be involved. Arrange for them to take leave for a few weeks or whatever time you feel is necessary."

"Who do I report to for this project?"

General Zhu answered, "Directly to me."

"Yes sir."

"Whatever you need will be provided. Use this email," he said passing a slip of paper to Ren. "Begin immediately."

As Ren began to stand, Minister Yen added, "I want strong leverage over the Minister. I do not want a casualty but someone who will see value of an alliance with me. One that is permanent and binding. Do you understand?"

"Perfectly sir, I'm quite confident this will be possible."

"See that it is Major. You will not fail in this assignment."

*Where had I heard that ... **You will not fail**...before?*

As Ren walked back down to the tree-lined street, he remembered the official who gave him instructions. *While undergoing interviews for his selection as Shadows Commander, he had been summoned to the CMC office building. While waiting for his meeting he observed the comings and goings of senior officials on their way to meetings. This one had been pointed out to him because of the attention he received as he passed through the wide hallways of the building. He was Senior Minister Yen, also Chairman of the Party Disciplinary Committee.*

He also remembered where he had heard the ***You will not fail*** caveat: from the founder of SEAL Team Six in Rogue Warrior.

Ren's early military school briefings taught him that the SCS (*State Council Secretariat*) had day-to-day oversight of the Ministry of State Security, the Police and other security departments. It was one of the most powerful in the country, reporting directly to the President. It often had a contentious relationship with the CMC (*Central Military Commission*) that controlled all branches of the PLA. Now one of the

255

leaders of the State Council, Minister Chang, his mentor, was his target.

Chapter 26

Later that afternoon Ren arrived back at his base, arranged two weeks of leave for the Shadows and bid them goodbye for some well earned personal time. He told them that he and Pei had been given a 'special assignment'…to prepare a briefing for senior PLA staff on the **Use of Special Operations Commandos in Developing Economies**…for presentation to General Zhu and his entire staff in one week. After that, they would also take leave.

"Sounds like fun Boss," Army hooted.

"Yeah, tell us what we need to do next time we find some poor natives pointing AK's at us boss." Brave added. "I got it boss, how bout' you call the briefing **Shooting and Looting for Non-Chinese Speakers?**"

Ren laughed along with them but it sounded good enough that it could well have been something that the generals would have them do. "Okay, guy's, get packed and get out of here. You're on your time now. Leave started ten minutes ago," Ren shouted over the chaos as lockers were slammed shut, bags packed and uniforms stowed.

Shortly after the last Shadow departed the barracks, Pei and Ren, also in civilian clothing, climbed into a staff car for a trip to the airport and then to the Special Administrative Region of Hong Kong.

*****

"How much do we have in our Ghost Shadow account?" Ren inquired.

"Do we include the total of Colonel Wen's three accounts and those of the Minister or just his?"

"For now, just his."

"As of this morning, $15.45 million." Pei reported.

"I was asking about the Shadow's account,"

"Oh, sorry. In that one we now have $4.5 million dollars."

"Can you transfer all of Wen's accounts to ours and still have it appear to be in his account?"

"Certainly, I can set up a ghost account that reflects his current balance should he check, but the actual control of the funds will reside in the Shadow's Account."

"Do that for now and prepare the same thing for the Minister's account that he oversees?"

"Hold on," she answered as her fingers flashed over the computer keys. "Looks like a bit over $325 million dollars spread over twelve accounts that we know about and can access."

"That's all of his accounts?"

"Only the ones that Colonel Wen had access to on behalf of the Minister.

"Okay, let's just deal with those for now."

"We can do whatever you wish with the twelve."

"Are you able to do the same type of Ghost account for all twelve?"

"I think so, give me a few hours and I'll let you know but it should work just as well for twelve as for Wen's three."

"Okay, finish the transfer of Wen's right now, then start on the Minister's dozen. Are there any others we should think about bleeding?"

"There are several other accounts that he appears to manage but we don't have the access codes or passwords for them and not even the identities of the true account owners. Just what looks like pseudonyms for them. It will take more horsepower than I have here to get through the protection to unlock that information. We can do it, but I need more help."

"Sorry, we have to limit the work to just us for the time being."

"I really think that when they discover that they have been hacked, they will quickly be checking all their other

258

accounts. Perhaps then we can get their passwords and sign-in information from the software we now have residing on their systems."

"Assuming that they do not realize that we have access via Wen's administrator software."

"Exactly."

"Make sure that when you make all the transfers to the Ghost Shadow's accounts we set up in Vanuatu we can transfer funds from there to London or the Caymans as we may need them for future Shadow's operations."

*****

By eight that evening both were tired. Ever since their initial deployment to Bangkok thirteen days ago they had been running on little food, power naps and pure adrenalin. Looking out of the rented Midlevels penthouse balcony, Hong Kong looked like a fairyland of lights, color and relaxation. After gazing at the mystical sight for a few minutes, Ren told Pei that they were stopping work for the evening and going out for dinner.

They quickly went to their rooms, showered, put on clean clothes and met in the spacious living room of the oversized apartment he had hastily identified on the Internet. Minutes later they were in a taxi winding down toward the high-energy streets and restaurants of Lan Kwai Fong.

"So this is what free enterprise looks like Western style?" Pei chided.

"Looks like the young people have fun, dance and drink. I'm sure they work hard to be able to live here, it's so expensive," Ren answered.

"Is this what everyone can look forward to back home?" Pei asked. "This is what we fight for...have class struggle so we can attain it?"

"We're tourists here...remember. One Country Two Systems for another thirty years. How different is this from

259

Shanghai or other cities where the young want different things than the Party offers?" Ren answered.

The glitter cast a pall over the night. What should have been pleasure turned to ash as they realized that everything they had been brought up to believe in was being discarded by the generation just below them in age and, in the case of Hong Kong, merely geography.

Learning of his mentor's unethical actions also made him sad. Stealing from those he was responsible for protecting was not acceptable. His actions doomed him from the start. At least he would not pay with his life for these actions.

*****

They found a small restaurant, ate well and taxied back to their building all within two hours. As they walked into the apartment, Pei turned and kissed Ren lightly on the lips and said, "Thank you for trusting me as much as I trust you."

Ren held her close, kissed her again and looked in her eyes. "You were special to me, from the first moment I saw you in training. How could I not?" He hesitated, holding his arms around her and said, "no more or we will not be able to stop." he added for both of them,

"Good night. Tomorrow I leave early for Hainan. If all goes well I will return late in the evening. Sleep well."

Pei did not move, rather she held out her hand and touched his arm. They moved together as their shadows blended in the darkened hallway.

Sanya, Hainan Island, China

As the beautiful young girl slipped out of the bedroom suite, Colonel Wen fell into a relaxed sleep. She had been a wonderful addition to the evening. She had been gratefully provided by the hotel management as a reward for him bringing the free spending Thai officers to this beachside resort. He dozed on, not noticing the larger shadow that moved across the highly glossed parquet floor. He rolled over, trying to drop off into a deeper REM sleep but it just would not come.

The ocean breeze wafted through the open doors of his bedroom that overlooked the small pool just outside his door. The flower petals that earlier in the evening had floated on the surface as the young girl surprised and relaxed him, now were settling to the bottom of the crystal clear water. Lights from the sides of the pool gave an ethereal quality to the enclosed courtyard that surrounded his villa. All he heard were cicadas, some mosquitoes and the quiet slap of waves breaking on the fine beach sand. Life was good.

Then, there was a noise, something that did not belong. Scratching at the door? Rustling on the patio? What was it? Just outside his consciousness. *Beautiful night, maybe she was still here, ready for another love session?*

He arose, walked to the door and looked out at the pool. She was not there. Ren was.

Before he could react, Ren had subdued him, dragged him to the pool and slid him into the water holding him down until bubbles stopped flowing from his nostrils.

After sanitizing the room of any evidence that he had visited and collecting Wen's smartphone, Ren slipped across the patio wall to the beach and then to the airport for the short flight back to Hong Kong. He was back to the apartment as the late night clubs on Hollywood Road were closing for the evening.

*****

The tragic drowning of Colonel Wen was described by the hotel General Manager as a sad affair. Possibly the Colonel had gone into the pool after drinking, fell asleep and

261

drowned. The hotel was cooperating with local authorities in this unfortunate accident.

Pei dozed, waiting for him to return. When he finally quietly opened the apartment door, she welcomed him with great tenderness. Hours later, as dawn broke over the densely populated, skyscraper filled horizon, they fell asleep in each other's arms.

Chapter 27

The Shadows trickled back to the post the day before their holidays were due to end. After two weeks of relaxation, Ren had devised a grueling schedule of requalification exercises to focus their energies and bring 'unit cohesion' back to the group that had just performed a major service to the country. They also began competitions to find a replacement for Rocky. That, everyone knew, would take time.

"So how did the presentation go?" Army asked.

"Oh, the presentation." Ren said, "It went well. General Chang thinks we all need more time in developing countries. It's the *wave of the future* for China he says. Expect to see it again and again."

Pei added with a smile, "We learned a lot preparing for the presentation. It was one of the best experiences so far in the Shadows"

"Really? More than killing those guys on the train?" Brave asked.

Pei smiled and said, "The best."

The other Shadows just scratched their heads and quietly muttered, "Just like a girl."

*****

What Ren failed to tell them was that Minister Yen was now in possession of a specially prepared IPad with all the account information that would make his role in dealing with the State Council much easier. How he chose to use it was of no concern to the Shadows. It was way above Ren's pay grade.

The Shadows account was securely protected and beyond the reach of party or PLA hackers. Never again would their operations be at risk because of poor decisions that could harm the team. How these funds would be used was unclear, but since money was a weapon of modern warfare, the Shadows were always going to be well armed.

The only thing Ren knew for certain was that the Shadows would continue to be the 'sharp end' of China's spear for some time to come.

"Strike First, Strike Hard, Strike Often" would continue to be how the Shadow's worked, lived and protected the country.

Acronyms/Terms

ABS	Advanced bomb suit
ADC	Aide de Camp-Military assistant
Bird	Satellite
BPP	Border Patrol Police Thailand
CF	Cluster fuck-major screw-up
CI	Counterintelligence
CMC	Central Military Commission-China
COS	Chief of Station-Country CIA leader
CR	Contact Report
CT	Computer Terrorism
DCI	Director of Central Intelligence USA
DDO	Director of Operations CIA - US
DDP	Director of Plans
Delta	Ultra Elite Special Operations soldiers -USA
EOD	Explosive Ordinance Disposal
Farang	White foreigner-European
Feebee	Slang name for FBI
FIR	Field Information Report
Flimsey	Intelligence report
G-2	Military Intelligence
GF	Goat fuck-Worst posssible screw-up
IC	Identity Cards- Malaysia
IG	Inspector General
ISAF	International Security Assistance Forces
ISOC	Thai Intelligence Service Headquarters
Katoey	Girl-boy transgender-Thailand
Kris	Ceremonial Knife
Lo Ban	Boss in Chinese
LZ	Landing Zone

MID	Military Intelligence Division-China
MIT	Turkish Intelligence Service
MSS	Ministry of State Security-China
NVG	Night Vision Goggles
OP	Observation Post
OPS	Operations
PBS	Public Security Bureau
PLA	Peoples Liberation Army
RECON	Conduct reconnaissance
SA	Special Activities -CIA
SCIF	Semsitive Compartmented Information Facility
SCS	State Council Secretariat
SDR	Surveillance Detection Route
SF	Special Forces
SITREP	Situation Report
SOG	Special Operations Group - Chinese
Soi	Small streets
SWAT	Special Weapons and Tactics unit
Tango(s) or T's	Terrorist(s) in phonetic alphabet
TDY	Temporary Duty Assignment
TSD	Technical Services Division

www.ingramcontent.com/pod-product-compliance
Lightning Source LLC
Chambersburg PA
CBHW072211170626
46813CB00003B/889